THE

WORLD

OF

LIES

Published 2018 by
The Oxygen Factory

ISBN: 978-0-646-98972-3

Cover art and interior illustrations
by Prashant Miranda

Cover and interior design
by Inkspiral Design

THE WORLD
OF LIES

STEWART SHEARGOLD

CONTENTS

CHAPTER ONE

THE BACKSTAGE DOOR

CHLOE WAS UP BEFORE FIVE to catch the early morning train. It left the station at six sharp and she disliked being late for anything. In any case her turbulent dreams had woken her well beforehand. She lay in the dark, listening to the rain pour down outside, and the sudden spray as cars sped through the waterlogged street. When Amanda knocked on her door at ten to five, Chloe was packed, dressed, and ready to leave. Amanda exclaimed at the figure sitting on the edge of the bed in the dark: her black curls brushed, her red pinafore straight, her shiny new black brogues catching the hall light, and even now, fresh from sleep, the furrow of a frown ready to begin on her pale, aristocratic face.

Chloe liked Amanda. They had been neighbours for seven years. Amanda had been a good friend to Chloe's mother. The two of them used to bake cakes for the Cancer Council morning teas and had a good-natured rivalry when it came to growing vegetables, seeing who could grow the rudest carrot or the most obscene capsicum. Chloe especially liked the card nights Amanda hosted. They started with the confusing game 500 which Chloe did not understand so she drew in her sketchbook. Then, after a few glasses of wine, Amanda and Chloe's mum became giggly and the card games simplified from Poker to Hearts all the way down to Snap! Chloe was invited to play this last game and usually won, due mostly to the adults' drunkenness.

These last three months with Amanda had been comforting even though Chloe was stuck with dull pains — a thorn in her stomach, a tightness in her chest. Aunt Lavinia had outright refused to allow Chloe to live with her and Chloe's cheating father until all his outstanding debts were paid. This meant her home was to be sold. It didn't help that her home was empty next door, and had people tramping messily through it with hopeful expressions. She knew the car from the real estate agency now — a bland white stickered sedan. She watched the prospective buyers walk up her path and disappear under the lintel. She put her ear to her bedroom wall and, using a glass as Bradley had shown her, heard them walking about in the upstairs rooms and talking in low, serious tones. During these times she wished she was a ghost and could flow through the wall to terrorise them. She had wonderful visions of her howling translucent figure chasing them down the stairs, watching them flee from her house with expressions of terror.

Sometimes she let herself in — she still had a key — and stood around in the dark, dusty rooms. Nothing remained. The walls were marked with pale stains where paintings had once hung. It made the feeling in her chest worsen and she had to leave.

She'd go out into the garden and remember with happiness those weekends when she and her mother got muddy planting new vegetables and herbs and flowers.

Everything was possible in their garden: blue cornflowers, broad beans, mint, passionflowers, carrots, daffodils, tomatoes, kale, bluebells, love-in-a-mist, lettuce, peppers, sweet william, tansy, potatoes, creeping thyme. It was ruined now; she'd ripped the flowers and plants from their beds one day in an alarming rage that had overcome her.

Then the worst thing had happened: she came home from school (where the other girls and boys avoided her, as though they could catch a little death from her) and saw the red SOLD sticker plastered to the sign on the front lawn. The alarm fizzed up inside her, as though she was going to vomit. She wanted to rip the sign down. She imagined the delight on her father's face, imagined him hugging her aunt, satisfied they had everything they wanted. Only Chloe was left. She knew what they meant to do with her — pull her up to the north, away from familiar comforts, where they could impose their will on her. Oh, it was so unfair!

But there was nothing she could do. Amanda had been kind to take her in for the time it took to sell the house. But Amanda couldn't adopt her; there were legal and biologically binding documents in place that said she was the property of her father. She wanted to run away, to escape, but the idea terrified her too. Where could she go? Who would help her? What did she think she could achieve by running away? The frustration and anger began to build in her, piling on top of the grief as though a mountain was stacking up inside her. She wondered what would happen when it got to the level of her mouth — would she overflow with poisonous, uncontrollable rage?

When the call came from Aunt Lavinia, Chloe was resigned to her fate, and she dressed and packed and sat on the edge of her bed in the early hours of the morning, waiting to start the journey into the north, to a new, difficult life.

The sound of the train rollicking over the tracks was gently melancholic. It was speeding her away from everything she knew, into the frightening unknown. The November fields went by, covered in glittering frost, while she was wrapped in the warmth of the carriage.

Rain spattered against the glass.

A new hardness entered her this morning. Her mother had told her she should be independent, her own person. Chloe might not have control over her fate yet, but she was determined not to let her aunt and father tell her what to do. She'd be difficult and disobedient if she had to. She would find a way to break out of these circumstances and escape.

The carriage was full but none of the other passengers looked interesting. They were reading or playing cards or moodily watching the rushing fields outside. The kind conductor who had shown her to her seat had not returned after bringing her lemonade, despite a promise to check on her. She fiddled with the walkie-talkie that Bradley had given to her, trying to get it to work, but she doubted that the signal coped over such a distance. Her last meeting with Bradley had been teary. She was certain she'd never see him again.

She must be halfway there. She'd counted six stations from London, with two further stops once they were in the countryside. It was hard to tell exactly where she was, the rain making everything out the window grey.

She took out her sketchpad and a set of pencils. Opening her pad to a fresh sheet she began to draw. Sometimes the urge to draw was so strong that she began without any subject in mind, and was stunned to see what her imagination came up with. This was one of those times. She let the pencils define shapes and then gave them textures, and very soon figures and forms emerged from the scribbles. Recently, she had begun to draw strange, fantastical things — castles and odd creatures and tall, forbidding women with striking features. She wasn't sure where these images came from, but when she was drawing them she felt happy. She stopped before finishing the drawing and put her pencils carefully away in their slender tin. The drawing she had started was of a crumbling palace, surrounded by overlarge flowers. Half of the building was made of metal and there was the face of a clock at one end. Each flower in the garden had a staring, hostile eye at its centre. Disturbed, she closed the pad and put it away.

At the next station a man boarded her car and, after glancing nervously at the ticket numbers slotted into the top of the seats, sat down beside her. He spent some minutes shifting in his seat to get comfortable and pressing buttons noisily to make the seat go back, which it did with a loud creak. He had a dark wood cane with a dog's head (a Saint Bernard, she guessed) that he rattled against the seat, slotting it firmly into a groove so it wouldn't fall. He smiled reassuringly.

Chloe thought he looked old-fashioned. He was dressed in a crumpled white linen suit with brown two-tone brogues, a brown vest, cream shirt, and a lavender paisley cravat. He was old, with a craggy face, and a shock of white hair to go with his drooping white moustache. He looked like a learned professor and he smelled of sandalwood and dusty books. But his eyes twinkled kindly when he smiled at her. When he spoke, Chloe was shocked at his deep smoky voice.

'Sorry for all the fuss. At my age it takes a while to get settled.'

Chloe smiled in return. She wasn't sure what to say. He was an adult and she didn't trust adults. They lived in a different world. She became self-conscious in his gaze, looked down, saw she had lead on her fingers, began to rub it off.

'You draw?' he asked.

She froze.

'I have been known to dabble myself, in ink. Though I'm not very good. You're probably much better than me.'

'Pencil,' she said quietly.

'Ah,' he replied. 'Then you are certainly more gifted than I am. I'm afraid I've only reached the scribbles-while-on-the-telephone stage there.'

He smiled again and his eyes crinkled at the corners.

Though he seemed kind she did not show him her drawings. He did not push this line of conversation.

'Are you going far?' he asked.

'Edinburgh,' she replied, knowing she should be polite.

'That's where I'm going. How nice to find someone to share the journey with.'

She did not reply.

'Of course, I am a silly chatterbox. Please say the word and I shall be quiet as a mouse for the rest of the journey.'

Chloe looked at him but he wasn't being sarcastic. Her stubbornness seemed unkind.

'You don't need to do that,' she replied. Then, believing he needed an explanation: 'I'm going to live with my aunt because my mother died.' Not her father. It was not his house. He was an attachment she would ignore. Every time she thought of what he had done, with her aunt, probably in her bedroom, definitely in her house, she felt sick, wanted to lash out, wanted to make him pay. Every time, that night she witnessed it and ran, like a tattletale, to tell it to her mother, to give the shock to someone else, she saw her mother's tears.

He said simply, 'I am sorry to hear that.'

She was grateful that he left it there.

'Why are you going?'

'I'm going to see my daughter. She lives there.' He paused and licked his lips. 'You see, I have to have an operation, and there's a good chance it could be tricky. I want to see her beforehand.'

Chloe knew what he meant. 'You might die?'

He smiled. 'There is the distinct possibility.'

She found this unacceptable. 'You should get a new doctor if he tells you that.'

The old man laughed, then a rattle at the back of his throat turned it into a cough that went on for a minute.

'Oh!' she cried. 'I'm sorry.'

He waved her concern away. 'It is age, my dear. It comes to us all.'

Chloe became glum, thinking of her mother's slack face in the long black coffin. The clods of dirt thudding unkindly on the wood. The headstone incapable of representing her life. Was death following Chloe?

A thought came to her: 'Is it cancer?'

'No. It's my heart.' He touched a hand to his chest in a gesture of acceptance.

Chloe suddenly wanted to do something for him. She rifled through her bag and pulled out her sketchpad. He looked enquiringly at it, as though this is what he had intended all along. She smiled at him, realising that she had not shown her drawings to anyone but her mother. Not even Bradley.

She opened the pad to her newest drawing.

'I did thi —'

There was a sudden screech of brakes, interrupting her, lifting them violently forward in their seats. Then a strange faraway bang from outside, like a muffled gunshot. Seconds later the loudest sound she had ever heard — a splintering, roaring crash of metal as the carriage smashed into something.

The world turned upside down.

Her stomach dropped as she was flipped out of her seat, falling to the ceiling. Screams echoed down the carriage. It moved across the ground at speed. The sound of shearing metal and broken glass was deafening. She was thrown down the carriage, her body battered by seats and people and luggage racks. Panic crashed through her. She grabbed wildly for a hold, her hand clasping something solid.

The carriage hit something hard, violently shifted onto a new course.

A screech of metal and the side sheared open, letting in freezing rain.

Chloe screamed as glass spattered her. People rolled around her, bloody and frightened. Her heart pounded in her chest.

She saw the old man, sitting in his seat, held in by a mass of luggage on top of him. She thought he was dead until his eyes fluttered weakly open. In that moment amongst the noise they locked glances.

Then the carriage split in two, the abrupt motion ripped her handhold away.

She fell. There was a hard smack. Then nothing.

She was walking, slowly and painfully, one arm — broken — cradled across her chest. She wandered through metal debris. The heat of many fires warmed her face. The smell of churned, wet earth and acrid smoke. Her head was one large bruise.

Rain poured into her eyes and ears. She was so filled up with wet she felt underwater.

She realised someone was holding her hand. A man with a mesmerising voice. He murmured to her.

'That's it. Keep it up. One foot in front of the other. Everything will be all right. Just keep hold of my hand.'

She was grateful she did not have to think. Someone kind was helping, taking her to a waiting ambulance that would ferry her to hospital where she could lie down and sleep for days. You don't have to do anything when you're ill. The pain in her arm was excruciating, but the pain in her head had numbed her. She let herself be led, dumb, from the crash site.

Only once did they stop, when she tripped on a root and collapsed. Her arm *screamed* as it banged the earth, making her breathless.

'Rest a moment,' said the slippery voice. 'There's a few minutes left.'

Holding her arm with her other hand, she gathered the pain to her chest, where it seemed less fierce. Ahead of her was a forest of dense pine and spruce. Below her was the chaos of the wreckage. She realised she was sitting at the top of a hill.

Away in the distance — hundreds of metres — she could see the bulk of the train, carriages piled on top of one another like toys a child had thrown in a jumble. She shivered. The shape it made was wrong. Her eye followed the devastation from the crash impact across the churned-up field, where carriages were littered in twos or threes, crackling with fire, lying ominously silent. Passengers wandered blankly across the field, numbed by the jolt to their strict, comfortable lives. It was like a scene in a painting, vivid but not real.

The man took her by the hand again, coaxing her into the forest. The rain pounded down on them. Her hair stuck to her face, irritating her.

Chloe concentrated on her feet — the new black brogues Amanda had bought for the trip up north. She didn't want to get them dirty, though they were already scuffed beyond repair.

The man murmured a rhyme that tripped lightly off his tongue.

'Oh, the thing it is the play
And the plot is there to lay,
I've got a girl to end all girls
And an ending to that world,
In just a few small minutes more
We'll be through the Backstage Door
And then the gaoler she will pay
For the Man will have his day!'

As they walked further into the forest, Chloe realised — slowly, each raindrop filling her with awareness — that something was wrong. She shouldn't be entering the forest with a stranger. The ambulance would not have parked so far from the crash site. What was happening?

As she thought this, the man began to speak his rhyme more loudly. It was less jolly and more sinister. She tried to pull away from him but he held her tightly. Looking up, as though she had not been able to before, she was horrified to see his hand had no fingernails. It was white and blubbery, like rubber. Desperately she tried to pull away.

'Now, now, my dear, there's really nothing to worry about. This is all happening just as it should.'

He turned his head, formerly in darkness, to her. Chloe cried out. It was a featureless white oval. It bobbed obscenely on his neck. She fell to the ground, trying to drag him down with her. He pulled her up with inhuman strength. She screamed as broken bone wrenched in her arm.

'Help!' she yelled, hoping her voice carried.

The man ignored her, pulling her on through the forest. The spruces uncaringly watched her progress. His white hand gripped her so hard she was getting pins and needles.

Abruptly he stopped, and she ceased struggling.

They were in a clearing. In the centre was a gnarled oak, which appeared out of place amidst the spruces. Its limbs were like devil's fingers pointing down at her. Cut into it in gold were the markings of an ornate clock, hands at ten to twelve. The man threw her to the ground. She scrabbled to get away from him.

'There really is no need for fuss
For very soon you'll be like us.'

'Who are you?' she snapped. 'What do you want with me?'

He scrutinised his hand, squeezed it into a fist. When he released it, she could see it was now pink, with delicate, rounded fingernails.

He stretched out a finger, as though it were a gesture new to him. He pointed it at her. 'I want you, my dear Chloe.'

As he said her name she was struck with panic. He intended to harm her. She pulled herself to her feet, ready to run.

Before she could, the man went to the tree and placed his new pink hand — the hand that had touched her — against the clock face. The carving in the wood was etched with white light, as though the tree was filled with it. The light traced the numbers and the minute hands. The man watched, and though he had no features, Chloe could sense his glee. There was an abrupt shudder from the ground and she stumbled.

He turned to face her, an air of triumph in his stance.

'She's all yours,' he said to the tree, though she sensed he was speaking to someone elsewhere.

Chloe thought, In the next second, I'll run.

Then, with a tremor, thick roots burst from the ground and shot straight at her. They wrapped around her legs and pulled her off her feet. She clawed at the mud but could get no purchase. The roots reeled her in like a flapping fish until she was at the base of the tree. Her arm struck the ground and she blinked to keep herself from passing out at the pain.

The man without a face made a gesture and the roots released her. He reached down and pulled her up. This close she could see rain pouring down his smooth white mask. His non-face frightened her more than anything she had ever feared.

'I've been looking for you for such a long time, Chloe Susannah Alexandra Jane Hattersley.'

Chloe looked past him and smiled. Behind him, she could see torchlight, and hear voices calling out. People were looking for her. Before she could shout out to them, the man stuck his wormy fingers into her mouth, gagging her. She spluttered in revulsion.

He wrapped himself around her, took her hand in his new pink one and pressed them both to the shining clock face in the tree.

Light flared around them. With a thunderous boom the clock struck twelve.

Chloe felt a small tug, then a more insistent one. Then the roots pulled them both into the earth. Mud filled her mouth, dirt closed over her eyes, and she was sucked under.

With the worms, she thought. Like mum.

SPRING

CHAPTER TWO

THE QUEEN OF SPRING

CHLOE WOKE TO A LOUD crash.

For a moment she was disoriented; the tail end of the sound lingered in her head. She blinked herself properly awake. But the feeling of uncertainty did not leave her. Slowly, she registered another sound — water splashing against stone.

It was raining, thin waterfalls pouring through holes in the ceiling. It was not the ceiling with the chandelier and rose-pattern she knew from Aunt Lavinia's guest bedroom. She sat bolt upright. It was not the bed she knew either.

It was a large bed, enough to sleep five or more people, and it filled half the room she found herself in. She was wrapped in heavy quilts and pressed against soft pillows. Lace curtains cocooned the bed and moved lazily in a wind that, she saw, when she looked up (for the bed had no canopy), blew in from the holes in the ceiling. Holes, she noted, punched in the arched dome so deliberately that the bed did not get wet.

The room itself was luxurious though macabre. There was the large bed she was in, a single chair beside it, and on it a candle in a glass burnt down to its wick. At the other end of the room was a dresser, flourishing with make-up, and a plain mahogany wardrobe with double doors in a corner. The walls were crowded with paintings, all indistinguishable, as the rain had bubbled and cracked the paint.

Behind her was a row of windows, high up in the wall. Green plants pressed against the panes.

It was clear this room was rarely used. It was dusty and decayed. One thing Chloe knew — it was not her bedroom in Aunt Lavinia's terrace.

So where was she?

She remembered sitting in a train, staring out the window at the fields racing past. She recalled the conductor being kind to her as she came aboard at King's Cross station. The station had impressed her with its gothic splendour and frightened her with its rush of people and their lost-looking faces. But the kind conductor had taken her hand and shown her to her seat in first class.

'Have you ever travelled first class before?' he asked.

Chloe shook her head. She remembered Amanda booking the tickets — "a last indulgence," she said, knowing that Aunt Lavinia disapproved of such extravagance.

'Well then,' the conductor said, 'it will be the most exciting trip you ever have on a train. The first time in first class.' He winked, and she was taken aback at such a familiar gesture. 'You must be a very special girl to someone.'

'I am,' Chloe replied glumly, thinking of what awaited her at the end of the trip. A draughty terrace house, a new school; her moody aunt; her jealous father.

The kind man asked for her ticket, took out a small device like a toenail clipper and punched a hole in it ('So you don't have to go through all the bother later,' he explained), and sat her down in her allocated seat. Then he realised she was in the aisle. 'Can't have that,' he said and quickly switched the reservation tickets. 'You've got to have the window on your first trip in first class.'

Leaving her, he explained he had other jobs to do to make sure the train left on time, and that he'd come back to check on her during the journey.

Chloe was pleased when he left. She'd wondered how much longer she could keep up the smiles; she had learned that adults liked them, and she could get her own way through careful use of them. But he talked down to her. She wasn't a simpleton; she could take care of herself.

Now she had a sudden disturbing thought: what if the conductor had been nice because he'd wanted to kidnap her? Had he drugged her (that lemonade he gave her midtrip!), snatched her away at one of the halfway stations and secreted her here? Why would anyone want to kidnap me? she thought. Unless it was something to do with her father. It was exactly the sort of thing he might try. But he was waiting for her in Edinburgh with her aunt. He'd won her back and needn't go to such trouble anymore.

She looked around the room again. Could it be one of the extremely aged houses in the Old Town of Edinburgh? Or a heritage-listed building, judging by the historical furnishings? Was the council about to refurbish it, or demolish it?

She sighed. It was no good sitting here and wondering. She would have to see if there was anyone else in this odd place, or whether she was stuck in this room, a prisoner.

She jumped down from the bed into a puddle of water. She was a practical girl who didn't mind getting her shoes wet, her new black brogues bought for the trip to Aunt Lavinia's. New shoes to step into a new life. Though she noticed now with dismay that they were scuffed and shabby. Disappointment ran through her at something so new and shiny being so quickly ruined. She frowned. What had happened to ruin them?

The floor was awash with puddles. She tiptoed carefully through them, using the ceiling rubble as stepping-stones.

She was drawn to the wing-mirror dresser at the other end of the room. The central mirror had been smashed and showed only a vicious splinter; the wing mirrors were gone, only the wood backing remained. Tiny bottles of perfume were arranged in neat rows along the top of the dresser. This had obviously been a woman's bedroom.

As she reached for a bottle there was a sharp pain in her right arm, below the elbow. It was a deep internal pain, at the level of the bone. She gently felt around it. There was bruising around the muscle, and she felt something shift as she rotated her arm. As though it had been broken. But she had never broken any bones. Frowning at this oddity she realised nevertheless that it was healing, so dismissed it and turned her attention to the dresser. Her reflection moved oddly in the broken glass.

Taking a bottle that glimmered blue, she unstoppered it. There was an audible *whoosh* and a strange scent suffused her senses. It was as though she was suddenly there — she could feel spray on her face, wind in her hair, hear a roar of water as it crashed ashore. Fresh salt air. She replaced the lid and the scent disappeared. The label on the bottle said, *Sea in Winter*. Intrigued, Chloe peered closely at other bottles — *An Autumn Storm*, *Tea on the Ice*, *The Duke's Velvet*, *Summer Bazaar*, *Blood of the Hunt*, *101 Spring Raindrops*. She wanted to open all of them. She reached out …

'I wouldn't, if I were you.'

'Who's there?' she replied, startled, for there was visibly no one in the room.

'Those are old memories,' said the voice, 'and old

memories have some darkness in them.'

Memories, she thought, looking over the bottles. Something tugged at her, enticed her; the pull of the dark. She reached out and pocketed a bottle.

Attempting to hide her theft, Chloe frowned. 'I demand that you show yourself this instant.' She blustered, 'What *is* going on here? Have I been kidnapped?'

'Kidnapped? Oh no, not at all. Though I couldn't possibly tell you why you're here. Not up to me, you see.'

'I see,' replied Chloe, bewildered.

'No, you don't, but that's quite all right.' The voice — female, elderly and cigarette-husky — sighed. 'You will find out all in good time. As for me, see the hand-mirror on the dresser, with the silver filigree? Pick it up.'

Chloe picked it up guardedly, as though something might leap at her from the glass. She looked into it. For a moment she saw nothing, and her heart beat in panic. Where was she? Why couldn't she see herself? Had she ceased to exist? Then the glass shivered like a stone dropped into a pond, and a face appeared. An old woman stared out at her: a wrinkled woman with deep-set blue eyes, dark grey hair piled high, and a friendly mouth. Chloe dropped the mirror. It splashed into a puddle and ripples bounced across the room. A ripple went through her too; she was certain she recognised the woman.

'Do you mind?' said the woman, her voice water-muffled.

Chloe delved into the water and picked the mirror out. 'I … I'm sorry,' she said. 'You startled me. I'm usually used to seeing myself when I look in a mirror.'

'Well the rules here are entirely different, so you shouldn't expect anything at all.' The woman in the mirror gazed fixedly at her for a second, eyes narrowing, and then her features softened. 'Poor Chloe, you must be in quite a state.'

Chloe frowned. She squared her shoulders, 'And just where am I? And who, might I ask, are you?'

'You are in spring, and all you need to know of me is that I am a friend.'

Chloe pouted. 'Spring?'

'Yes.'

'That would explain the rain.'

'Very probably,' said the woman.

'Then how did I get here?'

The mirror woman looked at her and sighed, as though this was a difficult question. Instead of answering, she gave Chloe a pointed look and said, 'You should go and see the Queen of Spring for an answer to that question.'

'The Queen of —'

'— Spring, yes.'

Chloe considered this for a moment. 'Fine. Anything to stop my feet getting wet.'

There was a complicated pulley system on the door. Looking over it, Chloe eventually found a brass knob in the shape of a closed flower and pulled it. Cogs whirred, and bars clicked upwards, slotting into grooves at the side of the door.

She opened the door and boldly stepped out.

She was in a long hallway carpeted in a strip of red velvet. Doors, spaced evenly apart, ranged the length of the hall. She could see the railings of a staircase at the far end. The walls were papered in a flocked green print with raised roses and spears; the persistent damp had soaked the walls and paper peeled in long strips. But the remarkable thing was the scene happening just down the hall.

Two slim girls stood absolutely still, as though in the aftershock of a violent storm. The girl facing Chloe leaned against a doorframe, eyes closed, apparently exhausted. She wore her red cardigan open, revealing a thin chest. Her waist was wrapped in what might once have been a fashionable tulle skirt but was now tattered ribbons. Underneath this she wore white stockings and cream shoes with a strap across the toe. Her face was a china doll's, snub nose raised, red lips pursed. Her hair stood upright as though in shock.

The other girl had her back turned to Chloe, but her posture was one of defiance — elbows bent, hands curled into fists, as though she were inwardly fighting for control of herself. She wore the same costume as the girl in red with the exception of a white long-sleeved blouse. Her skirt was ripped and trailed two lengths of soft ribbon, as though a bow had been hastily undone. Her hair also stood electric-shock upright.

Chloe took a step forward and time began again. The two girls were instantly aware of her. The red girl's eyes snapped open. They were an icy blue, full of wicked humour and contempt. The white girl turned her head to acknowledge Chloe, looking her full in the eyes with a disapproving stare. Absurdly, their hair did not fall back into place but remained upright.

They turned as one to each other and smiled covertly. They skipped up to her.

'Hello,' said the red girl. 'Who are you?' She peered at Chloe, unashamedly inquisitive.

The white girl clapped her hands in front of Chloe's eyes. Chloe flinched. 'I don't know you,' she said.

'That's because we haven't met,' replied Chloe. She was quite put out by their impolite manners.

The two girls turned to one another. The red girl began to skip around her. 'We know everyone in spring.'

'You're not from the garden,' said the white girl.

'No.'

'Perhaps a new kitchen maid?' suggested the red girl, skipping and circling.

'No.'

'You're on loan from another season. That's it.'

'I'm not any of those things,' said Chloe. 'I'm not sure what I'm doing here at all. I don't even know where *here* is!'

The red girl stopped her skipping circle. The white girl peered suspiciously at Chloe. 'Everyone here has a purpose. You must know what yours is.'

'Why?' asked Chloe.

'Just the way it is,' tinkled the red girl. 'The way the world works.'

'Otherwise you could be dangerous. And we can't have that,' said the white girl. Her eyes narrowed with threat.

'Well then,' started Chloe, folding her arms in challenge, 'what's *your* purpose?'

Both girls smiled. 'We're from the garden,' they stated in unison. 'We're here to bring a little wickedness to the days.'

Before Chloe could ask anything further there was a vibration from her pinafore. Both the strange girls took a step back, alarmed. Chloe pulled the mirror from her pocket. The old woman gazed back at her.

'Take no notice of them. They're Miss Chiefs, silly little girls who live in the hedgerows of the garden and come out to play tricks on people. Ignore them. They're troublemakers.'

'How dare you!' cried the white Miss Chief. 'We entertain people, we make them laugh.'

'You make them cry,' replied the mirror.

The red Miss Chief giggled. 'Only if they won't play.'

'Oh, get off with you,' said the mirror woman. 'We have an audience with the Queen.'

The Miss Chiefs gave each other a sly glance.

'She's in the counting house.'

'Counting out the one hundred and one raindrops for the Spinster.'

'She's in a terrible mood,' said the white girl.

'Disgracefully bossy.'

'She won't receive you well.'

'You'd be silly to try.'

'I hope you don't mean to question her.'

'She detests questions.'

At this Chloe interjected. 'But I have to find out how I got here so I can get back!' She looked into the mirror, 'You said she'd know.' The woman in the mirror opened her mouth to respond.

The white girl snatched the mirror away. 'How you got here is not her concern.' She peered into the glass and frowned. Obviously she couldn't see the mirror woman. She thrust it back at Chloe. 'It's what you're doing here now which is.'

'Oh, go away, you pests,' said the mirror.

The Miss Chiefs linked arms and walked off down the hallway. But their voices came trailing back like the ribbons of their wrecked dresses.

'Better find a purpose.'

'Or one'll find you first.'

'And that might not be pleasant.'

'Without a purpose … you don't exist.'

'And you wouldn't want that, would you?'

'Ta ta. See you in the garden.'

'Yes, do come out and play. If you're able.'

Their unnerving giggles filled the hallway.

The mirror guided Chloe through the crumbling palace (for it could only be that, not some grand manor house in the Old Town) — down majestic staircases, through opulent rooms covered in dust and cobwebs. Everywhere there were piles of rubble from where the roof had caved in, and the hissing of waterfalls as the rain streamed through the holes. They walked through halls hung with ancestral art — beaky faces stared solemnly at her as she passed. Shafts of light highlighted intricate, faded tapestries, or bluebells growing from cracks in the stones, or brutal metal implements on the walls. The longer the journey through the palace, the more anxious and doubtful Chloe became; nothing in this place was easily explained. She was out of her depth.

She thought of those unpleasant girls and shivered at their claim that she did not exist.

Finally, the mirror directed her to a rickety spiral staircase, and she climbed up and up and up, having to pause for breath many times on the way. Eventually she reached a simple wooden door at the top.

'Go on, knock,' said the mirror.

Chloe knocked. An imperious voice from within commanded, 'Enter!'

The room she entered was enormous. It was an attic, vaulted with dark beams, that appeared to go on forever. But then she realised that the room was hung with mirrors, their infinite reflections making it seem large when truly it was small. They threw back the light from hundreds of candles in glass jars, and the room blazed.

There was a wooden desk in the centre, covered in tiny glass phials (just like the phials she had seen on the dresser in her room). On the right side of the desk, the phials were full of a clear liquid and each was packed carefully into a small bookshelf, partitioned precisely according to their shape. On the left side of the desk there was a jumble of empty bottles.

It was the structure above the table that impressed; an enormous knot of chrome piping. It was like several tubas welded together. The large mouth of the machine pointed upwards to gather the raindrops that fell through a hole in the roof. Mechanics processed the rain as it passed through, with musical sighs and deep belches, before it dripped out a small outlet pipe into an empty bottle.

A woman sat in front of the rain machine, fitting the filled bottles into their velvet-lined spaces in the shelf. She wore a red gown with butterfly sleeves and a hooped skirt that billowed like a galleon's sail around her seat. Even from behind, Chloe could see the diamonds on her fingers and her ears. Her presence and composure could only make her the Queen of Spring. The Queen murmured under her breath, 'Ninety-eight, ninety-nine, one hundred, one hundred and one ...' and abruptly swigged the contents of a phial. She burped. Her movement was mimicked in the mirrors, making her seem ominously everywhere at once.

Chloe stood still for a moment to fully absorb this spectacle.

The Queen, becoming impatient, turned and, when she saw Chloe, gave a yelp.

Chloe jumped.

They stared at one another for a moment then the Queen said, 'I was expecting someone else. Who are you?'

Realising she was in the presence of a queen, Chloe curtsied. 'I'm Chloe.'

There was a pause. 'Chloe ... what?' the Queen frostily replied.

'Chloe Susannah Alexandra Jane —'

'No, no! Chloe ... "Your Majesty". You forgot to call

me "Your Majesty"!'

'Oh. I'm sorry, Your Majesty.'

'How am I expected to behave like a queen if no-one says, "Your Majesty"?'

'Wouldn't you just know?' asked Chloe.

'Don't be impudent!' snapped the Queen. 'And you forgot the "Your Majesty" again.'

'Sorry, Your Majesty.'

There was a sudden sparkle in the Queen's eye. 'Ah, I see. You're my new advisor, on loan from summer? Has the Spinster sent you to advise me in my daily routines, in my consultations with the other royal heads of the seasons? Come, quickly, answer.'

'No, Your Majesty. I'm not sure why —'

'No!' she screeched. Then: 'Chloe? Chloe?' The Queen frowned. 'I don't know any Chloes. Do you have any other names?'

'Yes, Your Majesty. My name is Chloe Susannah Alexandra Jane Hattersley.'

The Queen of Spring smiled, showing uneven yellow teeth. It marred her otherwise striking appearance. 'Oh, that's excellent! Four names. One for each season. We shall have fun with you.'

There was a mumble from Chloe's pockets. Chloe pulled out the mirror. 'Ask her about the dailies,' suggested the old woman.

Eyeing the mirror, the Queen said, 'A vain child, are you? After my own heart.'

'Your Majesty, I've been told to ask you about the dailies.'

The Queen's eyes narrowed. 'What do you know about the dailies?'

Chloe looked to the mirror.

The old woman smiled reassuringly. 'You do not know why you're here. The dailies should have recorded your entry into spring. They may help you to find out what you're doing here.'

Chloe relayed this to the Queen, who softened.

'Poor girl. You're confused. It's perfectly natural. I felt the same when I was first sent here. But you'll get used to it. I do wish the Spinster had told me you were coming. I could have prepared.'

'What do you mean I've been sent here?' There was another pause. Then Chloe remembered, 'Your Majesty.'

The Queen hiccoughed. 'My dear,' she explained, 'this may look like a crumbling spring palace, but the reality is that we've both been very naughty and have been locked up here in this season.'

Chloe looked at the mirror, but the woman glanced away. 'You mean this *is* a prison?'

'Oh yes,' replied the Queen. 'But as prisons go it's endurable.' Her eyes brightened, and she leaned forward. 'I've been here so long I can't actually remember what my crime was. But what was yours? Was it something ghastly, something petty and selfish? I bet an awful girl like you did something mean and spiteful, didn't you?' She smiled her yellow smile with such glee that Chloe was repulsed.

'But I haven't done anything!' she cried.

'You must have done something.' The Queen pressed her lips together at the tantrum. 'And now you are here we shall have to find a role for you. We can't have you wandering about without knowing what you're supposed to do.'

Chloe glared at the Queen. 'I can see you're going to be no help at all. I'm going to find my own way home.'

The Queen laughed. 'You're not. You're here forever.'

Chloe found herself staring into a mirror — a distressed

girl in a white blouse, red pinafore, and brogues stared back, black ringlets framing her pale face, mouth down-turned in sadness. She didn't like what she saw.

'Believe me,' continued the Queen, 'it has been tried before. You can't escape.'

Chloe made her hands into fists. 'Just you watch me.' She turned her back on the unhelpful queen and strode out, slamming the door.

The Queen's irate, self absorbed cry of 'Your Majesty! Your Majesty!' was soon lost to her as she fled down the stairs, trying to blink back tears, and failing.

THE SPINSTER OF SEASONS

CHLOE RETURNED TO THE RAIN-DRENCHED room she had woken in. It was, at least, familiar and the bed was comfortable. If she stayed there long enough she might discover how she had entered the season. She might find an escape.

She spent an anxious, watchful night in the room. The season kept up its steady stream of rain and, eventually, the waterfalls' *shoosh* sent her to a fitful sleep.

Next morning, the door opened on its cogs and pulleys and a tall, golden woman tick-tocked in. She raised golden hands and unnaturally long fingers reached out for Chloe. Chloe gasped.

'Oh dear — TICK — oh dear!' the clockwork woman said, her voice jangling, as though she had a loose part tumbling in her throat. 'I didn't mean to — TOCK — frighten you, Chloe.'

Chloe was wide-eyed.

'I'm here to dress you — TICK — for breakfast with the — TOCK — Queen.'

Chloe pulled the sheet down and sat up, curiosity getting the better of fright. 'Are you broken?' she asked.

There was a whirring sound and the mouth opened in a crude approximation of a smile. 'I may be a little — TOCK — old but I can still do my — TICK — job well enough.'

'You sound ill with those coughing tick-tocks,' replied Chloe.

Again the motorised smile. 'No. I'm not — TOCK — ill. I'm clockwork. How else am I to tell when — TICK — it is breakfast if not by the — TOCK — time?'

'Oh,' said Chloe.

'My name is Tokka,' said the golden woman.

Deciding the golden figure was no threat Chloe smiled.

Tokka came forward, cogs and gears grinding, until she was next to Chloe. 'I'm sure we're going to be — TICK — friends — TOCK,' she said, and reached out a golden hand.

Chloe, who was embarrassed at her former fright, marvelled at the intricate detail on Tokka's hands. They had patterns inlaid in them; lines spiralled down the fingers as though they might be part of some secret map when joined with the other hand. Remembering her manners, Chloe took Tokka's hand. The brass knuckles spun, and mechanisms closed the fingers around hers.

Feeling beguiled for the first time since she had arrived in this strange place, Chloe said, 'Yes, I'm sure we will be friends.'

Tokka helped her out of bed and took her to the wardrobe in the corner. She turned one of the knobs and there was a deep thud from within. Then the doors were thrown open and drawer after drawer folded out in a whirling wooden hurricane, until, with a final *clunk*, it stopped. Before them were the entire contents of the wardrobe, displayed as if on the branches of a tree.

Tokka looked Chloe up and down. 'Lovely as you are now — TICK — we shall have to choose something more appropriate — TOCK — for breakfast.'

Chloe thought she looked perfectly fine as she was and said as much.

Tokka winched her head back imperiously. 'Oh, no, you can't frighten the Queen — TOCK — like that again. You must dress appropriately — TICK — for the season.'

Chloe became stubborn. There was nothing wrong with how she looked, and she didn't want to pander to the Queen's ridiculous anxieties. She opened her mouth to argue.

Tokka held up an exquisite red gown.

Chloe was dumbstruck.

'This, I think, for — TICK — breakfast — TOCK.'

The breakfast room was in a long chamber that paralleled a terrace. With its many French doors, all with tiny square windows, it reminded Chloe of a greenhouse. This effect was heightened by the abundance of plants that grew from the stone floor, thriving in the wet that dripped in. She passed aspidistra, arum lilies, a carpet of bluebells, love-in-a-mist, dusky purple orchids, and large bush ferns willowing in the gloom; somewhere, there was a scent of jasmine. It felt as though the garden had crept in and was slowly consuming everything in its path.

A table ran the length of the room, covered in cakes and pastries, and seeded breads steamed fresh from ovens. Nuts and cereals were displayed in large white bowls. Jams and spreads were scattered across the table, though most were gathered at the Queen's end. Chloe saw the woman dipping a finger in each of them in a most unhygienic manner.

Tokka ushered Chloe to the Queen. At their last meeting the Queen had been seated and, as Chloe stood before her, she was startled by the monarch's height. This morning the Queen was dressed in a deep-blue velvet gown, with silver bracelets cuffed along her wrists and a chrome V-necked breastplate; her earrings were silver oak trees. Chloe caught her in mid-suck of a jammy finger.

'Your Majesty, I present a suitably attired — TICK — Chloe, for breakfast.' Tokka's gears ground into a creaky bow.

The Queen glared at Chloe, as though she had dared to interrupt the royal occasion of jam. She removed her finger from her mouth with a lip-smacking wet pop. Chloe was amused to see she had jam smeared on her cheek. The Queen loomed over Chloe and said, 'Well she certainly looks better. At least she'll appear to be one of us now, though, of course, she isn't.'

Chloe shot back, 'If you want me to appear like you, I shall need some blackberry jam to smear across my face.'

The Queen's eye's blazed. 'How dare you! I could have turned you over to the Spinster instantly. Instead I let you stay in my palace.' She harrumphed. 'And this is how you repay my hospitality. Ungrateful wretch!'

'Excuse me, Your Majesty,' said Tokka, 'but you do appear — TICK — to have some blackberry jam on your face. TOCK.'

The Queen stiffened, turned away, and took a small hand-mirror from her gown. As daintily as possible she wiped away the jam. She looked at it on the end of her finger and, deciding decorum was unnecessary, licked it greedily. Returning the mirror to her pocket she swept round to stare frostily at them.

'The Spinster is due any second. She'll know what to do with you. I find you quite impertinent. In the meantime, you may have something to eat. After all, that is what breakfast is for. Though I shall thank you not to have any of the blackberry jam.'

Chloe chose a seat not so far from the queen as to seem rude but also far enough to discourage easy conversation (not that she'd ever had an easy conversation with the woman). She looked over the gourmet delights on the table, wondering what to choose first, and was disgusted to see that much of the food was covered in a fine web. She hadn't seen it before as the light only caught it when seated. Glistening strands stuck to the danishes, a net of web encased the fried eggs, tiny albino spiderlings crawled in the bran. The only food the spiders hadn't spoiled was the jam. The Queen noticed Chloe's disappointment and smirked.

Chloe slumped in her seat. Tokka ratcheted over. 'Why does the Queen hate me?' she asked.

Tokka ground out a sympathetic frown. 'You do represent — TICK — a problem for her — TOCK. If you're a prisoner, then you might — TICK — be here to usurp her position — TOCK.'

'But I don't want to be queen,' Chloe said. 'I'm just a girl.'

'Are you just? TICK. There are many dangers here — TOCK — and not all of them come — TICK — without masks.'

Chloe glared at Tokka. 'I am *not* wearing a mask. This is my own face.'

'That — TICK — is what the Spinster — TOCK — will determine.' Tokka laid a hand on Chloe's head.

'Though you do seem — TICK — a nice girl. It would be a shame — TOCK — for you to turn out a villain.'

At that moment, a peal of trumpets rang out, loud enough to shake the foundations of the palace. Chloe was alarmed, but Tokka reached out to steady her chair as it wobbled on the stone. Pieces of tile shifted and slid through holes in the roof to crash down amongst breakfast. The Queen waved the dust away with familiar nonchalance.

'What was all that about?' asked Chloe.

'The Spinster arrives …' Tokka replied.

She was obviously someone of importance.

Something was happening to one of the waterfalls spilling from the roof. The stream was beginning to slow. As each drop hit the ground, it was thickening, becoming a hard shade of white. It was, she realised, turning to ice. Quickly, the ice travelled all the way up the fall to the hole in the roof, creating a shining pillar. It was all of a sudden quiet, and Chloe realised how loud the waterfall had been in the background. Then the pillar cracked, and like a living thing, tendrils shot across the floor, turning everything to ice in their path — chairs were encrusted, plants froze, one end of the table succumbed to the white frosting. It rippled across the floor in crazy-paving pattern, heading straight for the Queen. Chloe tucked her legs up underneath her.

'It's all right,' said Tokka.

The moment the tendrils reached the Queen they stopped. She eyed them, unconcerned. Then the pillar splintered, shards flying everywhere. Chloe covered her face with a hand as a bright light shone from where the pillar had been. A red stilettoed foot poked itself out of the rent, quickly followed by a short thick leg; a torso followed, ballooning with rolls of fat, and then a ruddy face with tiny, squinting eyes. For a second the figure appeared to be stuck in the ice, and she reached up, annoyed, and pulled a tall white wig through the rent. So the Spinster of Seasons made her entrance into spring.

The Spinster blinked, adjusting herself to the seasonal change. She glowed in the brilliance from the rent. It began to close behind her, and Chloe thought she glimpsed a vista of snow through it, before it crazed into ice again. The pillar quickly began to melt and soon the waterfall flowed freely, as though nothing had happened.

The Spinster was an enormous woman, naked yet covered in folds of her own fat, though it appeared she were wearing a skin-coloured gown. She wore only accessories — the red stiletto heels, which drew the gaze to her dainty feet, a necklace of vials which looked to hold strange coloured potions and organic matter, and a tall white wig common to eighteenth-century aristocrats. Her face was powdered an excessive white, with pantomime rouged cheeks; her lips were bursting with redness, her eyelids blackened with kohl. She patted her wig, making sure every hair was in place.

The Spinster fiddled underneath one of her folds and brought out a pair of opera glasses. She held them up to her eyes and peered about the room, taking in Chloe, Tokka, and the Queen. She tutted.

'Dear me,' she said, and her voice was immeasurably old and cracked, but kindly, 'my entrance seems to be a little off today.' She sucked in her lips and made a loud popping noise to make sure her lipstick was evenly applied. Then she hauled up her rolls, as if they were a trailing dress, and waddled across to the Queen. 'Good morning, my dear Columbine,' said the Spinster, giving two air kisses.

The Queen kissed back. 'Spinster, how good of you to come.'

The Spinster waved this platitude away. 'It was no problem. I was admonishing the Matriarch of Winter, and you know how she gets when her rule is questioned. I escaped two murder attempts while there. Dreadful woman.' She smiled and the powder on her face cracked. 'I have to say that this is quite my favourite prison season. I love how tragically romantic it is. You've done a lovely job, Columbine.'

'I try,' said the Queen.

'I wish the others were as compliant as you. Of course, the Duke is quite charming, though extremely deceitful. It's that unreasonable Summer King and that malevolent Winter Witch who cause all the problems. Typically, the most extreme seasons are the most trying.' The Spinster sighed. 'Speaking of problems …' She turned to squint at Chloe through her opera glasses. 'Is this the one?'

The Queen sneered. 'Yes. She just appeared, from nowhere, not a thunderclap or applause, not the slightest announcement.'

'No entrance? Most unusual,' said the Spinster. She appraised Chloe, looking her up and down. She wafted an almost overbearing scent. 'She doesn't seem to be a villain. I can tell instantly, you know.'

Chloe glared. 'I am not a villain. I'm a girl, and I have no idea what I am doing here in this horrid place. I just want to go home.'

The Queen took in a breath. 'You see, she doesn't have a role to play. She's … different.' She whispered the last word as though it were a terrible crime.

The Spinster smiled at Chloe. 'You don't want to be different, do you?'

'Of course I do!' Chloe replied.

'Oh dear.' The Spinster glanced askance at the Queen. 'She has quite a temper.'

'Her manners are savage,' added the Queen, licking a finger of jam.

The Spinster rummaged in her folds and pulled out a diary-sized book. She untied the string that bound it and flipped the dry pages until she found what she desired. She followed her finger down the page, reading intently. After a moment she tutted.

'No. No mention of a scheduled arrival in the manifests. It's most worrying.'

'I hasten to add that she knew of the dailies,' said the Queen.

'Really?' The Spinster's eyebrows flew up. 'Now that's interesting.' She peered at Chloe again, trying to discern her nature. 'Interesting and dangerous.' She nodded decisively. Taking a vial from her necklace filled with a pink liquid, she spilled a drop onto Chloe.

Chloe felt a thrill run through her body. She suddenly wanted to tell the Spinster everything she had ever known.

The Spinster smiled. 'What is your name, dear girl?'

'Chloe Susannah Alexandra Jane Hattersley.'

'Goodness.' The Queen gave the Spinster a nod.

'How did you arrive here?'

'I woke up in a bed in an upstairs room.'

'What do you last remember, then?'

'I was on a train to see my Aunt Lavinia. And my father.'

'Ah,' replied the Spinster, knowingly. 'So, if you know nothing about this season, how did you come to know about the dailies?' Chloe shuffled her feet. 'Come now,' cajoled the old woman.

'The woman in the mirror told me,' she said reluctantly.

The Spinster frowned. 'What mirror?'

'The mirror I found in the bedroom.'

'Show me.'

Chloe hesitated.

The Spinster inclined her head. 'Please.'

Chloe reluctantly took the mirror from her pocket and handed it over. The Spinster received it gravely. She turned her eyes from Chloe to the mirror. She stared into it. For a moment nothing happened. The Spinster frowned into the glass. Then her eyes went wide.

'What?' asked Chloe. 'What do you see?'

The Spinster was in shock. 'Oh my goodness.'

'What is it?' asked the Queen. 'Is it something very bad?' Her vindictive pleasure was obvious.

'It could be,' replied the Spinster, who was now gazing at Chloe as though she were a bomb about to explode. 'I fear, my dear, that you have entered this prison through a Backstage Door.'

The Queen dropped a jam jar.

Chloe frowned. 'What does that mean?'

'It means we must be cautious. You may not yet realise it, but you have started something terrible by your coming here.' The Spinster gave her a solemn look. 'The seasonal prisons are held in fragile balance by rules and regulations. When someone like yourself appears to be breaking those rules simply by existing, it does cause us to worry.'

Chloe was annoyed. She was being reprimanded for being herself!

The Spinster saw how glum she was and, with a knuckle under Chloe's chin, lifted her head. 'But you must not worry. This is our problem, not yours. You are here, and business must go on as usual. I will accept you as part of the workings of the prison, as it were.' The old woman's magnified eyes twinkled.

'Do you think that wise, Spinster?' said The Queen. 'She could cause great unrest and trouble in my palace.'

'I don't think she wishes that, do you, Chloe?'

Chloe shook her head. 'I just want to go home.'

Home? But where was home? Her home was gone. Yet it was not here. That she knew.

The Spinster nodded. 'Of course you do. I shall use all my considerable powers as gaoler to discover how you arrived and why you are here. In the meantime, you must go about and behave yourself.' She paused, raising a finger to her lips in thought. 'You must also come to the masquerade tomorrow night, where you shall be introduced into prison society, and therefore cause less alarm.'

Chloe realised what the Spinster was trying to do for her and thanked her.

'See, she has perfect manners.' The old woman turned to the Queen with eyebrows raised in challenge. The Queen frowned but said nothing. Noticing the hoard of jams, the Spinster plucked a jar of raspberry jam from the table and set it in Chloe's arms, much to the Queen's instant chagrin.

'Now, I have some business to do with Columbine. Tokka will take care of you. I suggest you go and play in the garden.'

'Why?' asked Chloe, not wanting to be separated from the Spinster's kindness.

The Spinster blinked. 'Because that is what young girls are supposed to do.' She smiled shrewdly and shooed Chloe out the French doors.

CHAPTER FOUR
THE GARDEN OF ENCHANTMENTS

THE RAIN HISSED DOWN ABOUT Tokka and Chloe. It dripped unceasingly onto the garden, the leaves and flowers sponging up the wet. The garden gave off an over-ripe scent. It was so *green* it almost hurt to look at it. Chloe imagined tubers and branches and stamens thrusting and rooting through soil and air; an unstoppable force growing and expanding, enveloping all who got in their way. The garden looked dangerous.

She sat down on a step, dispirited, placing the unopened jar of jam beside her.

Tokka noticed her glum face. 'It's perfectly safe. TICK. There is a gardener. TOCK. You just have to keep your wits about you.' Tokka whirred and, leaning down, said, 'At the bottom of the garden — TICK — you can see into the next — TOCK — season.'

Chloe lost her gloominess. 'Is there a way out?' she asked.

Tokka straightened. 'Well, I'm not sure about that — TICK.' Not wanting to dash Chloe's hopes, she added, 'Though anything is — TOCK — possible.'

Chloe jumped up. 'Then we must go!' She might not be

trapped after all. She reached for Tokka's brass hand. The clockwork woman pulled away. 'What is it, Tokka?'

Tokka lowered her head. 'I'm afraid the Spinster was — TICK — optimistic when she suggested I could — TOCK — look after you in the garden.' She rotated a hand in a gesture of meek acceptance. 'I am made of clockwork, and for tasks in the interior of the palace only. TICK. My metal cogs and wheels will seize up in the rain. TOCK.' The intricate workings behind her face pulled her mouth down, in almost exact imitation of Chloe's glumness a moment before. 'I would ask one of the — TICK — clockwork women made for exterior tasks — TOCK — to accompany you, if they were not occupied — TICK.'

Chloe thought, But I can't go into the garden alone! She had a premonition that something terrible would happen to her in there. But she understood too that Tokka could not venture out; the rain would trickle into her metal workings and she'd grind to a halt. Chloe did not want that to happen. So she strengthened her resolve and said, 'That's okay. I shall be perfectly all right on my own.'

Tokka gazed at her steadily for a moment, not entirely believing this, but nodded. 'Be careful, Chloe. This is a garden of enchantments — TICK — and there are many things in there that you should not touch. TOCK. But you will know that when you — TICK — see them.' She took Chloe's hand in hers and gently closed her brass fingers around the girl's. Then she turned and walked away.

Chloe was left alone in the rain.

For the first time since Chloe had arrived in this odd season, the weight of her predicament came crashing down upon her. She was alone in a strange place without any friends, and without a single idea as to what she might do next. She felt like a lab rat, running around in someone's game, trying to decipher what the rules were.

There was a muffled vibration from her pocket. She remembered the mirror. She pulled it out and looked at the old woman who appeared in the glass. It unnerved her how she could not see herself, but the old woman gave her a feeling of comfort.

'Silly girl, you'll always have people to look out for you,' said the mirror. 'You're very important to this world.'

'What do you mean?' asked Chloe.

'You'll see,' said the mirror. 'I'd like to tell you everything … but I can't.' She crumpled her face in annoyance. 'You'll have to find out by yourself. I can guide you, but I cannot tell you outright. It's the way this world works. To do otherwise might harm you.'

Chloe thought again of rules and regulations and was certain she was on to something. She registered what the mirror had said. 'Could you guide me to the bottom of the garden?' Chloe looked out at the mist creeping through the green.

'Of course.'

Chloe grinned, all worry gone, and darted down the steps. Within seconds her red dress was soaked, her black ringlets bedraggled.

The garden was a steamy, overgrown jungle, the plants and flowers lush with wet. Strange birds cried out, and insects chittered in the undergrowth. Chloe stepped lightly through the leaf-litter, afraid she might sink down covered holes.

The mirror guided her with ease, down overgrown

pathways, through tangled arbours where roses grew wild and thorny. Occasionally, flashes startled her, until she realised it was only a bird's colourful plumage or an insect's wings. The garden pulsed with life.

Eventually the path opened into a clearing. Chloe breathed a sigh of relief. The jungle had been oppressive. The clearing dipped into a two-tiered sunken garden, carpeted in a thin lawn. It was edged with miniature box hedges and beds of roses in single colours. They were in bloom and the rain brought out their perfume. In the upper garden, loveseats were arranged opposite one another and enclosed with large rhododendron bushes and lattice screens crawling with passionflower vine. In the lower garden there were a number of topiary figures. They stood in attitudes of alarm, hands raised to ward off something frightful. Chloe noticed that their faces, though made of leaf, were clipped so finely that she could make out despairing or startled expressions.

There was an unnatural calm about this sunken garden, as though it were stilled with a spell. There was a soft whispering on the edge of hearing.

'They are so well done,' she said admiringly. 'The gardener is very clever.'

'These are not done by the gardener,' said the mirror. 'They are criminals, enchanted by the garden. They tried to steal something from spring or attempted to break through the barrier. This is their punishment, to be turned into topiary ornaments for all time.' The mirror continued, 'Do not touch them. They are ever trying to break free of their enchantment and will drag you into their topiary prison.'

Chloe thought, If everything is a prison here, how am I

ever going to get out? But then she remembered the mirror's words: she was special. Perhaps she did have a purpose here, one that did not obey the rules of the seasons.

Behind the topiary prisoners was a hedge, metres high, with an arbour of roses announcing an entrance.

The woman in the mirror coughed to get her attention. 'The bottom of the garden. It is a maze that is said to reach into the autumn season. Many have tried to traverse it, to escape, but have never been seen again, in any other season, according to the Spinster. No one here knows what exists in the depths of the maze.' Chloe looked at the hedge with wonder and fear. 'Go on,' said the mirror, cajoling her. 'Climb up and have a look. I assure you it's safe.'

There was something too knowing in the old woman's tone. How did she know it was safe? How did she know the paths through the garden? She knew altogether too much that other people did not know. Chloe gazed into the old woman's eyes. She thought of herself as an expert liar when it was necessary and could usually tell when others were deceiving her. The old woman looked back at Chloe without guile, a gentle smile on her face, though Chloe sensed sadness underneath. Again, Chloe had the feeling that she knew this woman. Yet she could not place from where. In any case, the mirror woman had not deceived her so far, she had promised her help, and Chloe was inclined to believe what she said was the truth.

She began to climb the hedge and was surprised to find easy footholds (Had someone done this before, at this very spot?). It was higher than it looked, and it seemed as though the hedge deliberately impeded her progress; she caught her dress on twigs, and by the time she reached the top the hemline was ripped and trailing ribbons, and her legs and arms were scratched. She would come out in red weals. But then she reached the top and her breath was taken away, and it was worth all the trouble of the climb.

The maze zigzagged across the landscape for hundreds of yards and vanished into a misty haze at the edge of her vision. Beyond the haze, Chloe could see an entirely different season. An autumn forest — a riot of reds, oranges and yellows. Winds tossed the trees. She could hear their fluttering even at this distance. The sky was the colour of a purple bruise. In the distance Chloe could see a grey stone castle with battlements and keep. The woods writhed with tiny figures — warring or dancing — though she wasn't certain if they were people or not. It was so violently active and different to spring that she was unsure whether she wanted to leave this comparatively calm season. Yet she felt a strange urge, a tug at her body, as though there was something out there, waiting for her.

The whisperings surged about her.

'No, don't —' started the mirror, but that was all she could say before the hedge *moved* and a branch shot out and ripped the looking glass from her hand. Chloe heard the old woman cry out as the mirror fell.

She pulled away in shock as leaves rippled beneath her. As she fell she reached out but grasped thin air. Instead, she found that something inside the hedge had grabbed her ankles and roughly pulled her in. She squealed as the branches cut into her legs and threw up her arms to shield her face.

Then she was snatched away into the violently thrashing hedge.

She woke slowly as aches and tender bruises made themselves known. Her eyes adjusted to a dimly lit scene. She was still in the hedge, but the branches had been pulled back and shaped into a sitting room. There was a leafy lounge and a rickety table carved from the hedge wood, with two dining chairs that looked as though they were sharp and uncomfortable to sit on.

Along the walls, branches had been twisted and tied into shelves. In them were colourful gems, pieces of cutlery, a number of the Queen's glass phials, pieces of jade roof tile, bits of lace from dresses, dead roses, a cracked enamel tea pot, a steel spike from a portcullis, a dead sparrow, a ripped canvas depicting a severed head, a rusty mechanical crow, and a few tattered books. It was obviously a nest of some kind, with a magpie mind collecting every bit of tat and colour to furnish it. Throughout the room, thorned vines twisted with tiny white flowers with yellow centres. They smelled like rotten fruit.

Chloe, fully awake now, took note of these vines with alarm when she found that her wrists and her legs were tied to the hedge wall with them. The thorns poked sharply at her. She pulled at her restraints but they were tight and did not give. Oddly, she felt frustration rather than fright. She had reached the point where calamity and strangeness were now merely annoying. She wondered what sort of something lived here.

'Oh look, she's awake!' said an excitable girl's voice.

'Oh good, we can begin the interrogation,' said another.

Chloe managed to turn her head to the right, and saw, jutted up on their elbows, heads held by fists, the red and the white Miss Chiefs. Their hair still shot straight up, making them look permanently shocked, filled with electric malevolence. They gazed at her from a hammock made of vines. The thorns didn't seem to bother them.

'Not you again.'

The Miss Chiefs looked at one another. 'She's not happy to see us,' said the red girl.

'But we're happy to see her,' said the white girl.

Chloe frowned. 'What do you want with me?'

'We want to play,' they said in unison, and giggled.

Chloe supposed that their kind of "play" was not the kind she was going to like. 'You said "interrogation"?'

'Yes, I did,' replied the white girl slowly.

'You haven't found a purpose yet, have you?' said the red girl, and in a swift movement swung her legs to the ground and leapt out of the hammock.

'But you must be a criminal to be in this prison.'

'And criminals must be interrogated.'

'We'll get a crime out of you, yet.' The white girl smiled with such wicked glee that Chloe was a bit afraid. Perhaps they did intend to harm her.

They both came to stand in front of her. 'What shall we ask her first?' said the red girl, whom Chloe noticed gave some deference to her white sister.

The white Miss Chief looked for a moment perplexed. Chloe smiled with relief. She might have a little play herself.

'You're both useless,' she snapped. 'You wouldn't know what to do with a criminal if you did have one, would you? Have you ever actually seen one?'

White gave her a glare, which seemed her natural expression.

'Of course we have,' said Miss Red. 'We're criminals ourselves.'

'Rubbish!' Chloe snapped, and the Miss Chiefs flinched.

'You said you just play and cause trouble. That's not criminal.'
She sensed their doubt; their frowns became long.

'I've broken precious things!' yelled Miss White.

'We've made people cry,' suggested Miss Red.

Chloe looked down upon the Miss Chiefs with a superior gaze. 'Have you ever cut someone in half?' she said. This acknowledgement of the truth, at least as she saw it, made her stomach turn.

The girls blanched at this horrifying statement.

'Wait a moment ...' Miss White knocked her head to one side, as though that angle might show the truth of the situation. And for a moment she did pause. Then she yelled, 'She's make-believing!'

Miss White grabbed Red and swung her round, face to face. 'Don't you see. It's performance! She's being very clever, trying to trick us.' She turned and snapped at Chloe, 'You can't be a trickster! We're the tricksters of this season. You'll have to find another purpose!'

The red girl gave this some thought, then her face cleared of confusion. She swept round on Chloe. 'How dare you try to befuddle us! We're not stupid, you know.'

Chloe was not yet finished with her tease. 'I think you are,' she said with as much gravity as she could muster in her position. 'Because, you see, I can do things to you that you wouldn't think were possible.'

Miss White stepped forward, unafraid. 'Oh yes? Do tell us, please, what these awful things are.'

'Oh yes!' said Miss Red delightedly, 'I do so like awful things.'

Chloe straightened on her makeshift cross. 'When I said I cut someone in half ...' She paused. 'It was just me. *I* did it.' She caught both their eyes. 'By thinking it.' She remembered hiding underneath the hall table, her mother's red shoes beside her, as an argument spilled over in the kitchen. An argument she had caused. Ending with her father slamming the front door, and her mother crying into a mug of tea.

Miss Red clutched at Miss White's lacy arm. 'I think she's telling the truth.'

Miss White was silent for a long while, and Chloe could see her thinking this through. Then, abruptly, she smiled. 'Yes. I think she is.' Her smile had a trap in it. 'Which makes her, by her own tongue, a murderer, and a criminal.'

Miss Red's eyes lit up. 'Oh, so it does!'

'So we have the perfect right to interrogate her,' stated Miss White.

'Rules of the world,' replied Miss Red.

Chloe was alarmed at this sudden turn in proceedings. 'I'll think you in half!' she cried.

'Do it, then,' said Miss White, and she stepped up close.

'Cut her in half!' squealed Miss Red. 'Then I'll have two sisters.'

'Oh, no, you misunderstood. It was a couple I cut in half. Two people who were one.' She conjured up a nasty smile. 'Just like I might do to two sisters.'

That shocked them. The Miss Chiefs clutched each other protectively. Miss Red looked ready to cry and, suddenly belligerent, rolled her hands into fists. 'There's no proof! There's no *proof!*'

'*Snap!* Just like that. And you'll never see one another ever again.' Chloe relaxed her features, which were tight with play-acting. 'Let me down and I'll be reasonable. I might even forget about all of this.'

'No,' said Miss White. Her negative cut through the tension. Her sister peered with wonder at this bravery in the face of danger. Miss White puffed up her chest. 'I'm going to tell the Spinster we've discovered your crime and she'll be able to give you proper punishment!' She turned to her red sister. 'Watch her. I shall be back shortly.'

Miss Red clutched at her sister. 'Oh! But don't you see, she's already splitting us apart if you go.'

Chloe smiled a crafty smile.

Miss White shrugged her sister off. 'Don't be silly. I'm coming back.' She gave Chloe a glare. Whispering quickly to her sister, she went to the hedge and entwining both wrists with loops of the flowered vine, she spoke a single strange word. They shot up to her elbows, then to her shoulders and, locking thorns, interlaced at her neck. She turned and gave a comforting smile to Miss Red, said 'Ta ta,' and was pulled headfirst into the hedge.

Miss Red, distressed, gathered herself and sat down on one of the uncomfortable looking chairs. She refused to look at Chloe.

Chloe's arms were getting tired, and she was sure the vines were tightening, as the thorns were cutting into her. She tried squirming into new positions but nothing helped, though the hold around her ankles was looser.

'Look,' said Chloe reasonably, 'I'm not going to hurt you. Could you please let me down?'

'So you can run away?'

'Don't you want me gone?'

'No. I want you punished.'

Chloe decided to try something. 'I'm sorry about your sister.'

The red girl spun round. 'What do you mean?'

Chloe said, gently, 'She's not coming back.'

'She said you'd try to trick me.'

'It's not a trick.'

Miss Red faltered. 'I don't believe you.'

'Call her back, then,' said Chloe smugly.

Miss Red looked at Chloe, gleaning the truth from her fixed expression. Her face grew suddenly into a mask of rage. 'What have you done to her?!'

'Cut her off from you.' She shrugged. 'You gave me no choice.'

'You horrid girl! Make her come back!' Her anger brought her forward.

'I can't,' replied Chloe. She was playing this dangerously close to harm, but if Miss Red became enraged she might get close enough for Chloe to entrap her in the vines as well.

'Make her come back,' she said with a quiet controlled anger, 'or I will kill you.'

Chloe considered this. 'If you let me down I might think about it.'

But this pushed Miss Red too far. Ripping off a length of vine, she rushed forward, flailing the makeshift whip. She struck Chloe on her legs and her arms and her face. Each contact stung as thorns scratched deep and sharply.

Chloe closed her eyes and cried out in terror and pain.

'Murderess!' screamed Miss Red, 'vile criminal!' She whipped and whipped and whipped, drawing bloody welts across Chloe's skin. Her yells were wild and unhinged. 'Harpy! Killer! Witch!'

Chloe realised the red Miss Chief was right: she was

going to kill her. She hadn't meant to get caught up in this world. She wasn't even supposed to be here. Now she was going to die without finding out what she was doing here. She would never see her aunt or even her lying father again.

Then the whipping stopped.

Carefully, Chloe opened her eyes, thinking it a feint by the Miss Chief. What she saw was such a strange but happy sight that she sagged with relief.

Opposite, there was a ragged hole cut in the hedge, and standing in front of it was a boy. He was dressed in a dirty white shirt, and a leather jerkin fitted tight to his stocky body. He had a wide face with large, inquisitive eyes and his brown hair was short but had grown out over his ears and flopped casually on his brow. He had hair on his chin and jowls uncommon for someone so young; there was a ruddy wholesomeness to his features, as though he had been grown in the rich soil of the garden. Chloe saw, marvellously, that his ears were longer and furrier than a normal person's. Atop his head he had two small yellow horns.

He held in one hand a pair of gardening shears, which accounted for the tunnel of broken branches she could see behind him. In the other hand, he held the Miss Chief, the whipping vine tied around her wriggling body and gagging her mouth.

The boy looked up at Chloe with a curious gaze. 'You look like you might be in a spot of bother there, my lady,' he said, and he smiled such a warm, protective smile that Chloe knew everything was going to be all right.

The boy, whose name was Brandon Tuck, cut a way out of the hedge back to the garden. He took her hand and she followed obediently, eager to be free of that terrible place. She was taken aback when she saw that his calves were also covered in a light fur — though he wore short, dun-coloured breeches to cover himself — and that his legs ended in pointed hooves. He was embarrassed at her appraisal of him.

He shepherded her through the damp gardens at a steady pace, set on a known destination. He didn't speak but occasionally looked back to make sure she was okay and gave her one of his thrilling smiles.

Eventually they came to the very edge of the garden. Chloe could see a turret of the spring palace rising above. The familiarity of the building gave her comfort.

Brandon pointed. 'Here we are, my lady.'

Nestled on the edge of the garden was a redbrick cottage, with small wooden windows, a solid green door, and a chimney. Grey smoke plumed in the air and the scent gave Chloe an instant sense of goodness; this was a sanctuary.

'Who owns that?' she asked.

Brandon turned to her. 'It's my home, my lady. I live there with my father. He's the gardener.' He reached out for her hand again. 'I'll have him put on tea and we'll look at those cuts.'

Overwhelmed by a glowing, sleepy feeling, she let herself be led inside.

The cottage was exactly the sort of dwelling the Miss Chiefs had been trying to emulate, though it had a very different atmosphere. For one, there was a fire crackling in the corner. Its dancing light made the lacquered wooden walls glow and Chloe relaxed as heat seeped into her.

To her left was a lounge room, with a couch large enough to get lost in. To her right was a dining table with two thick nursery-like chairs, and on the table a steaming teapot and two cups painted with flower designs. There were paintings and lithographs of flowers — roses, hyacinth, African violets — in frames or on tables throughout the room. Shelves lined every wall, filled with gardening books. An archway in the centre led into the kitchen, from which delicious smells drifted. A staircase led to the bedrooms upstairs. It was such a picture, so quaint and comfortable, so much the opposite of the rundown palace that Chloe found herself smiling.

'Papa!' yelled Brandon as he motioned her in.

'Ah, you're back,' said a gruff voice from somewhere inside. 'There's tea on the table.'

'We have a guest.'

There was a surprised exclamation. 'Good lord!'

A tall, thin man wearing an overlarge checked shirt, blue overalls and grey woollen socks, rushed out from the kitchen, holding a spoon dripping something orange. He had messy black hair that stood up all over his head and a wiry moustache that moved when he spoke. He looked to Chloe like a kindly but mad professor, though he clearly had some of the same gentle features as Brandon, not least his large, expressive eyes. But where Brandon's were blue, his were a dark brown. He stopped when he saw Chloe and his eyebrows went up. Then he glanced at Brandon in admonishment. 'I thought you meant the Queen or the Spinster!' He eyed Chloe. 'Who's this, then?'

'I'm Chloe,' she said and then, perhaps because of the warmth, she felt dizzy, and put a hand to her head.

'Are you all right, young lady?' asked the man.

Brandon steadied her with a hand on her shoulder. 'No, she needs some of your special ointment, Papa.' His touch was tentative but assured. 'The Miss Chiefs had her in the hedge.'

The gardener frowned. 'Blasted girls, up to no good. Harassing everyone about their purpose, like irritating little security officers. I told the Spinster they should be locked up to save everyone a lot of trouble. But no; apparently we need disruptive elements. Keeps the system healthy, she says. Gives her something to do more like.' He huffed and stopped abruptly, realising he'd been complaining. 'But enough of my chatter.' He looked at Chloe's red weals. 'I'll get the ointment.'

A wave of dizziness passed through Chloe again and she stumbled. Brandon's firm hold kept her up. 'I … I think I need to sit down.'

He led her to the couch, where she sank into the fabric with relief. He then went to the table and poured her a cup from the steaming teapot. The sound of the splashing liquid was immensely comforting. He placed it in her hands and the warmth siphoned slowly into her. Her mother had always said, "There's nothing a good cup of tea won't cure." She sipped.

At the thought of her mother she felt sad. Her mother was gone. She was alone in the hard, selfish world, surrounded by people who wanted only to use her, make her conform to what they wanted. But that was the real world, not here, where the rules were so much more confusing. Even if the adults — most of the adults, she amended, thinking kindly of Brandon and his Papa — were the same.

Brandon gazed at her intently.

'I'm sorry,' she said. 'It must be the fire.'

'Oh no, that'll be Brandon's influence,' said the gardener, as he emerged from the kitchen holding a bottle of white ointment. He smiled, 'It's his enchantment, you see. It rubs off onto people when they're near.'

Chloe's eyes widened.

The gardener laughed. 'Don't worry. It doesn't harm. It's because of his innate goodness. The spell couldn't stop that. It makes everyone sleepy and trusting.'

Brandon had his head down, sheepish.

His Papa sat down next to Chloe. 'I keep telling him he should use it for nefarious ends, make the Queen fall in love with him, and convince her to let him travel beyond this season.' He registered Brandon's discomfort. 'But, see, he's too good for that, too.'

His eyes suddenly went wide with alarm. 'My goodness,' he said, 'we haven't been properly introduced. Where are my manners?' He reached out a hand. 'I'm Tom. Tom Tuck.'

Chloe shook his outstretched hand.

Tom held on to hers. 'Let's have a look at these cuts.' He gently took Chloe's arm, rolling back her sleeve. He winced when he saw what the Miss Chiefs had done, at the slashes of dried blood and the cuts from the thorns. He unstoppered the glass bottle. A pearlescent drop gathered at the mouth. He turned the bottle and let the drop fall onto her hand. He dabbed a finger in the milky ointment and began to delicately rub over all her cuts and abrasions. The liquid was oily on her skin and made her tingle. Already she could see it having an effect; the cuts lost their intense red and became, magically, a pale healing pink. She looked to

Tom, who was smiling beneficently at her. Brandon, too, gave her a look of reassurance. She felt luxuriously safe, and a hundred times better than she had in the garden. All her aches and pains ebbed away.

'That's amazing,' she said.

'The Duke makes it for me. He's an Alchemist, you see.' Tom studied her for a moment then decided to tell her. 'The Spinster lets me visit the autumn season, on occasion, to clip and prune the gardens at the Duke's castle. They are not as fine as the spring gardens, much too wild and grim. I'm always injuring myself, or the wood dryads are tricking me into nasty harmful games.

'The Duke, when he learned of this, invented an ointment for me, to heal my cuts and scrapes. He is a good man, despite his deviousness. And it is good to be able to see the other seasons first-hand.' Brandon hung his head, shame-faced. His father noticed and changed tack.

'There you go. All better.' He took her arm and gave it a small shake.

A sudden sharp pain made her gasp.

Tom frowned and inspected her arm. He took her elbow and slowly bent the forearm up. As it touched her shoulder she felt the pain stab her again. Tom gave her an enquiring look. 'Hmm. A break that hasn't healed perfectly. We shall have to keep an eye on that.'

Chloe was certain she had never broken her arm.

Before she could say so, Tom grinned. 'But you must be hungry. I was making pumpkin soup when you arrived. Pumpkins grown from the garden. You must have some.' He leapt up and went into the kitchen.

She turned to Brandon, whose mouth was downcast.

'You wanted to see the other seasons, too, didn't you?' It hadn't been difficult to guess that his enchantment was a punishment. 'Was it the garden that enchanted you?'

Brandon gave her a soulful look. 'It was the Spinster.'

Chloe was surprised, thinking the old woman an understanding type.

Brandon laughed ruefully. 'I tried to sneak across the seasonal barrier by hiding under one of her rolls of fat. I thought she would never know.'

Chloe smiled too. 'When was this?'

'Years ago, now.'

Chloe found herself becoming defensive. 'But that's unfair! Surely, you've been punished enough. You've learnt your lesson, haven't you?'

Brandon smirked. 'Perhaps.' Then he was serious. 'It wasn't the Spinster's fault. It was a spell that she had created as part of the security features, to stop people from crossing the barriers.' He frowned. 'It's a reminder that we can never leave, unless invited into the other seasons.'

A log settled in the fire; sparks fluttered up the chimney. It was becoming dark outside.

Chloe reached out a hand and placed it tenderly on his arm. 'Is there a way to reverse it?'

He was pleased at her touch. 'I suppose so. I mean, there must be. But the Spinster says she doesn't know how, or she isn't telling.'

Chloe was suddenly angry at his meek acceptance. 'It's ridiculous!' Brandon jerked at her raised voice. 'You're all enslaved by these rules and regulations, and as far as I can see they only work when the Spinster wants them to work.' She huffed in frustration. 'Everyone goes on about "the way this world works" and "keeping to the rules". Well, rules are made to be broken!'

'Is that what you think?' asked Tom, as he came through from the kitchen. He held a tray with three bowls of pumpkin soup, and three plates each with a steaming bread roll and a knob of butter. He set them down and the spicy, vegetable aroma played games with Chloe's senses. She realised that she hadn't eaten a thing today, after the aborted breakfast. She was famished.

'Yes, it is what *I* think,' she replied in a tone that brooked no argument.

But Tom shook his head. 'The seasonal rules are not decided on the Spinster's whim. This, my dear girl, is, unfortunately, a prison, and though it may not seem so, with its stereotypical seasons and its strange trappings, there are undesirable elements. Though they have been romanticised as kings and queens of their respective seasons, they are, still, criminals, despite what they may tell you. Each one is capable of the utmost harm and damage. We others have been put here to serve them and their environment, to make certain that they cannot ever commit this terrible crime again. It is not such a bad life.' Tom seemed happy with his lot and his fertile everyday existence. She was envious of that. Especially as hers was so muddled. For a moment, she thought he was going to add to this sobering statement, but he simply took up his spoon and slurped at his soup.

'Mm, it's good. Have some, have some.'

Chloe felt as though she had been cleverly talked down from a superior position and was annoyed. But she took up her spoon and began to eat. The soup was delicious, and it ran down her throat and made her stomach groan with pleasure. Realising how hungry she was, she decided to abandon her argument for the moment (despite knowing she was in the right).

She broke the crusty bread roll and it steamed pleasurably. She piled butter into the soft centre and watched it melt. Then she took a bite out of it. Butter dribbled down her chin.

Whether it was the gentle fire, the pleasure taken in fresh, tasty food, or the kindness of strangers, Chloe did not know, but at that moment she felt entirely happy.

Later, after the meal, Chloe asked Tom to tell her more of the world. They sat by the dimming fire and he told her about the wicked dryads in the autumn woods, and the generosity of the Duke; he told her of the rumours surrounding the evil Matriarch of Winter and how she ate the eyes of guests to see a way out of her season, only to be punished for it by the Spinster when she found her out. He told of the Karkarim — the metal eagles of summer, spies for the Summer King — and how it was said he was so large he had to be wheeled about in a bath all day by his servants to keep cool. He told her of the trains that ran through the seasons, always disguised, so people could only catch them at the Spinster's request. All these tales he told her and more, though as most of them were reported to him second hand she was to take them with a grain of salt. Her mind full of stories, and her stomach full of soup, Chloe found her eyes drooping. Tom noticed and wound up the tales. Though sleepy, Chloe did not want to lose the pleasure of the night and the company, and so mentioned the Queen's masquerade and made them promise to appear at the event. There was some fuss about the need for invitations, but Chloe, superior with fatigue, waved their objections aside. It was decided; she would arrange everything. But now she had to sleep.

'You can sleep in my bed,' Brandon said, offering it up without hesitation with one of his beautiful smiles.

Chloe knew she should be polite and object, but after today's events she was exhausted. She let herself be led up the wooden staircase to the bedroom. She took in that it was plainly a boy's room, full of wooden toys — trains and puppets and an astral mobile — before she gratefully flopped onto the single bed, closed her eyes and fell asleep.

Brandon removed her shoes and pulled the quilt over her. He reached out and gently stroked her face. Chloe murmured. Brandon watched her for a while, then, rummaging in an inside pocket of his jerkin, he pulled out Chloe's mirror. He peered into it but saw nothing now. He laid it carefully on the bedside table. She would be pleased to find it in the morning when she woke. 'Good night, my lady,' he whispered. 'Sweet dreams.'

He lingered a moment longer, wondering whether he should stay by her side, but then turned and went out, closing the door.

CHAPTER FIVE
THE MASQUERADE

The Queen's masquerade party was in full swing by the time Chloe made her entrance.

All day Chloe had watched from the staircase as clockwork servants went to and from the kitchens with platters of meats, cheeses or sweets. They set tables with delicate cutlery, and arranged flower displays in alcoves around the large ballroom, the roof of which had been shored up against the rain. They brought in tall candelabra to illuminate the room. Paintings of the Queen in various attitudes — in ball gown, hunting regalia, even a provocative nude — were hung in direct line of sight of the entry. A stage was erected at the far end of the room and a string quintet, immaculate in black dinner jackets, vests and bow ties, appeared late in the afternoon and began to warm up.

Four suckling pigs were assembled on spit-roasts at the side of the room, overseen by two fat cooks in white aprons. The heady smells emanating from the kitchens made Chloe's mouth water. It was going to be a night of decadence.

It was just after lunch when Tokka came to collect her from her lookout on the stairs. 'There you are, Chloe. TICK. It's time for you to change — TOCK — for tonight's performance.'

'Performance?' she asked, allowing herself to be led away.

Tokka's eyes went up in an amused expression. 'Of course. TICK. Everything is a performance to a drama queen. TOCK. I think I can give the Queen of Spring such a title.'

Chloe smiled, thinking it appropriate. 'You certainly can.' Remembering her promise, she asked, 'Have costumes been sent to Brandon and his father?' Tokka assured her they had.

Tokka took her back to the room she was beginning to believe was her own. She unfolded the wardrobe to display a selection of dresses. Many of them had not been there previously and Chloe wondered who arranged and organised the contents of the wardrobe. Eventually she chose a blue ensemble, a fitted blouse with frilled sleeves and a hoop skirt. The skirt was embroidered with gold stripes that made her seem much taller and more distinguished. At the Queen's request she had been allocated a necklace of diamonds surrounding a tiny mirror, to appear "less provincial." Chloe would have bridled at such condescension if the diamonds hadn't been so spectacular. They glittered expensively on her neck. She begrudgingly had to compliment the Queen on her good taste.

Her hair took more than two hours to style. Tokka first washed it, using a large porcelain bowl, then curled lengths of it with a heated iron. She then deftly wound these into tight buns. By the end, she looked a lot less like a little girl and far more mature and aristocratic. She topped the whole outfit off with an orange butterfly mask.

It was drifting into evening by the time she was ready to present herself to the Queen. She took the mirror along for comfort. (She had been overjoyed that morning to discover it by the bedside, and thanked Brandon for finding it. She felt disconnected without it, unable to believe in herself.) The woman in the mirror, however, stayed silent. Nevertheless, Chloe felt she needed it close, and found a place for it under her skirt, snapped to her thigh by tight elastic.

The Queen of Spring was in her chamber — the best-appointed room of the palace — gazing into her dresser mirrors. She measured every angle of her figure for imperfections. For a second there was something in the tilt of her head that reminded Chloe of her aunt when she dabbed perfume behind an ear. A jolt of unease went through her.

The door was open, so Chloe walked in. The Queen took a moment to notice her in the mirrors.

'Didn't your mother teach you to knock first?'

'Not when the door is open,' Chloe snapped. How dare the Queen speak ill of her mother.

'It's perfectly obvious that your mother didn't teach you any manners at all.'

Chloe glared.

Before she could argue the Queen said, 'Well then, come into the light and let us see you.'

Chloe stepped forward.

The Queen appraised her. Then she gave a quick clap. 'Excellent. You're much improved and eminently presentable to the masses. Appropriate for you to be a butterfly after such a transformation. It amazes me what Tokka can do.' Smirking at Chloe's ill-concealed annoyance, the Queen continued, 'Now go and amuse yourself for a while. I am not yet ready to face my guests. I have my Mask of Lies to fit. Tokka will collect you when the Spinster arrives.'

Chloe curbed her anger. It would do no good to provoke the Queen and ruin her own night of pleasure. She satisfied herself that the woman's time of embarrassment would come.

She turned to walk away.

The Queen pointedly cleared her throat.

Chloe faced her again and dragged out a smile. She bowed. 'Your Majesty,' she said, 'I shall leave you to put on your face.' Then she whispered, though it carried easily in the large chamber, 'Both of them.'

She returned to her lookout on the staircase. Guests began to arrive, coming in from the garden. Tokka told her that the Spinster had opened a gateway in the barrier to let the prisoners through, and that it was strictly marshalled. Chloe went down to the barrier to witness the first arrivals. Clockwork women (dull-grey versions made for the outdoors) clustered around the hedge, ticking in anticipation. As if at some determined hour, the hedge burst into life. A huge form, covered in ivy, pushed itself from the barrier, clanking noisily to the lawn. Behind the green disguise it sparkled silver. Chloe was amazed to see that it was a train. She remembered what Tom had told her the previous night. The Spinster must have sent this one to pick up the guests for the masquerade.

There was a thought at the back of her head that sounded like a bell. Something she should remember about trains. But try as she might it did not come to her. Instead, she focused on the guests. And what guests! There were wolfish, hairy creatures standing upright and growling every time they spoke. There were tiny dark men with turbans, and women in bright saris. There were stick-thin dryads made of oak, the whorls of age showing on their bodies. There were upright reptiles, their hides glistening. She felt dizzy with the spectacle. She followed them all back inside, taking a watchful perch on the staircase.

The string quintet played a moody pavane that relaxed her. A man dressed like a poet, in a green velvet frock coat and paisley cravat, danced abstractedly to the music.

The vast ballroom was now full of conversations and tinkling glasses. The waiters were painted red and naked but for a vine leaf. They carried drinks or hors d'oeuvres on their chests or heads, much to the amusement of the guests.

Expectation began to grow. It would soon be time for her entrance. Anxiety came over her. How would she be received? She hoped it was the Spinster and not the Queen who presented her to the guests. She'd feel more confident if Brandon and Tom were here. She had been keeping an eye out for them but had yet to see them arrive. Then again, she had not chosen their costumes, had left that decision to Tokka, so they could well be present, and she had not recognised them.

There was a peal of trumpets. The chatter and laughing faltered. The music slowed and petered out. Chloe peered through the bars of the staircase. The guests were looking upward, towards her! She realised there was a soft tinkling, like glass chinking together, on the edge of hearing. Turning, she followed the eyes of every guest to the large mirror at the centre of the staircase. It shimmered like liquid, and a picture was appearing from within. Chloe smiled; it was the Spinster, she was sure of it.

A pure note was building in the hall, coming from the mirror. Each guest calmly watched as the glass bulged and a Spinster-shaped figure stepped out, shimmering with silver. As the glass split, a note of such intensity resounded in the room that it made everyone feel a brief potent happiness. But Chloe stopped smiling when she saw that the figure was two-dimensional. Something had gone wrong. As the note faded, there was an inelegant sound like a belch, and the figure ballooned into fatness. The silver gloss drained to reveal the Spinster's ancient features and her rolls of fat, primped into the very image of a ball gown. Her red stilettos and her red lips were prominent, as was her white beehive. She patted her hair into place and, lifting her opera glasses to peer at the crowd, gave a small curtsey.

The guests applauded her impressive entrance.

'Thank you, thank you,' said the Spinster, appreciatively. 'Welcome   friends, creatures, servants, and royal heads of the seasons. I shan't make a big speech for this is the Queen's party and I shall let her greet you. But I do wish to remind you that all animosities should be put aside whilst here, and that anyone who breaks the rules of this temporary accord shall have me to deal with. Though my exterior may seem a kindly old woman, I can devise the most terrible of punishments.' The crowd was subdued by her seriousness. 'But now, please drink up and be merry, and enjoy yourselves!'

The guests gave her light applause then turned to their drinks and conversations. The quintet began to play something sprightly.

The Spinster smiled at her subjects and then looked up at Chloe. Her glance was shrewd — a woman in charge. She stepped up the marble stairs to the girl. 'Well, my dear, you certainly seem regal in that dress. I'm sure your introduction will be a great success.'

With that acknowledgement Chloe became worried. With her introduction she might be ensnared by the season, might become a prisoner like all the others. She blurted out, 'Spinster, how are your investigations going? Have you discovered why I'm here?'

The Spinster gazed at her gently. 'You are not a prisoner, Chloe. There is no need for you to be concerned on that count.'

'But have you? Tell me, Spinster.'

The wise woman pursed her lips together, thinking, and made a decision. 'Very well, you have a right to know what I believe, if only for your own safety.'

'Safety?' she replied, alarmed.

The Spinster sighed. 'I have gone through the recent dailies, all those that may have recorded your arrival. I have found nothing, nothing at all. I considered that the recording devices may have been faulty but discovered since that everything is and was previously working. There is not a single record of your entrance into any of the four seasons.'

'Then how did I get here?'

The Spinster became guarded. 'As I did not sanction your arrival, I believe that someone else has lured you here through an unknown Backstage Door.' She bent down to Chloe and whispered, 'I believe that you have come here at the instruction of The Man with 8 Faces.'

Chloe blinked. 'Who's he?'

The Spinster's eyes were dark. 'He is an upstart, a nuisance, a man who delights in trouble, confusion and chaos. He is a subversive, theatrical player who loves to cause mischief and disruption to the seasons.'

'Can't you imprison him?' Chloe asked.

The Spinster laughed humourlessly. 'I would indeed, if I could catch him. He is a master of disguise. One never knows whose character he has appropriated. Somehow, he simply arrived, as you did, without an entrance, and has been a thorn in my side ever since.

'First, it was just silly games. He would open a rent from summer into winter and cause a lake to melt or bring icy rain to the hottest day in summer. But now he has begun to steal personalities and use them as skins to infiltrate the seasons and corrupt their rules from within.

'He is planning something against me. I know it.'

'And you think I have something to do with him?!' asked Chloe, distressed.

'My dear, I know you are innocent. But your entrance has caused some disruption, which is exactly what he would do. He may have some use for you that you do not know of, which is why it is safer for you to integrate with the season and obey the rules. Which is why tonight is important.'

A weight settled upon Chloe. She felt herself part of something larger than she had comprehended. The description of the Man with 8 Faces alarmed and excited her. Someone who could steal a personality and step into it like a costume was someone who was unidentifiable. She was thrilled that the Spinster's barriers could be overcome; it meant there was a way out. If this man had brought her into the season, perhaps he could get her out?

'Please, Chloe, I do not want you to worry. I didn't tell you this to frighten you. You are perfectly safe here, with me, tonight.' She paused. 'But just in case, always ask a stranger's name. The Man cannot take over a personality so completely until he has the name. It is the hardest part to own.' She leaned down and spoke quietly. 'If the stranger cannot immediately give you his name ...' She straightened. 'Beware!'

Realising she had created an air of anxiety, she smiled. 'Now, come along. It's time Columbine made her entrance. She lingers too long to make herself presentable. And the sooner this is over, the sooner you can enjoy the party.' The Spinster took her hand and slowly they made their way up the staircase.

It took forever for the Queen to descend from her bedchamber. She refused to be rushed by the Spinster. When she did she was wearing her Mask of Lies, a porcelain likeness of herself that changed emotion like the theatrical Janus face. Chloe wasn't sure if it represented her true feelings. It was eerie to watch the porcelain move after the Queen had smiled or frowned beneath it. She clearly wanted to remain aloof and superior to her guests.

Her presence — after four hours of the festivities had passed — was greeted by a cheer. Trumpets sounded, and the Queen drew herself to her full height to make her speech.

'My dear friends, welcome to my modest little party.' Her guests tittered. 'It is so rare that we are allowed such a decadent pleasure, and I thank the Spinster for arranging this.' The Spinster gave a mild bow. 'But tonight is not simply an occasion for pleasure. I have with me a guest who has come from a season outside the prison ...' She let the statement hang and her guests oohed with wonder. She gestured for Chloe to come down from her position on the staircase.

With each step, Chloe felt human eyes and reptile eyes and hungry wolfish eyes rove over her and appraise her strangeness. She felt as though she were walking up to the front of a school assembly and everyone was waiting for her to trip. She concentrated on getting to the Queen's side. The Queen's mask turned slowly into a smile, which was probably a lie. She took Chloe's hand, squeezing it uncomfortably hard.

'I present to you, prisoners and servants of the four seasons, Chloe Susannah Alexandra Jane ...' She stopped, gave a noise of embarrassment, and glanced down at Chloe.

'Hattersley,' Chloe finished, unimpressed.

The Queen's mask frowned. 'Hattersley!' she cried. She raised Chloe's arm in victorious mimicry.

There was a deluge of applause and whistles and mutterings. Chloe felt approval flow through the audience, and she gave them one of her meek smiles.

'I am certain she will amuse,' finished the Queen. 'Now, please, enjoy the delicacies and drink, for the night is young and we should be decadent and indulge in all its pleasures before its end.' The guests cheered at her encouragement, and the party started up again.

As soon as attention was diverted from her, the Queen threw off her hold of Chloe's hand. 'There, they have accepted you. You are now one of my subjects. Go now and do as you wish.' She waved Chloe away, snatching a champagne flute from a waiter.

And just like that Chloe belonged to the prison season of spring. After such anticipation it was an anti-climax to be thrust aside. She wondered whether she should be pleased or upset.

Chloe wandered the incandescent ballroom, watching the masquerade play itself out. She drank a number of flutes of what turned out to be honeyberry wine and became tipsy. Everything was pleasant and softened.

The man on the dance floor winked at her and she smiled in return, but she didn't feel like dancing. She saw Tokka across the room, but the clockwork woman was overseeing events in the kitchens and did not smile back. She searched the room for Brandon and finding no one who could be him, felt hurt that he had not come. She caught the eye of the Miss Chiefs, who'd wandered in from the garden and looked to be up to no good. They gave her unkind sneers. She watched the Spinster introduce various guests to the Queen — a Viceroy with a gold turban so fat on his head it seemed he'd tip over; a lean wolfman who wore a red cape and carried a cherub mask; a skeletal man in a tuxedo with a plate of glass for a head that showed clouds; a squat woman with a dress like an icicle, and a machine connected to her that occasionally puffed out mist, presumably to keep her cool in the warm room.

Though people had shown curiosity toward her, no one had spoken to her. At first, she thought it was deliberate, but the guests smiled courteously when she went by. Yet every time she went close, with the intention of starting a conversation, they turned away. She felt rejected, so drank more honeyberry wine, which made her tipsier.

The great noise of the masquerade and the strangeness of the creatures, and their curious yet aloof glances, began to press upon Chloe. She felt nauseous and searched out a lounge, one of those at the edge of the room where guests reclined and chatted.

She took off her butterfly mask and took in deep breaths and, after a moment, felt better. Realising she still held the glass of honeyberry wine, she put it down on the table in front of her. No more of that.

As she did so, she registered that there was a figure seated beside her. She had not heard him sit. She was relieved to see that it was the man in the green velvet jacket, who had been dancing, who had smiled at her.

'I'm curious,' he said, parting thin pink lips.

Chloe blinked to clear the fug from her head. 'Curious?' she asked.

'Why have you not introduced yourself?'

'I ... I didn't know I had to.'

He was amused. 'The Queen did not tell you, then?'

Chloe frowned at this, another of the Queen's attempts to confuse and belittle her.

'I did try,' she said. 'But they were all so rude and

turned their backs.'

'Perhaps you frighten them,' he suggested. 'After all, you don't come from here.'

'No,' she said. 'I come from … somewhere else.' Sadness entered her: this man was right; she did not belong here, despite the Spinster's efforts to assure the people that she was no danger.

Chloe looked at the man beside her, noticing the gleam in his eyes from the candlelight, the way his long dark hair framed his pale features. 'Why aren't you frightened of me?' she asked.

He smiled again. 'You are just a girl, a little lost now, but I'm certain you will soon find your purpose.'

'Purpose,' she said, annoyed. 'Why is it so important that everyone should have one here?'

He leaned forward, and the lounge's leather creaked. 'Look out there,' he gestured at the masquerade, where the guests ate and danced and chatted in a great cacophony. 'What do you see?'

Chloe, head full of cotton wool, didn't see his meaning.

'Theatre,' he explained. 'And everyone must have a role to play, whether it is to rule, as the Queen nominally does, or to ensure security, as the Spinster would have you believe, or to serve, as the clockwork women do.' He slid closer along the leather and it squeaked again. He spoke low: 'Some of us are required to create the drama — a little conflict, a smidgen of chaos.'

Chloe turned to him, catching his eye. 'Do you mean me?'

The corners of his mouth turned up. 'Perhaps. For the Spinster, it is especially worrying for a person to appear without an obvious reason for existence.' He flared his eyes. 'I hear you didn't make an entrance at all.'

'I woke up in an upstairs bedroom,' said Chloe.

'You woke up ...' he said. 'But where did you fall asleep?'

Shockingly, Chloe could not remember. Had she simply fallen asleep in the upstairs bedroom? Did she truly belong here? Why could she not remember? She hoped that it was only the intense, syrupy wine that was befuddling her senses and not some magic of the season. Were the rules seeking to classify and catalogue her, give her a motive, a reason, a character?

The velvet man saw her worry. 'It's all the more worrying after this business with the Man with 8 Faces.'

Catching on his name, Chloe asked, 'Who is he? How did he get here?'

'No one knows. He appeared in much the same manner that you have. So you see why there is some caution around guests?'

'But I'm not like that at all.'

'Of course not, I can see that,' he murmured gently. 'Let's not discuss such irksome things.' He presented her with his palm. 'Please, will you take a dance with me?'

Though she wasn't certain it was a good idea, her head thick and her stomach roiling, she placed her hand in his. He led her onto the dance floor. He whirled her about as the quintet played a reel, a jig, then a dirge that made her want to collapse into deep slumber. The man in green velvet held her, one hand upon her back, and his eyes held hers throughout each dance. The people and creatures watched them avidly, until there were only eyes and eyes and eyes.

Exhausted, her head pounding, she extricated herself from his grasp.

'Are you all right, my dear?'

'I need some fresh air.'

That was only the half of it. The air was too warm,

the light too soft and unfocused, the dresses rustling on the dance floor were putting her to sleep. Beneath all that, she felt that something was wrong.

The velvet man insisted all she needed was another dance. But she did not want to dance anymore, and quickly threw off his reaching hand, running from the room.

Chloe pushed open the terrace doors and went out into the cold night.

The garden had undergone a change for the Queen's masquerade. Many of the plantings had been cut back so that a parterre lawn was revealed. This was furnished with steel benches, and poles were planted around the lawn with lanterns atop. They gave off a fogged glow.

She had been shocked by the velvet man's insinuation: that perhaps she did belong here and was simply confused. She racked her brain as to where she had fallen asleep; she was almost sure that it hadn't been upstairs. But almost wasn't good enough.

The night suited her mood. The rain poured down, saturating her, ridding her of tiredness, making her head clearer. It struck every plant in the garden. She looked up. Far off, toward autumn, there was lightning, then sky-cracking thunder. Grey clouds massed. A wind was coming, tunnelling through the garden, fluttering leaves, slanting the rain. The palace waterfalls would be great deluges now, spilling across the floors. She hoped the plugs in the ballroom roof held. An image of the soaked queen flashed through her mind and made her smile.

A sudden gust of wind blew her over.

There was a muffled voice from within her gown. She had forgotten she still carried the mirror! She stuck a hand down her dress and rummaged, finding it stuffed in the elastic waistband of her petticoat. The woman in the mirror was annoyed when Chloe looked into the glass. She almost expected her to spit fabric.

'I thought you'd forgotten about me,' said Chloe, delighted to have her friend back.

'Quite the opposite,' the woman snapped. 'You'd forgotten about me. You'd become too involved, ensnared by the season. I warned you about that.' Her tone was stern, that of a teacher reproaching an inattentive student.

'I'm sorry,' replied Chloe. 'I didn't realise.'

'We need one another more than you might think.'

But Chloe suddenly snapped, 'Stop that! I'm fed up with your cryptic statements. I'm fed up with everything about this season! The Spinster says one thing, you say another. I want to see Aunt Lavinia. I wouldn't even mind seeing Dad. Am I ever going to get back?' Abruptly she burst into tears. She had been trying to hold it in, trying not to show how afraid and frustrated she felt, but it was no good.

'There, there. Let it out. There's nothing wrong with a good cry, my dear. But you must never forget about me.'

There was a soft tap on her shoulder. Startled, she leapt out of her grief. Standing behind her, gazing at her fondly, was Brandon. He was dressed as a woodcutter, in baggy green overalls and a red-checked flannelette shirt. His horns and hooves were not so incongruous in this natural wood costume.

Yet her vulnerability made her defensive. 'Where the hell have you been?' she yelled.

He took a step back and frowned. 'I'm sorry. I tried to get here earlier. There was a disturbance at the spring/autumn seasonal barrier. I had to go and help Papa.' He smiled one of his disarming smiles.

Chloe chewed her lip, not wanting him to get the better

of her. But those eyes were too innocent and warm to pour scorn on. After a pause she asked, 'Disturbance?'

Seeing she was intrigued, Brandon explained. 'It was amazing,' he started. 'Somehow the Spinster's gate was corrupted, and autumn was leaking through into spring!' He raised his eyebrows. 'It even affected the wind. It's been blowing a gale. Didn't you feel the force of it just now?'

'Yes. I thought it was normal.'

'Absolutely not. The Spinster arrived and everything! She had to summon up a spell to stop all the fuss. The hedge maze was thrashing, and the wind kept blowing us all over. It was really scary but really exciting, too.' He leaned inward, secretly. 'During it all the Spinster dropped her eyeglasses.' He produced her opera glasses from a pocket of his overalls and waved them about.

'Dropped?' asked Chloe.

Brandon averted his eyes. 'Yes.'

'Ha!'

'It's true!' He glanced quickly at her. 'I only want to borrow them.'

'Why?'

He smiled at her and, disturbingly, she felt soft and compliant, like a flower bending to his hand. 'I want to show you the way out of spring.'

She grabbed Brandon's hand, looked him in the eye and said: 'Show me.'

They ran through the garden, happily getting mud-splashed. Their clothes were soaked to the skin, their hair plastered to their foreheads. The broad-leaved plants nodded at them as they dashed by.

Chloe, still tipsy, staggered after Brandon, who led her down paths only he could see. The garden heaved around her in the dark, like a malevolent presence. But she wasn't frightened; Brandon was a protective figure before her. She was exhilarated by the experience. Perhaps it was because of the drink, but she marvelled at how flighty she could be with her changing moods. Appropriate for such a season, she thought. And then was immediately worried that she had thought to equate herself with the season yet again. She remembered what the mirror had said. Concentrate on running, she thought to herself — the wind in her hair, the cool rain on her brow. She let Brandon lead her to the edge of the season.

There ...

There was no deliberate gateway into autumn, no shimmering porthole. She only knew it was the gateway due to the grey clockwork servants clustered around the hedge. They had shepherded the guests into the masquerade and remained to police the barrier in case anything undesirable attempted to come through.

Brandon handed her the Spinster's glasses. 'Look,' he said.

She put the all-seeing glasses to her eyes and gasped. It was as though she had a compound eye and could see in four directions at once. Directly in front she saw the hedge in spring. But beyond that, as though the horizon had been brought forward, and lay a yard or two away, she saw the shimmering edge of the autumn forests. Her peripheral vision was screaming for her attention and she knew that if she turned right she would see the frozen lakes of winter. If she turned left she would see summer dunes. The glasses should have disconcerted her, but she had an immediate aptitude with them. A part of her mind was worried at that but was quickly overruled by awe. The Spinster truly could see everything.

And before her, in front of the clockwork servants, she could see the place where she might step through and into the autumn storm. The temptation was like a hook pulling irresistibly at her. She took three steps forward. A clockwork servant stopped her. Chloe reluctantly removed the opera glasses, and everything spread back into place like a jumbled puzzle suddenly smoothed out and completed. The sense of disappointment was, for a moment, breathtaking.

She turned to Brandon and was enveloped in his smile. 'See,' he said.

Chloe registered the firm hand on her shoulder. 'I must ask you — TICK — not to venture any further. You do not have the requisite permission — TOCK — to enter the autumn season.'

'How do you know I don't?' she asked.

'The Spinster has imbued me with the necessary means — TICK — to recognise the proper codes of ingress and egress. TOCK. You do not have the code for proper entry — TICK — into the autumn season. TOCK.' Its clockwork features ground into a frown. 'In fact, you do not possess the correct codes — TICK — for residency within the spring season. TOCK.' Its hold tightened on her shoulder.

Brandon leapt to her defence. 'She is a guest of the Queen of Spring!' he cried, taking hold of the clockwork servant's arm. 'She has all the rights of residency whilst in this season because of such a status.'

The clockwork woman ticked over for a moment. Then, seemingly mollified by the truth of his statement, let Chloe go.

'Apologies, my lady,' the woman said. 'But there have been a number — TICK — of illegal people trying to — TOCK — enter the season tonight.'

'Really? What happened?'

The clockwork woman's face clicked and ratcheted, as though processing whether she should tell. Then she said, 'A guest tried to enter the season without the proper — TICK — invitation. He was turned into topiary — TOCK.'

Seeing her chance to learn something, Chloe asked, 'How do you know who has permission to come into the spring season? I mean, you must have some way of discovering which guests have been invited to the masquerade ...'

The clockwork woman ratcheted. 'Of course. TICK. Invitations were issued with a vial — TOCK — containing one hundred and one drops of spring rain. TICK. Guests were to drink this — TOCK — and the seasonal barrier verified their veracity as they arrived.'

'So the weather disturbance ... was it that a guest was trying to attend without an invitation?'

The grey woman click-clacked: a sound that emulated wariness. 'TICK. How do you know of the prior disturbance? TOCK.'

'It's a small season,' replied Chloe smartly.

'The gateway was breached,' stated the servant, matter-of-fact.

Chloe licked her lips and said, carefully, 'Was it the Man with 8 Faces?'

There was a pause. The clockwork woman looked gravely at the little girl. 'The Spinster — TICK — seemed to think so.'

Brandon touched her on the shoulder. 'Be careful, my lady. He could still be around.'

'It's okay, Brandon,' she said, reassuring him, only to throw him with her next comment, 'I want to meet him.' She felt a shiver go down her spine, as though her wish had circumvented a rule and allowed a meeting to take place that never should have.

The air became suddenly still

The clockwork woman clicked rapidly upright and began to scan the hedge maze to either side of her. 'The barrier is —'

That was all she said before a twiggy claw erupted from the hedge, wrapped itself around her body and pulled her into the maze. There was a shower of ripped leaves about them. The other clockwork servants clustered around the hole and raised their hands, as though to ward off evil. Chloe remembered the patterns on Tokka's hands.

Chloe felt a gentle tug on her very being that was not unpleasant. Following instinct, she walked quickly through the entrance of the hedge into the maze. Brandon shouted at her, but his voice was dim and insubstantial behind her. She must be passing through the seasonal barrier. She was on a threshold where the two seasons were striving to become one — spring rain lashed the hedge and autumn wind drove it back. The cloudy autumn sky seeped into spring. All this was happening around her while she remained in a bubble of calm.

She could feel eyes on her.

'Show yourself!' she cried.

The hedge burst outward with a terrible splintering and woody claws reached for her. Not expecting this, Chloe screamed and turned to run, only to find that something was still connected to her and pulling her forward. As the claws jaggedly embraced her, a voice commanded, 'Stop!' and they halted.

A figure came out of the shadows. Chloe saw his eyes first. They were eyes quite inimical to kindness, drinking her in like prey. The shadows spilled from him as though he had been covered in a cape of them. For a terrible moment she thought it was her father — that arrogant strut, that disdain. But then he moved into the light. It was the man from the dance floor, with the long hair, the poet's face and the velvet jacket. But he was so changed as to make Chloe think him a completely different person. Perhaps he was, she mused, remembering the stories of how the Man with 8 Faces could steal people's skins and 'inhabit' them. Perhaps the man on the dance floor had been his mask for the night, his lie. There was nothing kind about him now.

He stopped an arm's length from her and smiled. Chloe shivered at the intent in that smile.

'Are you the Man with 8 Faces?' she boldly asked.

'I am a man,' he said, and his voice was like silk. 'I have but this face … Chloe.'

As he spoke her name a spiral of fear went through her. She was certain she had heard his voice before. It made her think of dark woods and cold water. There was something incomplete about him, as though he was only covered with a thin sheen of respectable humanity.

'Did you bring me here?' she demanded.

His eyes blazed. 'Here? Now? Yes.'

'Why?'

He smiled coldly. 'You're the key. You break all the rules.' The hedge-claws clattered in anticipation of attack. 'I'd like you to be part of my new play.'

Chloe glared at him. 'I don't think so.'

The man locked her gaze in deadly earnest and declaimed:

'This is not something I would ask,
I want you for my greatest mask.
With no crime, you have no flaw,
And thus, can find the Backstage Door …'

His rhyme dazzled Chloe for a moment, but it also

made him childish and ridiculous. She laughed.

The Man frowned, furious to be mocked by a powerless slip of a girl. He reached out, and as though she were on an invisible wire she was instantly pulled to him.

She tried to drag her feet in the mud but there was a desire within her that made her body bend to his whim. He gripped her hard when she was within his grasp, twisting her arm so that a brittle pain shot through her bones. There was a memory that went with the pain, and it had to do with the Man. It was as though they were connected, there at her right arm, her right hand.

He caressed her cheek. She cried out and now he laughed.

'Take her,' he commanded and stepped away, though she still found herself held in the air by his magic.

The wooden claws wavered and then the hedge bulged, and the claws became hands, then arms, and finally four figures pushed outwards into strange existence. They were skeletal thin, their faces smooth and oval, bobbing like moons. Their bodies were twisted and inelegant, branches shoved together in crude approximation of a humanoid form. One of them brushed past the Man as it stepped from the hedge and it began to change, cloth flowing over it, becoming pants, frilled shirt, velvet jacket, until it was dressed in exactly the same style as him.

The four figures reached out for Chloe, their twig fingers scratching her skin. As they touched her they began to change. She felt pieces of herself snatched away, as though she were being pulled apart from the inside out. Memories swirled and ripped away.

… her mother, lying in bed, her breaths so small; the long black box; the red dress she wore to the school play; her aunt's secret smile behind her sad mask; her father's hand like a claw on her arm. A look; a touch; a growing anger inside her ... a journey to the cold north ...

The figures' sharp features began to blur and smooth, turn flesh-coloured. Twigs became eyes, an ear, a mouth. She recognised the colour of her own eyes on the new face before her. When she realised what was happening, she went to scream. But she no longer had a mouth.

A voice, somewhere nearby, shouted, 'Chloe!'

Who was Chloe? There was a vibration from her skirt. She pulled out the mirror. There was an old woman in it.

'Quickly, Chloe, point me toward the Blank!'

Oh, that's right, she thought, *I'm* Chloe.

The Man tried to grab the mirror but Chloe — somehow knowing what the old woman meant by Blank — thrust the glass right into the face of the creature that was now half-wood, half-Chloe. The Blank looked into the mirror and hissed as its features drained away to become smooth again. The Man snarled in anger. Striding forward he reached out and snatched the mirror from her. But all her features had returned, her character was no longer in doubt. She could breathe again.

Before anything else could happen, a bright light erupted on the scene. The stillness of the threshold was broken, and violent winds and rain poured in.

An ancient voice said, 'That's quite enough of that.'

The Man looked up, annoyed.

Chloe was snatched from his hold and pulled roughly back into a soft pillow. Glancing up she saw the Spinster looking down upon her. She was lying in the folds of the old woman's skin. The Spinster gently extricated her.

The Man with 8 Faces sneered. 'My dear Spinster,' he said, and somehow his mellifluous tones carried through. 'You were almost too late.'

'This is one game you're not going to win,' she snapped.

'This isn't a game and you know it.'

'It's always been a game to you,' said the old woman. 'You always want to better me.'

'Better you!' he cried angrily. 'I want what you denied me!'

The Spinster stared at him coldly. 'You shall never have what you want whilst I still live.'

The Man gave her a cocky smile. 'You won't kill me, Valinia,' he said, the familiar use of her name startling both the Spinster and Chloe.

The Spinster glanced over her shoulder and nodded.

Brandon came out from behind her, carrying a tapered glass bottle. It held a bright, throbbing light.

The Man's eyes went up.

Brandon threw it.

It passed through the barrier and broke at the Man's feet. A light bloomed that was so intense everyone had to shut their eyes. They felt the heat from the spring side of the barrier. But the Spinster peered through her returned eyeglasses at the light and spoke a single word. Chloe heard the Man cry out. The light faded. They were all slightly pink with sunburn.

The Spinster stepped forward. There was a solemn moment when nobody spoke. Then the old woman frowned. 'Blast!'

Chloe looked. She found she had suddenly acquired the ability to see the edges of the barrier, shimmering and sheer as a beetle's wings. Beyond it, in the autumn maze, the hedge-claws had twisted to form a wooden cage. But inside the cage there was only a limp skin, like a deflated balloon, with blank eyeholes and long brown hair. It was draped with a velvet jacket.

The Spinster turned to Chloe and looked her over carefully. 'I'm sorry,' she said.

Brandon touched her shoulder. 'Are you all right?' he asked. She felt his concern pour through her.

But amidst her tired, confused thoughts there was one that shone out. She had to let the Spinster know. Chloe looked up, into the wise features of this woman wed to the seasons, and said, 'I know what my purpose is. I know why I'm here.'

CHAPTER SIX
THE FACE LIKE A CITY

'How dare you! You awful girl, causing a death in my palace!'

The Queen of Spring was putting on another performance. She blazed down upon Chloe, her eyes sharp.

'Calm down, Columbine,' said the Spinster.

'Calm down! *You* told me her disruption could be controlled. And look what has happened — she brought *that* man into my palace, and murder has been committed. I shall be spurned for months.'

Chloe was woken by Tokka. She came to groggily, her head pounding with the after-effects of something that hadn't been honeyberries. The clockwork woman asked her downstairs, where the Spinster and the Queen required her presence. Her manner was formal and subdued. The golden woman helped Chloe dress and shepherded her through the palace. Chloe asked, 'Are you all right, Tokka?' The clockwork woman nodded, urging her on.

Of course, she knew now why her behaviour had been so cautious. She was to be blamed for another crime she had not committed. In her current state, with her head throbbing like an engine, she couldn't have been more irritated by the Queen's claims of murder.

She gritted her teeth during the woman's tirade but could stand it no longer. The anger shot up her throat. 'Oh shut up, you dreadful woman! How dare you blame me when you haven't got any proof!' She paused for breath.

'You're useless! You have no idea what is going on, and at least now I do! All you do is screech about how everything disrupts your day. I did not murder this person, and until you find evidence that I did, stop blaming me for all your problems!'

She had aimed her rage at the Queen. Now she took note of the effect of her words. The Queen was still as a statue, her eyes wide as though she had been struck. The air vibrated with tension.

The Spinster placed a hand on Chloe's shoulder. 'That's enough,' she said in a stern tone, but she did not mean it.

The Queen took advantage of the pause. She swung round and slapped Chloe across the face.

Chloe felt a sharp pain on her cheek and fell to the floor at the force of the blow. Instinct, after shock, told her to play it for all it was worth. She sniffed and let the tears flow.

The Spinster, quick as a magician, took one of the vials from her neck and, speaking a strange word, threw the contents at the Queen. A blue gel splashed her face. The effect was immediate: her arms were pinioned to her sides; every part but her eyes was stilled. 'That was utterly uncalled for, Columbine!'

The Queen tried to speak but her lips were pressed together by the spell. Chloe stopped crying and sniffed away her tears. She glanced at the Queen and, without the Spinster seeing, smirked. The Queen's eyes flared.

The Spinster said to Chloe, 'I'm sorry, my dear. I sometimes forget that Columbine is a criminal and is capable of harm.'

For a moment, Chloe considered continuing the act. But she played it straight. 'I honestly didn't have anything to do with the death.'

The Spinster sighed and patted her shoulder. 'I know that, my dear.' Her brow furrowed, 'Though, once again, I'm sorry to say that the death has come about from your presence here. We know the Man with 8 Faces wants you, and we know he will use his Blanks to infiltrate and lie to get to you. We may have stripped him of one skin — the man in velvet — but he can still inhabit the skin he jumped into, our dead guest, and undermine us from within this very season!'

'But surely it's simple?' asked Chloe. 'When this dead guest turns up we know it's not him but the Man, and you can trap him.'

The Spinster was silent for a while, and when she spoke it was with a weariness that was disheartening. 'It isn't simple at all, Chloe. The Man covers his tracks well — we have no idea who the deceased guest is.'

'So he could be here now and we *wouldn't know*?'

The Spinster nodded solemnly.

'No. I don't believe it. There must be a way to discover who this guest is. Isn't everything recorded here?'

The Spinster's attention was piqued. 'The dailies? I suppose they may have recorded something. I'm only doubtful because I know the Man of old.' She clapped her hands together. 'Yes. Yes! It's worth a try.'

Chloe smiled. The Spinster returned the smile. A measured smile, thought Chloe, could get you anything.

'What about her?' asked Chloe, motioning to the irate queen.

'It'll wear off shortly.'

'She'll be even more furious when it does.'

The Spinster grinned in complicity. 'Yes, she will,' she replied. 'So we best solve the whole annoying puzzle before she's free.'

She took Chloe's hand and led her into the secret depths of the palace.

They travelled staircases that descended deep into the earth. Flambeaux lit the darkness. Their shadows flickered like moths on the stone walls.

'Where are we going?' asked Chloe, her curiosity giving way to trepidation.

'Down,' replied the Spinster. She held tight to Chloe's hand.

'Down?'

'That's where the morgue is,' said the Spinster. Chloe frowned; the Spinster noticed. 'This *is* a prison. Some of my charges are here for life. All eventualities are catered for.'

They went down, step after step after step, until, finally, Chloe felt flat stone beneath her feet. The Spinster let go of her hand. Instantly cut off, Chloe felt the blackness close in. The Spinster spoke a word in the dark — '*Illumine.*' Flambeaux flared around the edges of the room.

Chloe looked up, and up. They were in a grey stone chamber. The walls were indented with hundreds of square-shaped holes that looked to go up forever. In the lower squares, she could see skeletal remains. Beyond the chamber she could feel a gentle air flow and sensed that tunnels wormed through the darkness. It was not simply a morgue, but great and ancient catacombs. The prison had been here for a long time. Chloe shivered.

In the centre of the chamber were three stone slabs. Two were empty. On the middle slab was an ugly, misshapen body. No attempt had been made to cover it. The Spinster took Chloe's hand and led her towards it.

'I thought we were going to look at the dailies?' she asked. There was something wrong about the shape of the body that scared her.

'Afterwards,' replied the Spinster. 'I need you to have a look at this.'

'Why? I didn't murder him!'

'So it was a him then?'

'What? No!' Chloe pulled her hand from the Spinster's. 'Are you trying to trick me?'

The Spinster gazed kindly at her. 'My dear Chloe, I know that you didn't murder this person. I'm simply hoping that since the death was, in a sense, caused by your presence in the season, that bringing you here might spark some latent remembrance.'

Chloe narrowed her eyes. 'Why would I remember something I didn't do?'

The Spinster sighed. 'Out by the spring barrier, the Man sampled you. You're linked to him. You may feel some of the things that he has done.'

She remembered the cold, numbing feeling she'd had when the Blanks tried to erase her. She wondered what sort of link she had with the Man with 8 Faces. Would he know what she was thinking now? Could he get into her thoughts and puppet her? She shivered at such terrible ideas.

'I ... I've never seen this before,' said the Spinster, gazing warily at the body. 'The hollow he leaves behind. He usually hides it too well. He only wants the skin, you know. Rips it from you. You become nothing ... Blank.' The Spinster blinked out of her reverie. 'Please, Chloe. Will you have a look?'

And then Chloe realised how powerless the Spinster felt. The Man with 8 Faces had easily penetrated her season. Not a single alarm had gone off. She was worried. The least she could do, after the Spinster's kindness toward her, was to try and help.

She went to look at the body.

It was wrong. Though the general shape was humanoid, the fingers, the toes, the limbs, the torso, everything was just a little too elongated. The body was made of compacted mud, as though it were a golem—a base structure for character to be imprinted upon. But it was the face that was most disturbing. All normal features were gone. Instead, tall spikes rose from it. Looking closer, Chloe made out a design to the spikes. Some were squat, others tall and long, others had cupolas or domes or spires. Chloe looked at the Spinster, who was standing there, her features set in worry.

'It's a city,' she said.

'What is a city?' asked the Spinster.

Chloe was taken aback at the question. 'Surely you know.'

'No. I do not,' replied the Spinster tartly.

Perhaps they don't have cities here, she thought.

'A city is ... a large place with lots of people ... who

live there. You know … with suburbs and shops and houses. There are poor areas and rich areas, and places to buy food and clothes …' She trailed off at the Spinster's uncomprehending expression.

'We have only the palaces and the seasons here,' said the old woman, simply. 'There is nothing else.'

'Then you're right,' said Chloe, disheartened. 'This must be because of me. I'm the only one who knows about cities here.' Shadows rippled across the hideous body and made her shiver. All of a sudden, she had an idea. 'I wonder …'

The Spinster heard the hope in her voice. 'Yes?'

'If the Man can rub off onto me, I suppose that I can rub off onto the Man.'

'It's certainly possible,' agreed the Spinster.

'So, if the Man has stolen this person's identity, all we need to do is find someone who knows what a city is.'

The Spinster clapped her hands with delight. 'Chloe that is an excellent idea! I knew I could rely on you. You're such a clever girl.'

Chloe swelled with pride. 'I have my moments.'

'I can set up a program within the dailies. We can search for any reference to "city" from any guest at last night's party.'

Chloe was pleased they were finally getting somewhere.

The journey to the library was the direct opposite of the one taken to the morgue. After retracing their steps, they ascended the grand staircase in the main foyer and kept going up and up and up. The Spinster made deliberate, careful decisions whenever she came to a fork.

Eventually they came to two enormous gold and

verdigris doors. In contrast to much of the palace they were in fair condition. The wrought-iron designs were painted with a fresh gold leaf, and even the verdigris complemented with a distinguished decay.

'Here we are,' said the Spinster happily. 'My library'. The library was her domain, off limits. She had to be watchful, she explained to Chloe. The Queen had attempted to break into the library before, to find evidence of her, the Queen's, crime and build a case for her innocence.

'But she can't be innocent, can she?' asked Chloe.

'Certainly not!' replied the Spinster. 'She wouldn't be queen otherwise. The most criminal personalities are the strongest. They're the ones who demand their stories be told over all the other stories in the library. They're the ones who shape the seasons with their desires.'

'Will she ever remember her crime?' asked Chloe.

The Spinster peered down at her imperiously. 'Only at the end of her reign. And only if she is rehabilitated by good behaviour.' She paused and added gravely, 'I'm afraid I don't hold out much hope for her.'

Chloe thought about it. 'What happens if she does remember?'

The Spinster sighed. 'Then her time as queen will be written into a storybook, where her good example can be used for other criminals.'

'She'll become a story?' asked Chloe, concerned that reality could become a fiction so easily.

The Spinster was defensive. 'A lesson learned,' she said. She turned back to the library door and sent out a command.

There was a click from within and wheels began to turn

behind the doors. They parted with a reluctant creak, and slowly began to reveal what was within. Chloe wondered whether anyone, apart from the Spinster, had been allowed a glimpse into the secure workings of the prison before. She felt a glow of pride that she might be the first, though this was quickly dampened by the reason for her being there.

'Come along,' said the Spinster and took Chloe's hand. For the first time the woman's smile was forced.

The library was enormous and bewildering. Staircases branched from one another in many directions, creating impossible paths like the MC Escher print that used to hang on the wall of her father's study. Chloe's eyes began to hurt as she tried to decipher the mad geography. The staircases went up into the barely visible roof. Fortunately, there were tangible floors, each one with many bookshelves, stacked with hundreds of books of all shapes and sizes. She saw silver ladders on rollers on each floor, some moving by themselves. Chloe couldn't help but gasp at the immensity and precision of it all.

'Where are the librarians?' she asked.

'I am not always here to take care of things. Robots file and address the various issues of daily running. I do employ a small number of clockwork servants to do the more arduous tasks and to care for the older books and dailies here.' She sighed, ruminatively, 'Despite the wonders of technology, there is no substitute for the personal touch. And some of these records are so very old that a careless hand could destroy them simply by turning a page.'

There was a metallic clicking and twittering above them in the shelves, creatures talking in binary code. 'There, do you hear that? That's them muttering. Probably arguing over the placement of a particular book. They get so fussy and proprietorial. I occasionally have to reprogram them when they become too big for their own boots. I once had one try to ban me from using my own library because I had a book out a day too long!' She smiled, reminiscing, then snapped back to business. 'Yes, well, let me access the daily for last night's masquerade.'

The Spinster walked into a patch of dark. Chloe followed. Underneath, where four sets of stairs converged, there was a long desk with a clockwork woman behind it. She was writing with deep concentration in a leather-bound ledger. She glanced up as the Spinster waddled up to her.

'My dear Spinster. How wonderful to see you.' Her tone was cloying.

The Spinster pulled out a pair of pince-nez and placed them on her nose. She leaned over the desk, causing rolls of fat to bulge on the desk top.

'I would like to look at last night's dailies, specifically the Queen's masquerade. From say, 4 of the evening clock to say 6 of the morning clock.' She peered down her nose at the clockwork librarian, her eyes distorted and demanding behind her glasses.

The clockwork librarian ratcheted her head to the side. Chloe thought it a supercilious gesture. 'Those records are still being transcribed. Not every characterisation and action has been analysed.' She looked pointedly back down at the leather-bound book.

The Spinster breezed past the unhelpful comment. 'That's perfectly all right. We are capable of analysing the scenes ourselves. Indeed, that is exactly what we wish to do.'

The librarian fidgeted. 'But —' she started.

'The book, please,' said the Spinster sweetly but with iron underlying her tone.

The clockwork woman pursed her lips and, reaching out, she closed a book she had before her and handed it to the Spinster. It was a thick tome with a heavy spine; it gave off an evocative scent of dust and mould. The Spinster tucked it under her arm, the book almost disappearing, and thanked her. Turning away she motioned Chloe to follow.

'You see what I mean,' she nodded backwards, when they were far enough away to discuss the difficult librarian. 'Think they own the place. Get far too bossy and unhelpful. Then again, I suppose it isn't their fault entirely. One does get ingrained within the season. That's how they were designed.'

'Really?' asked Chloe, intrigued. 'By who?'

The Spinster did not reply. Chloe decided, for once, not to make a nuisance of herself. She presumed she would learn a great deal from what was about to occur here, in the secure heart of the season.

The Spinster climbed a short staircase and went immediately to another impressive gold and verdigris door at the top. It opened into a round chamber, lit softly with wall sconces. In the centre a shaft of light picked out a single lectern with a book on it. As Chloe looked, it flipped a page, though no one was present to turn it.

'That is the storybook, or daily, for today,' explained the Spinster. 'Go and have a look.' She gave the girl a nudge.

There was a silence here that was like the reverent atmosphere of a cathedral. Chloe's footsteps struck out loudly on the marble floor. When she reached the lectern, she had to stand on tiptoe to see.

'Don't touch it!' said the Spinster behind her.

Chloe looked up and saw that the book was writing itself in an elegant looped hand, with calligraphic flourishes on the letters that started each paragraph. Peering closer she could read the last few words ...

"Chloe looked up at the book on the lectern and saw that it was writing itself in an elegant looped hand, with calligraphic ..." She stopped. She spun to look at the Spinster, who smiled and nodded. Chloe turned back to read more. "Peering closely, she could read the last few words ..."

The Spinster placed a hand on her arm. 'That's enough,' she said, and pulled the girl away.

'But —'

'No, Chloe. It would not have told you your future in any case. It would have repeated that moment forever — of you staring into the book and it writing of you staring, and only when you had moved away would it begin to write your drama again. There are fail-safes to guard against knowing too much about your future. Besides, that is only *your* timeline here in spring. The book writes simultaneously of what each character in the season is doing. You only saw yours.'

'Can't I read anyone else's?'

The Spinster frowned. 'These are security records, my dear. Only the librarians and I have access to everything that is written. Though there are times when I must let others access certain volumes.'

She took yesterday's daily record from under her arm and pointed. Chloe saw that there were many alcoves that led from the chamber, each with a single red door. The Spinster clip-clopped toward one. She opened the door and went inside.

The room was a mirror image of the chamber outside but smaller. Chloe could feel the claustrophobic proximity of the walls around her in the dark. It was lit with a single point of light, and that was centred on the lectern in the middle of the carrel.

The Spinster stepped across to the lectern and placed the heavy book on it. The book opened with an ancient tearing of the pages, despite having been written just yesterday. Artifice and charm, thought Chloe, then frowned. She had never known what the word "artifice" had meant before now. Even her language was being sieved through the season, or perhaps it was a result of the Man tasting her. The Spinster saw her indecision.

'It was your idea,' she said, and held out a hand.

Warily, Chloe took it.

The Spinster began to read.

The party was in full swing around them. The red-painted waiters contorted themselves into impossible shapes, balancing goblets and platters of food on their heads or their backs. The string quintet played their moody music. The guests mingled and chatted and drank.

Something Chloe couldn't quite explain had happened. The room had blurred and warped as the Spinster read, but only for a moment. As she spoke of "trumpets", Chloe believed she'd heard the brassy sound. She'd whipped her head about as someone said something loudly in her ear. Music suffused the chamber. And then the room dropped last night's party on them.

'This is impossible!' exclaimed Chloe, wide-eyed.

The Spinster peered through her pince-nez and sniffed, 'Evidently not, as we are clearly here.'

'But ... how?' she asked.

'These are the dailies, my dear. Everything is recorded here and, when it is put together and catalogued by the librarians, we are able to revisit past days. Primarily for security purposes, you understand. Though there are times when I like to come here for pleasurable reasons.'

'But isn't this dangerous?' Chloe had not moved for fear of putting a foot wrong; she had read stories of people erasing their own futures by tampering in the past.

The Spinster laughed. 'Dear me, no, you cannot interact with any of the people here. It is a recording, a vividly real one certainly, but a recording nevertheless. We are of course still in the carrel chamber in the library. Think of it as a television program you have recorded of an entire day, one you can enter, in three dimensions, with colour.'

Chloe thought for a moment. 'Can you fast-forward and rewind?'

'Of course. Some days are duller than others and you wouldn't want to have to watch the entire thing in order to get to one moment at the end.'

'Okay,' replied Chloe, not entirely convinced, 'Show me my entrance.' The Spinster pursed her lips. Chloe realised what she was thinking. 'Oh! I meant my entrance to the masquerade.'

'All right,' the Spinster said. 'Prepare yourself. This bit is usually quite nauseating.' She looked down at the book, licked a finger and flipped a few pages. 'Ah, here we go.' She pushed her pince-nez up the bridge of her nose and peered closely at the text.

'"It took forever for the Queen to descend from her bedchamber. She had refused to be rushed by the Spinster. When she did she was wearing her Mask of Lies ..."' The Spinster stopped and frowned. 'No, no, too much introduction.' She scanned the book. '"Her presence — after four hours of the festivities had passed — was greeted by a cheer ..."'

The party around them abruptly stopped, all sound and movement paused. Chloe turned her head from side to side to make sure she hadn't been affected. She carefully reached out and touched the wooden dryad near her. It felt as real as last night.

The Spinster scanned the book and muttered, '"Trumpets sounded ... the Queen ... ah! The Queen drew herself to her full height to make her speech."

The scene slammed into fast-forward, figures squeaking and rushing by crazily. In quick succession she saw: herself on the staircase searching the crowd for a glimpse of Brandon; Tokka leading her away to dress; the man on the dance floor who looked like a poet and who would later try to kill her (she shivered); clockwork servants running madly from the kitchens at collision speeds. Turbaned Viceroys and Miss Chiefs and vulpine creatures all raced by.

Her head full of whirl and incident, she shut her eyes.

'"My dear friends, welcome to my modest little party,"' read the Spinster. '"Her guests tittered. It is so rare that we are allowed such a decadent pleasure, and I thank the Spinster for arranging this."'

Chloe realised that she could hear properly again. She opened her eyes and saw that the scene had slowed down to a pause. There was a jump and every figure shifted sharply into rewind. The Spinster tutted and flipped a page.

The party started again.

'... such a decadent pleasure, and I thank the Spinster for arranging this.'

They were at the bottom of the grand staircase. Chloe looked up and saw the Queen above them, making her grandiloquent speech, and herself standing further up, looking queasy. The Spinster stood behind Chloe's earlier self. The old woman bowed to the crowd at the Queen's statement.

'But tonight is not simply an occasion for pleasure. I have with me a guest who has come from a season outside the prison ...' She let the statement hang and her guests oohed with wonder.

Chloe looked up at her Spinster, the real one in the here and now. The old woman gazed back with a sardonic expression.

'Okay. I'm impressed,' she said.

She watched herself come down from the landing and stand beside the Queen, who took her hand, and her mask turned upwards into a lying smile. Chloe had been preoccupied last night and had not realised how disrespectful the Queen's mask was to her audience. It was a disturbing sight to see its porcelain features crack into false emotions.

'I present to you, prisoners and servants of the four seasons, Chloe Susannah Alexandra Jane ...' The Queen stopped abruptly, gave an exclamation of embarrassment and glanced down at Chloe.

'Hattersley,' Chloe finished.

The Queen's mask frowned. 'Hattersley!' she cried. And she raised Chloe's arm in victorious mimicry. There was a deluge of applause and whistles and mutterings.

Chloe found herself in the curious position of being able to watch her own past reactions. Not surprisingly, she found it disconcerting. She watched as she gave one of her meek smiles and discovered that it was not at all how she had imagined it; it was simpering and false. Then, after the applause and acceptance, the Queen threw off her hand. She saw her face fall at being disregarded. She hardened at the Queen's cruelty. She determined to find something incriminating against the woman.

'Are you all right?' asked the Spinster, pausing the scene around them with a wave of her hand.

'Fine,' she said levelly. 'We've wasted enough time here. We're supposed to be searching for someone who knows about a city.'

'You are perfectly right, my dear. Let's find this killer and prove your innocence.'

The Spinster fluttered her fingers and closed her hand into a fist. The scene around them disappeared, leaving them in the small library carrel, alone. Chloe blinked back her wonder at the fantastical feat she had just witnessed. There was a smell of ozone in the air; she pinched her nose.

Fussing and muttering to herself, the old woman rummaged in her folds, then with a triumphant 'a-ha' pulled out a peacock-feathered quill. She handed it to Chloe.

'Could you write it, please?'

Chloe turned to the book on the lectern and wrote both "city" and "cities" in the white space at the bottom of the page. She watched as the ink sank in. She handed back the quill.

The Spinster smiled her thanks. She touched the

unfamiliar word with a long red nail and said, 'Complete daily search.'

The party flickered back into existence around them, though this time there was white noise and indecision to the picture as it skipped forward and jerked awkwardly back. A barrage of conversation was thrown at them:

'... one's *sanity* good to have these parties now and ...'

'... I *certainly* wouldn't have thought it of her ...'

'... affair was *sordidly* done, I ...'

'... some *Sai Tea* — TOCK — madam?'

'... such a *pity* that, pity that, pity that, pity that ...'

The scene ground to a halt, whispering static.

'Oh dear,' said the Spinster. 'It seems to have stuck. I thought this might happen. It is an unfamiliar word.' She waved her hand and the scene disappeared.

Chloe's face fell. The Spinster patted her on the shoulder, 'It was a good idea, Chloe. But the Man is a clever opponent, he doesn't leave clues.'

Chloe suddenly brightened. 'Yes he does!' she exclaimed. 'He left the body. Surely that's all we need.' The Spinster raised an eyebrow. 'Go back to the scene of the crime.' Chloe took a deep breath to harden herself against the gruesomeness of the situation. 'Take me to the exact point last night when the body appeared.'

The Spinster considered the request gravely then nodded. 'As you wish, my dear,' she said and clicked her fingers. Pages began to flick rapidly back through the party.

They were on the terrace. Rain poured incessantly down onto the parterre garden, soaking the grass. From the French doors behind them oozed amber light, and the sound of voices and slow music.

Chloe was getting rained on and wasn't pleased. The sooner this is solved the better to get out of the wet, she thought. 'Where is the body?'

'It is beneath those rhododendrons,' said the Spinster, pointing to a clump of the bushes to the left of the terrace.

Chloe went immediately to them and, pushing through the clusters of pink flowers, she peered in. She saw the disfigured body at once, and a shiver went through her at its wrongness. The face was as before, exactly like that of a city, and proof that this body had something to do with her. She did not feel the need to touch it. Quickly, she surveyed the ground around it but could see no footprints. There were no marks at all apart from the sodden earth cratered by raindrops. The body was not going to give up its clues easily.

Chloe sloshed back to the Spinster, who assessed her face for some progress. But Chloe could give her nothing. She frowned and thought hard. Then she said, 'Can we go back to the point before the body is placed there? Perhaps we shall see someone put it there?' She did not sound optimistic and the Spinster mirrored her doubt with a sympathetic frown. But she raised a hand and ran her fingers through the air in what must have been a "rewind" motion, for the scene paused — music silenced, raindrops stopped — and then flew into reverse. With another gesture the Spinster stopped it and then played on. Apart from a stronger wind nothing in the garden appeared changed.

'According to the daily, the body appears within the next ten seconds.'

Chloe dashed down to the rhododendrons. Careful not to alert anyone who might be around, she parted the bushes and looked into the dark interior. And gave a startled cry when the ground heaved and pushed the body out of the earth.

She felt something in her head switch on, and her vision kaleidoscoped, zooming far and then near again. The wind rose in crescendo and there was a dramatic thunderclap at the bottom of the garden. For a small moment, Chloe saw herself at the barrier, with the Man sampling her through his Blanks. Again, she felt the discomfiting sensation of being drawn from her body. She almost retched.

She shivered and was slammed back into her body.

Lightning flashed and in the actinic burst she saw, on the face of the body, her own, contorted with pain and spasms. She threw herself back, branches flinging into her face. But the body did not wake, come after her like a horror movie; it just lay there waiting to be discovered.

The Spinster came across at her cry, mincing inelegantly as her stilettos sank into the lawn. 'What is it, Chloe? Who did you see? Tell me!'

Chloe did not immediately answer but went back to the terrace, where it was dry. The Spinster followed.

Chloe turned to the old woman. 'The body just appeared. No one left it at all. It just appeared!' She shook her head. 'But it can't just appear like that, can it?' Though she was unfamiliar with the rules of the prison, surely there should have been a warning.

The Spinster's face went through a variety of emotions but settled finally on sheepish ignorance. 'I'm not sure,' she finally admitted. 'It's highly likely, since it appeared in such a way, that whoever this was, was inhabited somewhere else by a Blank and this shell, this waste product, was placed here later.'

Chloe gazed up at the Spinster. 'One of his Blanks must

have prepared this character earlier. The Man simply jumped into this skin when you attacked him and left the dead body behind.' She gulped, 'Because he sampled me, he must have left behind the idea of a city in this body.' She frowned as a thought stumped her theory. 'From what you've said, the Man cannot inhabit two people at once?'

'That is correct. He cannot. But his Blanks can steal characters for him and they can only ape something living. And then he can take on the skin they have stolen for him.'

Chloe paced and dripped along the terrace, the cogs in her mind clicking rapidly. 'Then it must have been a Blank who killed this poor person and hid in the skin, so the Man could jump into it as an escape.' As she said this, she remembered the Blank who had brushed by the Man and changed. The Spinster nodded gravely, eyes downcast. 'But —'

'Yes?'

'What are the Blanks?' Chloe asked.

The Spinster's reply was grim. 'They are creatures he created, things of earth and wood. They can take on human form, and they can, through his evil ability, steal flesh. He grows stronger with every skin they take.'

Chloe was suddenly reminded of the conversation between the Spinster and the Man at the barrier. There had been a familiarity between them. Chloe realised there was history there. She caught the Spinster's eye. 'What happened between you and the Man?'

The Spinster flinched at the question. When she spoke, her voice was deep with remembrance. 'He stole something from me.'

'What?' asked Chloe carefully.

But the Spinster took a breath and came back to the

present moment. 'Something I can't get back,' she said.

'But surely you want to —'

'No, I don't!' snapped the Spinster. 'He took it! He destroyed it! I can't get it back!'

Chloe flinched at the Spinster's tone. The Spinster was immediately sorry for her outburst and reached out to squeeze Chloe's shoulder in apology. Chloe touched the old woman's wrinkled hand. With that gesture, when her mind had shifted away from the puzzle, the answer sprang into her mind. She gasped.

'Chloe?'

Her eyes widened. 'You said before that the Man doesn't leave behind clues, that you'd never seen a body like this before. So why now? Because we were *meant* to find it. Because it's a decoy!'

'But we cannot find him until we discover the identity!'

'No, there's no way of knowing who this is or when the Blank stole the skin. He's got us running around in circles.' For a moment she wondered where these instinctive judgements were coming from. They had such a truthfulness to them she knew them to be correct. Was it an effect of the Man's sampling? Had he given her a special intuition? Was he feeding her every thought, reeling her in to trap her? She shrugged those thoughts away.

'What do we know?' Chloe grasped the old woman's hands, imploring her to believe. 'We know the Man was in the dancing man with the velvet coat.'

The Spinster gave a slow smile of understanding. 'We need only to follow him throughout the party and see who he had contact with. You're right. He's far too vain not to give something away.'

Back in the carrel, circled in darkness, Chloe felt the weight of her deduction. The Man was still in this season, piecing together some plot to ensnare her. Until they knew who he was impersonating they could do nothing. The feeling of helplessness was so intense it almost made her cry. But she was determined not to be unsettled.

The Spinster wrote feverishly in the margins of the storybook. Flashes of the party bloomed into existence around them — snatches of dialogue, a flourish of music, laughter, noise — before running on to the next scene. She searched out their quarry.

Then it stopped. The scene crackled with static. Sounds and images were rolled back and forth.

The Spinster looked up from her examination. Her eyes were heavy with drama, her lips pursed solemnly. 'According to the dailies, the man in velvet spoke to four people.' She let the statement hang then said, 'A clockwork servant, where he remarked upon the quality of the wine; a member of the string quintet, whom he complimented; Columbine, and ... yourself.'

Chloe looked at the Spinster. 'It's not me. I swear.'

'I know,' the old woman replied and nodded.

Chloe had an idea. 'Where were these three people when the body in the garden appeared?'

The Spinster turned back to the lectern and interrogated the storybook. The room spun images around them. There was the clockwork servant, dutifully removing the spring raindrops from guests as they went back to their own season; there was the band member, walking back to his house in summer, discussing the merits of his playing with a fellow musician; there was Chloe talking to the man in velvet about her purpose; and … But the book had trouble discovering the Queen at the exact moment of the body's appearance. It paused and then ran hurriedly on to find her chatting to a Viscount, only to skip inelegantly to her berating a waiter over the toughness of the vol-au-vents. It skipped and rolled them through a number of scenes. Finally, it ground to a stop. The Queen's Mask of Lies loomed out at them, large and disproportionate to her face, as though to mock.

Slowly the Spinster turned to Chloe. With a gravitas that Chloe realised was hiding her worry, she said, 'At the exact moment the body appears in the garden, the Queen cannot be found. She disappears from the masquerade for precisely ten seconds.'

Chloe was pleased that she now had evidence against the queen. But she also realised the predicament they were in. They had to tread carefully.

She looked at the Spinster and said, more gleefully than she intended, 'I think that's out of character, don't you?'

CHAPTER SEVEN

THE QUEEN'S TRICK

THE QUEEN OF SPRING WAS sitting at her dresser staring into a mirror. She had drunk a number of vials of distilled raindrops to dampen her anger. Her head was awhirl. How dare that girl come into her palace and cause such disruption! And how dare the Spinster side with her! She was the Queen of Spring and, despite the Spinster's authority, it was her rule here. She might be reminded constantly that she was a criminal — she only had to go to the bottom of the garden to look into autumn — but damned if she was going to have her behaviour curbed in her own season.

She looked into her mirror and frowned at the face that glared back. She thought she detected new lines of age around her eyes. She pouted. 'It's that rotten girl. I hate her. I hate her! I want her gone! Gone, do you hear?!'

'I couldn't agree more,' her reflection replied. 'Get rid of her.' The Queen gasped, and then smiled in drunken delight. Her reflection stared at her counterpart. 'You are queen, after all.'

'It's not fair!' she slurred. 'She simply arrived here, with no crime attached. And now the Spinster prefers her to me. She's got the run of the season. It's not fair!'

She slammed a hand down on the dresser, making the vials jump.

'No, it certainly isn't,' replied her reflection. 'She commits the most heinous of crimes by existing here.'

'No purpose at all …' the Queen agreed.

'We should do something about that.'

The Queen narrowed her eyes guardedly for a second and was quiet. Then she leaned forward; her reflection mimicked the gesture. The Queen did not speak until she could see her breath on the glass. 'I have done something about it,' she whispered.

Her reflection's eyes bugged. 'Really? Do tell.'

The Queen was not so tipsy that she had lost her guard. 'One moment.'

Reaching into her décolletage she drew out a silver pocket-watch. It ticked slowly, with great pauses between tick-tocks.

'What is that?' asked her reflection.

The Queen gave a feline grin. 'It is a gift, from the Matriarch of Winter.'

She touched the top button of the watch and held it away from her as though there was something dangerous within. The hunt case flipped open.

'What are you doing?' asked her reflection.

The Queen smiled.

The watch stopped ticking. But then with a great belling, time rang out from it in greater decibels than such a tiny thing could be thought to contain. A wash of time flooded over the Queen, spreading out into the room. Everything in the bedchamber froze — the rain trickling down the wall stopped still. There was silence for two tick-tocks more. Then the watch hood clicked shut over the time-face.

Sound and time began again, the rain a pleasant trickle, a music box playing down the hall.

'There.' The Queen folded the watch away inside her gown.

'What have you done?' asked her reflection.

For a moment the Queen wondered why her own reflection shouldn't know what she herself was thinking. Then she dismissed the worry. 'I have tricked the dailies into recording a loop of prior time until I decide to resume it. I have used it often to gain some peace from the Spinster's prying eyes.'

'That is very clever,' replied her reflection.

'Indeed,' smiled the Queen. 'Only in-depth analysis of the dailies will reveal the deceit.'

'We are completely safe from prying security systems?'

'I haven't been caught yet.'

Her reflection leaned in. 'Then you must tell me what you've done about that dreadful girl.'

'I've been far cleverer than anyone would think me.'

'You have?' entertained her reflection.

'Since the Man with 8 Faces is intent on getting the girl, I thought I'd help him do so.'

There; she had said it; the secret was out. It was good to be able to tell someone how clever she had been.

'I invited him to my masquerade. Let him in using the pocket watch. Completely fooled the Spinster — she has no idea.' She laughed giddily. 'You know, he's not as bad as she says. I let him use my form for ten seconds in order to infiltrate, and he didn't do anything ghastly.' Her smile slipped. 'Well, apart from stealing the skin of the dead guest. But they're probably someone common, of no consequence. And, anyway, he's promised to break into the library to discover my crime, so I can present a case for my release.'

She realised that her reflection had been silent throughout all this. She glanced up to see her counterpart sitting back, arms folded.

'I am very disappointed in you, Columbine.'

The Queen of Spring was shocked out of her drunkenness. She gazed at her mirror image and leapt back as it *changed*. Her black loops of hair untwisted, shooting up into a tall white beehive, her body swelled into fatness, her cheekbones sagged with age. This new reflection stared back with tiny, angry eyes.

The Queen slipped off her chair, and glass crunched. She whipped her head around and found the flesh and blood Spinster standing in the doorway. The little brat was peering around her ample bulk, smiling at the Queen's shock.

'Sp-Spinster!' Her mouth fell open, then abruptly her whole body convulsed with anger. 'How dare you trick me!'

The old woman's features creased with fury. 'How dare *I*?' she replied, her tone threatening. She clicked her fingers and the knot of time unfurled with a resounding *TOCK*. 'How dare you consort behind my back with that Man! You selfish, traitorous woman, do you realise what you've done? You've upset the nature of this season. You've let in corruption.'

The Queen spat, 'Rubbish! The Man has been wronged.'

The Spinster glared, refusing to be drawn into an argument. 'I can think of no punishment worse than the one you have made for yourself.'

The Queen picked herself up, straightening her dress. 'What do you mean?'

'You have let the Man use your form. You vanished for ten seconds during the masquerade. You allowed him to escape my punishment and take on another body.' She continued coldly, 'Now he has sampled you, and you are prone to his attack, his imitation. You are your own worst enemy.' The Spinster shook her head ruefully. 'Was it worth it, Columbine? Was all this —' she gestured at the luxurious surroundings, the damasks and lace, the perfumes, the concessions to royalty '— not good enough for you? Are you obsessed with ruin?'

The Queen stuck up her nose. 'Is it any wonder when you clothe me in it? This crumbling palace, every corner decaying, every room filled with dust. You've made me so much a part of this place that ruin is all I am, and all I can do.'

The Spinster was harsh in her reply. 'You are mistress of your own season. What you make of it is entirely within your personality.'

The Queen bridled. The rain and the ruined palace was nothing to do with her. It was that girl who had brought about this. She glared at Chloe. The Spinster noticed.

'You blamed Chloe for your own murderous deed. How could you? She is just a girl.'

'Oh no, she isn't,' the Queen replied. 'Whatever she is, she's *wrong*.' She took a considered breath. 'She was ruining what I had. I wanted her gone.'

Chloe came forward. 'But that's all I want, too. I want to go home. I want to go back to the city.'

The Queen paused, and the room filled with tension; the Spinster stiffened.

'City?' said the Queen. 'What is "the city"?'

Tension ebbed. The Spinster and Chloe locked glances.

'Look at you both! Disgusting conspirators! This is my palace! My season! I demand you get rid of her! She is a stripling, an insignificance! Why do you protect her? Let the Man have her. What can he do if allowed her? She is nothing.'

Chloe blanched at the Queen's insults but stood calmly by the Spinster.

'Since the Man is after her and not you, Columbine, I imagine Chloe is worth a lot more than yourself. And since she is a far better person than anyone you could ever dream of being, I find it not only a duty but also a happy circumstance that I can protect her.' She drew a long weary breath. 'This is not something I am prepared to do for you anymore. I am sorry. You have proved yourself untrustworthy and a threat to the season. You are, once again, an accessory to murder. Evidently you have not learned anything. Sadly, I must enforce stricter imprisonment upon you.'

The Queen went white. 'No, please, dear Spinster, we have been friends for so long. I'm sure a lighter punishment can be substituted.'

The elderly woman did not reply but began to search among the vials on her necklace.

Realising she was serious, the Queen doubled her plea. 'A month in the garden as a topiary statue! Two months! Plant me in the garden, let it rain on me. You know I despise the rain. Make me endure the most dreadful of tortures. Put me in the dark.'

The Spinster plucked a chosen vial from her necklace, her face betraying nothing.

'Please, Spinster!'

The Spinster removed the glass top of the vial.

The Queen, knowing the terrible consequences of the action, dropped to her knees. 'I'll do anything,' she said.

For a moment the Spinster appeared to reconsider. Her head lifted, eyes measuring her charge for a spark of goodness. Then her eyes glazed, resolved to carry out her task.

The Queen gave a despairing cry.

The Spinster flicked her wrist, and a drop flew from the tip of the glass stopper. Before it hit the Queen, the Spinster spoke two words, barely audible and with great sadness.

The drop hit the Queen full in the face. Her mouth opened. As Chloe watched, colour drained from the monarch's form and ran like paint to the floor. Her features cracked and crazed, turning to glass.

'Perhaps you shouldn't watch this,' the Spinster suggested. But Chloe craned forward to see, and the old woman did not stop her.

The Queen was riddled with hairline cracks, across her face, down her arms, even her dress was cracking.

'I'm sorry, Columbine,' said the Spinster. She nodded once.

The Queen shattered into shards of glass.

Chloe reached down and picked one up. 'Don't cut yourself,' said the Spinster. In the glass, Chloe could see, quite distinctly, the Queen's eye; she was crying piteously.

'Was that really necessary?' Chloe asked.

The Spinster squeezed the little girl's shoulder. 'You defend her, after all her spite toward you?'

'I do. She seems so sad about it now. Surely she doesn't need to be in pieces?'

The Spinster took a deep breath. 'You are kind, Chloe Hattersley. It is better than she deserves, but I shall do it for you.' The Spinster waved a hand.

The glass pieces rushed into reverse and quickly formed the wailing queen. She was surprised to be reformed, though still of glass. 'Unfortunately, I cannot let her be so mobile.'

'Then put her in the mirror,' suggested Chloe and pointed to the dresser.

'Yes, that would be appropriate. The mirror shines back her duplicity.' She made a strange gesture.

The glass queen disappeared. The mirror crazed with cracks, and then the image of the Queen formed behind them. She had stopped crying, and now felt around the edges of her new prison. Slowly, the cracks in the mirror healed, until the glass was smooth once more.

'There. It is done.'

Chloe went to the glass and touched it. The Queen on the other side placed her hand against Chloe's. An understanding passed between them though no words were spoken. The Queen's glare was less antagonistic.

There was a sizzle of ozone between their fingers, and Chloe felt a presence in her head, scrabbling about in her thoughts. She tried to shrug it off. She heard her name called from far away and looked into the mirror ...

Chloe ...

... where the Queen had transformed into an elderly

woman, with black ringlets and kind eyes. Familiarity flooded through her. The woman in the hand mirror. Chloe remembered. Mirrors within mirrors. When had she lost the hand mirror? During her battle with the Man at the season's barrier. He must still have it and be using it as a conduit to find her. She tried to wrench her hand away from the glass, but a force restrained her, threatening to pull her in. The woman in the mirror said her name again and this time it was strong and motivating.

CHLOE …

'Chloe. My name is Chloe Susannah Alexandra Jane Hattersley!' she shouted. She pulled with all her might and felt her hand becoming unstuck. The woman in the mirror cracked and crazed and chipped and …

There

… was the Man with 8 Faces, leering, inviting her in, knowing she could not resist him now he'd had a taste of her. He had taken on the form of the man in velvet again; though he did not possess the skin he could obviously hold the image.

She could feel him pulling, wanting her.

She summoned all her strength and ripped her hand from the mirror. She cried out, leaving shreds of skin behind.

The image of the Man grimaced and faded back into the Queen. She was still, an ornament; yet those ten seconds when the Man had used her body meant she was one of his possessions, even if she was behind glass. He could always use her.

The Spinster was at her shoulder. 'What happened?'

'Mirrors within mirrors,' replied Chloe, breathing hard. 'He's got mine. He can see me through that.' Then she started, realising who'd left the missing mirror by her bed, days ago. 'Oh no.'

'What is it?'

'I just had a terrible thought. Though I really hope I'm wrong.' She looked into the mirror. The Queen had faded away, and her reflection gazed back at her. She did not blink, scared that it might begin a life of its own, or transform into something unspeakable.

'I need to see Brandon,' she said.

CHAPTER EIGHT
THE STOLEN SKIN

CHLOE RACED THROUGH THE GARDEN, refusing to cry. Her body thrummed with tension. She had a feeling that the season was placing a character upon her. Well, she would not be typecast! And certainly not as a simpering girl who cried at every turn. She agreed with the Queen in one respect wholeheartedly — she did not belong here. It was the one thought that kept her sane amidst the dangers and the oddities.

The sky was dimming with afternoon, and dark clouds swelled. A storm was coming.

Chloe ran instinctively down the garden paths. Only when she got to the door of the red brick cottage did she stop.

Should Brandon be under the Man's influence she was walking into danger. She wondered if he took her to the barrier to deliver her to the Man, to give him the mirror so he could look into her. Had it all been planned? But he was the only person she trusted. When had the Man stolen his character? Had she ever met the real Brandon? Surely that dreamy smile, that care he had shown toward her when he'd rescued her from the Miss Chiefs, was real? But she didn't know, so there was no point in wondering.

She shook her wet black ringlets. What she was about to do required something of the season — it required a performance. She almost wished she hadn't stopped the Spinster from coming with her; but she wanted to do this unmasking herself.

She knocked on the door. After a short moment, Tom opened it. 'Speak of the devil! Chloe! My dear girl, do come in, it's awfully wet outside and look at you …' He ushered her in. It was warm in the house, with a fire crackling away in the lounge. 'We've just been talking about you.'

'Oh?' she said as innocently as she could. 'Nice things, I hope.' Her eyes darted around the cottage, looking for Brandon.

'But of course. I don't imagine a bad word could be said of you.'

'The Queen has managed plenty.'

'Well, she's a common criminal, so I wouldn't listen to anything she says.' He shepherded her into the lounge.

'Where's Brandon?' she asked, forcing her eyes to light up.

There were footsteps on the stairs and Brandon came clomping down from above. The boy looked cheekily at her, and she tried to steel herself against his good looks and the thrill she got from his hairy legs and hooves and perky little horns.

'Some tea is in order, I think,' Tom suggested, and raised a bushy eyebrow, 'and a towel. You're wet through.' He went into the kitchen where she heard him bang and bustle about, muttering to himself all the while.

Brandon looked at her, hands behind his back. His smile was shy, dimpling his cheeks. She refused to find him irresistible, knowing he was throwing his magical enchantment around her; yet she must act as if she was being drawn into his web. How difficult this acting is, she thought; it takes more than an easy black-and-white lie.

'I knew it was you as soon as you knocked,' he said.

'Really? Do you have magical powers now?' she asked.

He hung his head. 'No.' Then he smiled, and she simply utterly *would not* let it affect her! 'We were talking about you and when there was a knock, well it just had to be you. We don't get any visitors.'

She decided to take the familiar tone of the conversation down a notch. 'What were you saying about me?'

'Nice things. Honestly.'

She suddenly registered his hands were behind his back. She tensed in case she needed to run. She looked at him and thought, try the direct approach.

'What are you hiding?'

This time his smile was too conniving. He pulled out a silver insect. It sat in his hand, segmented, with wings of silver mesh. Chloe wasn't sure how to react. Then its antennae twitched, and she flinched. What was it? Was it going to sting her into a stupor and then he could sample her again? What would he say to Tom? That she had fainted and must be taken to his room? Was Tom part of this? Was he a Blank? She mustn't let the silver wasp touch her.

Brandon took a step toward her.

She backed away.

He frowned. 'What's wrong?'

She must play along, mustn't let him know that she

knew who he really was; the deceitful lie inside the boy. She berated herself for not coming up with a more solid plan; what was she going to do when she unmasked him? He was the Man with 8 Faces. He had flummoxed the Spinster often enough. She could hardly be a threat to him. But she had the advantage — he needed her; that was her purpose here in the season. He would not want her damaged.

'My lady?' Brandon took another step forward, reverting to servitude to cover offence.

She stopped the smile that played around her mouth, then, in the spirit of performance, she let it go.

She motioned to the insect. 'What's that?'

Brandon, bless him (No! Keep alert!), noticed the reason for her anxiety. 'Oh, don't worry. It isn't going to harm you. It's a dragonfly.' He held it out to her. 'I made it for you. So you could have a piece of me with you all the time.' He gave a gentle push and it fluttered from his palm with a metallic beating sound and flew toward her.

She held out her hand, thinking that this couldn't possibly be a trap, she must have been wrong, that the Man could never think of something this sweet. For a second after it landed she realised how foolish it was of her to drop her guard and waited expectantly for the sting. But the insect settled, buzzing contentedly.

'Are you sure you're all right?' His concern was so touching, so all-consuming, that she submitted.

'I'm sorry,' she sat on the lounge. 'I've had such an awful day.'

Brandon gently squeezed her shoulder.

'Tea!' cried Tom, coming out of the kitchen with a tray containing a towel, a teapot and three tulip-shaped cups.

'That's what's needed to combat awful days.' He placed the tray before them and began to pour.

The splash of the tea, the warmth of the fire, the gentle buzzing of the dragonfly all made Chloe drowsy. She fought it off.

'Now, what was so awful about the day?' Tom asked.

Chloe mentally put her mask on. 'Well, waking up to be accused of murder was not a nice start.'

'What?' said Brandon, his eyebrows leaping up.

Tom frowned and handed her the towel.

Chloe handed the dragonfly to Brandon and took the towel. She began to dry her hair. 'The Queen said I'd killed one her guests at the masquerade and was completely horrible about it. But then the Spinster and I went through the dailies and proved that I couldn't have because the body just appeared which meant the Man must have done it. He stole the skin and deliberately left the body as a decoy. But the clue was that the face looked like a city, because he'd sampled me at the barrier the other night, so I'm part of him now and everything he does. So the Spinster and I concocted a trap for him.' She stopped her deliberate ramble and waited. She folded the towel into a square and placed it on the table.

'I see,' said Tom and sipped his tea carefully. 'And what might this trap be?'

Brandon frowned. 'What's a "city"?'

Abruptly, Chloe realised. She tried not to let her alarm show though it felt as though her heart had turned into a locomotive and was barrelling through her chest. It wasn't Brandon. It was Tom. She slowly turned to the gardener, who put his cup down, his every move considered. His eyes were cold and dark.

'That was clever.' Tom nodded appreciatively. 'That was the trap, wasn't it? My fault, really. I do get so caught up in a role.'

'Papa?'

Chloe took Brandon's hand. 'That's not your Papa. That's the Man with 8 Faces.' He stared uncomprehendingly at her. 'I'm sorry, Brandon.'

The boy looked at his father, wishing him to deny her statement. Tom stood up, towering over them. She mimicked the movement. Now she had unmasked him, she did not know what to do.

He looked into his son's face and laughed. 'She's absolutely right, Brandon, my boy. I'm afraid that you're an orphan. Your father died —'

'Died?' snapped Chloe. 'You killed him.'

The Man paused, annoyed at her interruption. Then shrugged. 'Fair enough. The correct word for the correct deed. Words are, after all, most important for the play. Yes, I *killed* Tom, or rather I had one of my wonderfully adaptive Blanks kill him, so I could use him as an escape. I had a feeling that the velvet man was a short-lived persona. He brought too much attention to himself. And I needed to blend in. Not a bad performance, though? I mean, you, Brandon, thought I was your Papa, for a whole day. Come on, what do you think? Be honest.' He grinned manically.

'You get a great big nothing from me,' said Chloe.

'Nothing!' roared the Man in the gardener's body. 'I had you running around in circles today. I had you thinking it was Brandon here —' Brandon looked at her, hurt — 'I fooled my own flesh and blood! That alone gives me at least a fair review.'

'No. You can't be him … he can't be you. He's my Papa, he's not just some *skin!*' Brandon was in shock.

The Man licked his lips. 'If it's any consolation, I killed him for his character as well. Trapping girls with kind words is hard to do without a kind face.'

Brandon leapt forward, his face transforming into a grimace.

The Man raised a hand, as though his wrist had dislocated, and Brandon's lunge stopped mid-air. The Man stroked the boy's cheek. 'Flesh of my flesh, you must obey your father.'

'Let him go.' Chloe's tone was dangerous. 'You are *not* his father. He's nothing to you.'

'But he's something to you, isn't he?' His eyes narrowed.

'He's my friend.'

'My dear girl, you don't have friends here. You can't. Because you don't belong here.'

'But I do have a purpose. Don't I?'

He tipped his head to one side, scrutinising her greedily. 'Yes. One.'

'What do you need me for?'

'You're my way out of this tricky little prison.'

'How?'

The man laughed. 'What a clever girl you are, keeping me talking, hoping for a rescue attempt. Did you think the Spinster would save the day? I'm afraid she's preoccupied. You must have read a lot of mystery novels. Such a mind. Such —'

Chloe threw her tea at him.

He yelled, threw his hands up to his face, trying to

claw the heat away. It broke his concentration and Brandon dropped to the floor.

Chloe raced forward and grabbed his arm. He turned and growled at her. 'It's me!' she cried. His features softened. 'Come on!' She dragged him to his feet. Hauled him to the door.

The Man snarled behind them with Tom's voice. '*Chloe. You can't escape. I can find you anywhere.*' He came forward, unseeing, reaching out for her. She struggled with the latch on the door. When the Man heard it lift, he hissed, making Chloe's heart pound. She ducked under his arms. But Brandon stood his ground. The man who had been his father brushed against the boy who had been his son and held on.

'Brandon!' Chloe yelled. She grabbed his hand and pulled.

'Blanks!' The Man shouted.

At the command, the front door bulged, and a form loomed from the oak. It narrowly missed Chloe. She leapt back. *They can only take on the form of something organic.*

'Brandon! Where's the back door?'

Brandon wasn't listening to her. He wasn't even struggling in the Man's grip. The Man dug his fingers into the boy's shoulders. Eyes closed, Brandon gritted his teeth in pain, but accepted his fate.

The Blank at the front door stepped from the oak and cast its oval face about to sniff Chloe out. Before she could react, it shot out a withered arm and latched onto her wrist.

The numb feeling took her over again. She looked down to see the Blank's hand become smooth wood, and coloured flesh pink. She was being pulled from her body.

'Brandon ...' she whispered.

Brandon's eyes snapped open. Quickly, he reached into an inside pocket of his vest and pulled out a thin decanter. Inside, a bright liquid shone. Brandon unstoppered it and threw the contents. The liquid splashed onto the Man's face — an incandescent blot.

The Man *screamed*.

The Blank instantly retreated into the wood of the front door.

The Man was bathed in golden light. It flowed across his skin like oil, eating him up. Chloe realised it was pure sunshine from the summer season.

Before the Man could recover, she grabbed Brandon and pushed him out the door. He gave a last forlorn backward look at the figure of his father as it burst into flame.

The night was a thrashing animal, alive and pungent. The storm had broken. Plants snatched and grasped at them. The rain pounded down. Lightning lit up the garden in lurid flashes, and Chloe had to stop herself from thinking she was seeing things in the seconds of light. There were Blanks out here.

She dragged Brandon down muddy paths, barely able to see where she was treading. All she wanted was to get away from that terrible scene. The image of Tom burning was etched unbearably on her retina. She hoped she was heading in the direction of the palace. She must get back and tell the Spinster. Brushing a leaf out of her face she felt a thorn in her palm, a throb of poison pump into her skin. She cried out, stopped, slipped and fell into the mud. She pulled Brandon down with her.

They sat in the dirt, the rain their entire world.

After a while, Brandon spoke. His voice was broken.

'We can't stay here.'

Chloe replied. 'We need to tell the Spinster.'

'I mean we can't stay in this season.' Chloe shivered, the mud soaking into her dress. 'The Man will keep looking for you. He won't give up. He'll keep killing, stealing skins so he can trap you. He knows where to find you. It isn't exactly difficult.' Brandon sighed in the dark. 'Do you want to cause more deaths?' He said it lightly, without blame, to provoke her into seeing reason, but it was still unkind.

'But we can't,' she replied, reasonably.

'We can,' he said. 'I let the Man sample me. And while he was looking into me, I looked into him.' He moved, and Chloe heard the rustle of fabric. Something sloshed in his hand and a glow lit up their faces. 'I still have this. The Spinster gave it to me to defeat the Man at the barrier. That's how I knew it would probably stop …'

'I'm sorry, Brandon.' Chloe squeezed his arm.

He breathed hard again and went on. 'It's summer sunshine. It will take us through the barrier. We just need to mix it with some raindrops. That's the key, elements from each season. Though since no one but the Spinster has summer sunshine no one can get into that season.' He returned the light to his pocket.

'We have to tell the Spinster what's happened.' She couldn't just leave.

'The Spinster will stop us, put everybody here in danger.' His voice turned hard. 'We have to do this ourselves.'

'We put ourselves in danger by leaving. At least here she can try to protect us.'

'I've heard that summer is a big season, with lots of

people. We can hide out there.'

'But —' Chloe resisted, frightened more of the other seasons than this one she had now found a place in, had found friendship in.

'We have to!' Brandon snapped.

The night sparked electric blue around them. Plants loomed large over them.

Chloe stared into Brandon's eyes as the night lit up. She couldn't tell if he was crying or it was the rain.

'All right,' she said.

He stood up and reached for her hand. She took it. He pulled her up.

A flash of lightning bathed the garden in light. It illuminated Brandon's tight smile, the wild night, and the Blank standing directly behind him.

Chloe's eyes widened, and she turned her upward movement into a backwards one, tilting Brandon to fall towards her. He saw her alarm.

'Run!' she yelled.

He didn't bother turning, knowing there could only be one thing to frighten her.

'The maze,' he said.

They ran.

The garden flashed around them. Every movement picked out in the infrequent light was a danger. Chloe started at misshapen branches that leaped out at her, and plants that moved into her path. Her heart beat insensibly. The rain washed away any sense of a path, but Brandon led them on. He brushed aside leaves, his direction unerring, his pace fast. Chloe kept a firm hold of his hand.

Then they shot out of the garden and were at the maze.

'I think the barrier is somewhere around here,' he said, looking around.

'I can find it,' replied Chloe. Brandon stared at her. 'When the Man sampled me … something happened.' That was all she was prepared to tell him for the moment.

She walked forward and closed her eyes. She let a single thought ring out — *summer*. She opened her eyes. Her vision kaleidoscoped, shooting forwards and backwards like a zoom lens on a camera. She gasped as dizziness overtook her. How did the Spinster manage? she wondered. Then Brandon put a steadying hand on her shoulder, and she calmed. She looked at the maze and, simply by thinking it, looked *through*, finding herself moving rapidly forward as though flying, even as she was standing still. But there was nothing but endless deceiving avenues that way. Her peripheral vision blinked, and she turned. A scent of spices, a flush of heat on her cheek.

'That way.' She pointed right.

They raced the length of the maze, trusting to her new ability. She was invigorated and terrified by it. As they passed a section of maze heat bloomed over her body.

'Stop!'

She grabbed onto a branch, felt herself go forward into the green interior. There, only a few pathways in, was the summer barrier. She could taste the scent of the season on the other side, feel its delicious warmth. She hadn't had sun on her for so long it felt like the first time. She luxuriated in it, gathering it into her skin.

'It's here.'

'So are the Blanks!' Brandon replied, shaking her out of her entrancement.

What she saw made her shrink against the hedge. The garden had grown limbs and reached out to attack them. Branches shot toward them, pinning them in a cage of thorns. Brandon rummaged in his jerkin, brandished the bottle of sunshine. The bright light throbbed at another dark thing it could eat. The limbs pulled back.

'Quickly,' said Chloe. 'Unstopper it. Let in the rain.'

'What if we have to measure it?'

'Too late for that,' she replied and snatched the bottle from him.

With a shattering thunderclap the rain *stopped*. Brandon and Chloe looked at one another, shocked. The season dripped. There was something unnatural about the lack of the constant, evocative rain. It was like someone had taken off a mask and everything Chloe had known here was false, and this was the dreadful truth underneath.

A laugh echoed from the garden. Chloe turned to face it. A Blank came out of the dark. It was humanoid, with two legs, two arms, and a smooth oval face. It was dressed in a dark blue pinstripe suit. In a hand it held her mirror. It brought it up to its non-face. In it was the Man, having reverted to his understudy — the man in the velvet coat, with his cruel smile and mirthless eyes.

'You thought it that easy to be rid of me?

But losing is not in my vocabulary.

And escape is certainly not available in yours,

So why don't you surrender to my worthwhile cause?'

Chloe glared. 'I might surprise you with my performance.'

'I had a formidable leading lady once,' said the Man wistfully. 'She'll never be bested.'

'I've learned a few things since I got here.'

Brandon grabbed her arm. 'Forget him. We have the sunshine. Let's go.'

The Man coughed. 'I'm afraid you'll find it's not as easy as you think to open the barrier. If it were as easy as collecting the rain, why, anyone could do it. Why don't you come quietly. I assure you I'll be gentle when I rip your skin off.' He pursed his lips, trying not to laugh at their predicament.

Chloe took two steps forward. 'You think you're so clever, don't you? The master of the seasons, hiding under all those masks.' Another step. The thorny limbs wavered at her golden approach. 'You know what I think? I think you're nothing! Why do you need all these masks, all these people? Because you have no character, because you are absolutely nothing yourself!'

The Man's face in the mirror grimaced. 'Why do you think I was able to bring you here? Because you're a cruel, nasty, unkind little liar! You're exactly like me on the other side of the glass. If I'm nothing, then you are too, young lady!'

While the Man ranted, Chloe surreptitiously unstoppered the bottle. 'I think you'll find that you really shouldn't have chosen me,' she said.

She shook the bottle and held it out in front of her. Sunshine blazed across them all, and Chloe felt her skin burning in the heat. The Man, his Blank, and the reaching limbs pulled back into the darkness.

With their attention averted, Chloe raced back to the maze. She gave the bottle another shake for good luck and threw the contents at the wet hedge. It splashed across the leaves and began to burn a path through.

'But what about the raindrops?' asked Brandon, frustrated, looking at the empty bottle she had thrust at him.

Chloe gave him a wicked smile. Delving into a pocket of her dress she took out the vial she had snatched from the dressing table in her chamber. She looked at the label — *101 Spring Raindrops* — and knew that there was some other force at work that was helping her. These weren't just any raindrops, but rain that had been distilled by that strange tuba-like machine she saw in the tower in her first meeting with the Queen.

She threw the contents of the vial at the hedge. Leaves burned away, turning to ash. The mixed sunshine and rain hit the barrier and ran across it, splintering it. There was a pause.

Then, with a crack, the barrier split open.

Inside, she could see pink-veined walls, pulsing and throbbing. The barrier was alive! On the other side summer beckoned — with sun-baked dunes, the smell of exotic spices, and cupolas and minarets brimming in a heat haze. She turned to Brandon. He gave her an unsure look.

The garden erupted in a mass of thorny limbs that came straight for them.

Chloe grabbed Brandon and pushed him into the barrier.

She turned back and saw the Blank with her mirror rushing forward. The Man inside snarled, 'I'll find you, Chloe Hattersley!' It threw the mirror at them.

She leapt into the barrier, into the slimy organs and veins. Spring closed with a solid suck behind her.

As if, she thought, a camouflaged animal had digested her in a clever trap.

SUMMER

CHAPTER NINE
THE COLLECTORS

WHEN SUSANNAH ALEXANDRA JANE HATTERSLEY opened her eyes, they filled with sunlight. After the days of constant spring rain, the warmth on her face bewildered her. She raised a hand to shield her eyes. Peering through her fingers, all she made out was a blur. She sat up and let her eyes focus.

She was in a large red tent with a tiered roof, like a general's war tent. Strips of silk — Chinese yellow, royal blue, jade Buddha green — dropped from the ceiling and moved languidly in a mysterious breeze. It was stifling inside the tent, a dry heat pressing against her, making breathing hard. Sweat covered her forehead and her cheeks.

How had she come to be here? Her mind struggled to fit sense together like a key finding difficulty with a lock. She had a terrible feeling of loss, as though a deep part of her was missing.

She remembered being enfolded by organs, wrapped tight with veins, pulled in a tug-of-war between the seasons: a leg to winter, an arm to summer, her head to autumn, heart to spring. A malevolent voice hounded her down the pink corridor:

"I'll find you Miss Hattersley
Of that you can be sure.
You cannot hide away from me
I breach the season's law!
So let us play this children's game
For by its end I'll own your name …"

The Man with 8 Faces! Was he here? Had he followed her through?

One thing at a time, she thought. Taking a steadying breath, she focused on her surroundings.

Large earthenware pots covered the floor, and were so closely packed that Susannah could barely see the path that led to the door outside. Vertically stacked carpet rolls ran around the tent walls. Behind the heat, there was a pungent muddle of spices. The foreign scents could only be coming from the pots.

She jumped down from the bench she had been lying on, noticing that someone had placed a sack underneath her, and a rolled-up cloak as a pillow. The floor was sandy beneath her bare feet. Feet? Someone had taken her shoes! Her lovely new black brogues bought especially for her trip up north. North, into the heat? Wasn't the north known for its colder climate? Well, it was no good to bemoan the loss of new shoes now. She wriggled her toes through the gritty red sand, determined to make the best of an as yet uncertain situation. Someone had also removed her red pinafore. She was clothed in a green cotton dress that cut sharply across her chest and possessed a strange triangular tail.

Closer to the ground the spices were stronger. Susannah peered into one of the pots. It was full of wood-like seeds. She brought out a handful. She sniffed them, taking in the sharp aroma of liquorice. She tipped them back into the pot and went to investigate another. The second pot was full of curled yellow pieces of bark that gave off a citrus scent, the third a strange paste as black as treacle with a sticky sheen. That one smelt unpleasant and made her nose twitch and her eyes water. The final pot she decided to look in was full of an ochre powder that looked like dirt but smelled powerfully sharp. She didn't touch it for it had a heat coming off it that reminded her of the fierceness of chilli, and of the time when she had wiped her eyes after helping her mother make dinner one night. Where had that been?

She remembered a house with a long corridor from the front door to the kitchen, and a red wall; there was a hat rack with a lady's sunhat on it, and keys in a bowl on a hall table. A pair of flat-heeled woman's shoes was upturned under the table, as though kicked beneath with careless haste. Susannah remembered this image clearly but couldn't remember where this house was. She was filled with sadness. Did it mean something terrible? Perturbed by these random imaginings she struggled to hold doubt at bay. She was not in the house with the red wall; she was in a red tent that was obviously a trader's storehouse, filled with rugs and spices. In any case, she'd spent too long here. She must find out exactly where she was in the summer season.

She headed toward the open doorway and the light.

The hanging strips of silk began to waver in agitation. Susannah stopped, but she had already betrayed her position. Yellow silk whipped out and wound itself around her arm. Susannah tugged back but the silk was immensely strong. As she pulled back, a blue strip entwined itself around her waist, as red silk ensnared her legs. With a slight tensioning the silks contracted, and Susannah's feet left the ground. She gave a short squeal at being unexpectedly airborne. She didn't fight the silk. She had a feeling they weren't intending harm, merely that they were keeping her from leaving.

Like a security system, she thought.

At least her entrance into summer hadn't been as distressing as her entry into spring. Perhaps the Spinster's barbarous descriptions of this season were exaggerated. At the thought of the old woman she felt her heart sink. She wished the Spinster were here. She wished she could have warned her about the Man, but the longer she spent in spring the more of a danger she was to everyone there. Besides, the Spinster could look after herself. Unlike ... She thought of Brandon. Brandon! Where was he? Had he come through with her, or had the barrier separated them, shunted him off into a different season? Her mind slammed into focus. The first thing to do was find him.

There was a skittering from the doorway.

Susannah stiffened.

The noise sounded again, a rasp of flesh.

She looked down at her feet. There, still, but standing alert on two back feet, was a green and yellow lizard. It cocked its head to one side, regarding her in a very human manner, and a pink tongue flicked out of its mouth to taste the air. It wasn't frightened of her at all. She felt her shock fade. She wondered how she could entice the lizard to free her from the silks.

A shadow fell across the doorway.

Susannah tensed, and the silks tightened, perhaps sensing an escape attempt. A figure was silhouetted in the entrance, his shadow stretched searchingly into the tent.

For a moment, Susannah thought he was going to move on, but then the tent flap was pushed aside, and he entered. He walked straight to her.

He had dark skin, a sullen Arab look, and large brown intelligent eyes. His soft lips were pinched in a smile that Susannah imagined might be an indication of wickedness. He was dressed in a simple white robe, like a very long shirt, with five buttons down the chest. Tied around his waist was a green silk sash embroidered with gold designs. His head was wrapped in a green scarf patterned with the same designs.

He looked directly into her eyes and smiled. 'You are awake,' he said, his accent thick with sand and heat.

'Obviously,' replied Susannah. 'Would you mind getting me down?'

The man reached out and stroked the coloured silks holding her. They gently eased their tension and dropped her to the ground. Susannah nodded thanks to the man. She noticed how tall he was now that she had to look up to him.

'Who are you?' she asked.

He studied her before replying, holding out his hand for the lizard. It leapt into his open palm, raced up his arm, and darted onto his shoulder, where it peered inquisitively at her. 'My name is Zahir,' he said with a small bow. 'I am at your service.'

My service, thought Susannah. Well then, she might exert her authority. 'Where are my shoes?' she demanded.

'They are lost. Do you not remember?'

'Hardly. I wouldn't be asking you otherwise.'

'Please, let me explain. But first, surely you would like a drink, some food?'

Susannah's natural suspicion fought with her sudden wish to eat. But Zahir had not harmed her, and the silks had probably been there for her protection. She gave in to hunger. Give him a smile, she thought. Zahir smiled back, pleased.

Motioning for her to wait, he left the tent but was gone for only a few moments before he returned with a small basket of food. The lizard had vanished, but she could hear noises from the basket.

At the back of the tent, behind where she had been lying, there was a flat expanse, the sand covered over with rugs. There were piles of glittering objects everywhere — Susannah made out lanterns and musical instruments and gilt-edged mirrors, beautiful glasses and bowls and ornaments and clocks, all haphazardly scattered. It was like Aladdin's cave.

'What is this place?' she asked. 'What exactly do you sell?'

Zahir frowned. 'I don't sell anything.' He puffed out his chest. 'I'm a collector.'

'A collector of spices and rugs?' she asked.

'A collector of everything,' he replied.

'But *why* do you collect it?'

Zahir's confusion cleared. 'You are new to the season, otherwise you would know.' He motioned her to the rugs, folding himself down beside her. 'I collect all this so that I can be interesting.'

He opened the basket he had retrieved, and delicious smells rose from it. He shooed the lizard from the basket. It shot out onto the rug and looked at him with displeasure.

Susannah realised how hungry she was; she hadn't eaten

properly since the Queen's masquerade. She really should be searching for Brandon. But it would do no good to wander through an unfamiliar city on an empty stomach. She'd have to humour Zahir.

'Can't you be interesting by yourself?' she asked.

His eyes widened with alarm. 'Certainly not. Only the King is interesting in this season, with his numbers, and his guards. Anyone found to be more interesting and popular than him is taken to the castle dungeons.' He proffered a thin piece of bread. 'Or worse — the tower!'

I see, thought Susannah. Another despot criminal who thought he ruled the season. She would have to arrange a visit to see the King. He'd most likely know a way out.

She took the bread and, looking into the basket, saw small silver bowls filled with spiced meats and curried vegetables. The aromas were tantalising. Her stomach groaned. She spooned some of the rich, dark meat onto her piece of bread.

'He must be very boring, if he's frightened of everyone else being more interesting than him.'

She bit into the bread. The spices ran down her throat and set up a famished tingle. She greedily scoffed the rest.

Zahir sat back. 'I have never heard anything like that said before,' he said guardedly. Then his smile came out like the sun from behind a cloud. 'But I have thought it myself many times.' His eyes twinkled. 'We are interesting enough, with our Changers.'

'Changers?'

Zahir reached out and the lizard walked onto his arm. He brought the animal to his face and gazed into its eyes. Abruptly his eyes clouded white and the lizard twitched.

Then its head snapped round at her, and she could see that it was looking at her with the same focused gaze that Zahir had used. Its long, thin tongue whipped out at her. Then the white dissolved from Zahir's eyes and the lizard jumped into the sand to resume its animal habits.

Susannah decided it was time for some proper answers. 'You said you were going to explain,' she looked down at her curling toes, 'how I lost my shoes.'

Zahir looked embarrassed. 'I had gone collecting in the desert beyond the red walls. There are so many things out there in the desert that people just throw away.'

He paused to bring out a gourd and two glasses from beneath his white robe. He poured a yellow liquid into each and held one out to her. She took it, sniffed, decided it wasn't alcoholic, and gulped it down. It had a sweet aniseed flavour.

He continued: 'I have to be careful out there. The Karkarim, the machine eagles of summer, the King's spies, fly the desert at night and swoop down on anyone who displays suspicious behaviour. Simply being out in the desert at night is suspicious ...'

'Did you find me in the desert?'

'Yes.' He nodded, excited. 'It was a miracle. The air *opened* as though it had been cut.' His face contorted with frightened memory. 'I saw pink organs as though the inside of the air was a living thing, and then you and a young boy were thrown from this strange cut in the air.'

Brandon had come through with her! What had happened to him? 'The boy, was he hurt?'

Zahir was shamefaced. He tried to delay by pouring more of the sweet drink into her glass, but she covered it with a hand. She looked at him pointedly.

'I don't know,' he answered. 'The Karkarim were there so swiftly.'

'They attacked?'

'No, they were simply curious. At first.' He paused. 'You had landed further away from the boy, quite close to where I was hidden, behind a dune. The Karkarim were more interested in him. I was able to pull you some way toward the dune before they noticed.'

'Then they attacked?'

'Yes.' Zahir licked his lips. 'But I was able to distract them. I used your shoes.'

Susannah was confused. 'Didn't these eagles see you?'

Zahir smiled cannily, and Susannah was reminded of her first thought of his wickedness. 'I have a cloak that looks to the eye in the dark like a small mound of sand when I am curled up beneath it. I simply covered us both. Eventually they went back to the boy.'

Susannah was annoyed that he had not attempted to help Brandon. But she did not know how dangerous these Karkarim were. Perhaps Zahir could have done nothing. He had protected her from them, and that was a kind enough act.

'What did they do with the boy?' she asked carefully.

'I can only think they took him to the castle. To the King.'

'Right. Then that is where I'm going, too.' She couldn't leave Brandon in the clutches of a mad king. Who knew what terrible things he was doing to him right this minute? There was not a moment to waste.

Zahir smiled strangely at her. Susannah didn't like it.

'You can't leave. I found you. You're part of my collection now.' His smile took on an unhinged quality. 'You're going to make me the most interesting man in the entire kingdom.'

'I thought that wasn't allowed.'

'Only I shall know,' he said. 'But that is enough.'

'Then there's hardly any point, is there?'

'Don't worry. I shall look after you. I shall clean you and dress you and feed you. You'll be my most prized possession.'

Just like a doll, a plaything, she thought, alarmed at how quickly the season was transforming her into the desires of the Man. Could Zahir be a disguise? Had he found her the moment she leapt? She remembered that connection they now shared. That connection she had wished to break or upset by placing an entire season between them. Well, she had already escaped three attempts on her character by the Man with 8 Faces, so why imagine she couldn't now?

She reached out, grabbed Zahir's cheeks, and pulled.

He yelled and took hold of her wrists.

Susannah pulled harder but felt only flesh beneath. Nothing gave. Zahir made an unpleasant high-pitched squeal. If it was a mask it was a good one.

Susannah let go.

Zahir fell backwards.

She ran.

Knowing that the silks might try to stop her, she didn't bother running through the pots and rugs at the front of the tent. Hoping she was right she threw herself down, burrowing into the sand at the base of the tent.

'No, you cannot leave! You're my prize!'

Zahir's hand grabbed her leg. She kicked and felt her

foot connect with his nose. He cried out and let go.

There was a scratching at the back of her head as the lizard thrashed at her.

Suddenly there was light.

She wriggled under the silk and pushed herself upward into the bright, hot season.

The noise struck her first. The city was alive with a clash of sounds — hawkers crying, entreating for a sale; hymns and prayers rolling musically down the many laneways from mosques and cathedrals; bells tolling over one another in the glassy sky.

She ran past stalls bristling with scimitars, swords and daggers; stalls packed high with towers of fruit; another with colourful parrots squawking on their tethers and lizards basking in their sun-shot cages. One stall was a garden of herbs spilling out into the path she ran down — the scent of rosemary, coriander, mint; the creeping thyme tripping her up.

People in coloured djellabas or skins or dirty rags seethed in the laneways; there was barely enough room to squeeze between them all. Animals — donkeys, camels, orange-faced monkeys, mongrel dogs and ratty cats — hung about the food stalls for scraps of meat and someone's sympathy. Susannah kept away from them, wary they were people in animal clothing. Watching her.

The stench of it all! The spice of cumin and saffron, fish and meat stews mingling with the putrid dung piled in corners. Gusts of wind brought scents of fresh oranges, or smoke from a fire. The air was hot; gulping it down was like eating it. Somewhere the smell of water on stone.

The sun pressed down on her, its heat so intense it was like being inside a clay oven.

This was a city that was, to her mind, full of the interesting, and a great threat to the King. She wondered as she ran, her feet stamping the dusty pathways, if the people were deliberately disobeying him by being so interesting. But then only she, as a newcomer, found it interesting; this was merely the routine of life here.

Her heart pounding, she sheltered in the cool doorway of a mud-brick hut. Tables out the front overflowed with leather-bound books. She had run so far that Zahir should never find her. Though the sand was hot, she was glad that she did not have her shoes — they were an obvious print to follow. She looked around to make sure there was no pursuit; a fleeing girl was, after all, an interesting thing.

The shop she had sheltered by was on top of a hill, overlooking the city. It was a wondrous city, bristling with steeples, onion and turnip domes, and copper and verdigris towers. The ancient pathways, bounded by high red stone walls, seemed a vast canyon.

Turning, she looked up at the fortress above the city. It was hewn from the mountain and glistened with bronze-tipped minarets and solemn battlements. The city grew outward from it like spilled seed. She could see guards in red livery pacing the outer walls and shrank further into the shadow of the hut.

The smell of books enticed her in.

Inside, it was cool; a breeze rippled the pages of the books. Susannah relaxed, the sweat drying on her forehead. The hut teemed with books on every surface. There was not a path to be seen amongst them.

She was startled by a whirring sound and, turning, came face-to-face with a fan. She stood in front of it as it blew cold, refreshing air across her face.

'You do not like the heat either?' said a voice with a plummy English accent.

Susannah whirled about.

Standing before her was a man in a white linen suit and a colonial hat, with wire-frame glasses and small eyes that crinkled in amusement behind them. Despite the heat he wore a paisley cravat. It was his white moustache that held Susannah's attention though, as it grew wildly beneath his nose and down around his mouth, and then kept going until it tangled into a dense beard. He held a curved wooden cane that he leant on heavily. She had a feeling that she knew him, from somewhere just out of reach of memory. His deep smoky tones were comforting and yet also gave her a sense of panic — an image of churned earth and fire came to her: some accident?

He gazed at her with soft, pink eyes. 'Are you lost?'

She must have looked crestfallen. 'Yes,' she admitted, 'I'm lost, and I don't know how to get home.' She sniffed. 'And I've lost the only person who wanted to be my friend.'

'Oh dear.' The man in white leant down, both hands balancing on his cane, and peered over the top of it at her. 'I've just made some tea. Would you like some?' He stopped and frowned. 'Do girls drink tea these days?'

'Yes. I drink tea,' she said. Then she remembered the last time she had sat down to tea, and what had happened. The guilt welled up in her over the murder of Brandon's father. No matter how it had come about, it was her fault.

She had offered an apology to Brandon, a meagre thing, and he had accepted it. But she still wondered about his forgiveness. She could not have been so kind.

The man in white raised his eyebrows at her hesitation. 'I have lemonade, if you don't want tea. Made from real lemons, I'm assured.'

'Lemonade, please,' said Susannah. A cool drink was more appropriate for this climate.

'Now come and sit down and tell me how you got lost.' He sat in a wing chair, the arms piled high with books, and gestured her to another. She had to move a bundle tied together with leather cord before she sat. 'Who knows, I may be able to help.'

'How?' she asked.

'Well, there are a number of books in here on cartography.'

'Cartography?'

The man in white leaned forward. 'Maps,' he said.

Susannah's eyes went up. 'Maps ... of the seasons?'

The man in white smiled. 'Of the seasons ... under the seasons ... and, perhaps, beyond the seasons.' He paused briefly to gauge her reaction. 'Would you be interested in maps like those?'

'I didn't think anyone knew what was beyond the seasons?' She was tentative with hope but guarded against giving too much away.

The man in white reached for a silver carafe and poured a glass of pale yellow liquid. He handed it to Susannah. She took it but did not drink. She would not drink until he answered. He took his time and, going back to the occasional table beside him, he took a floral-patterned teapot and poured himself a cup of sweet-smelling tea. He dropped a slice of lemon into it. He raised the cup to his nose, sniffed, and sighed contentedly.

'The Spinster has some knowledge of the world beyond the seasons,' he said and sipped.

Susannah tasted her lemonade. He was right. It was good. It was sharp and had a refreshing tang.

'I have met the Spinster,' she said carefully. 'She is a wise woman. She can cross the seasons.' She paused. 'It's strange that you're not surprised by another world beyond the seasons. How come?' The man in white's attitude alarmed her. Only someone with criminal access to the seasons' workings could know so much, and there was one criminal who she did not want to come across. At least not yet, while she was unarmed.

The man in white placed his cup on the occasional table and sat back in his armchair. His face was open and friendly, his eyes bright and unconcerned. He gestured at the piles of books around him. 'I read. A lot,' he replied. 'In fact, I have read every book in this hut, and more besides. I absorb their fictions, their stories, their facts, their lies. It is not difficult for me to believe in other worlds when I have experienced so many within the pages of these books.' His grin widened beneath his moustache. 'It is also not difficult for me to see that you are a girl out of your depth. You do not belong in this season, so you could only have come from another or ...'

'I came from spring,' she said.

'But you are not a prisoner?'

'I don't think so. I remember some things, but I don't remember that. Are *you* a prisoner?'

'Not all of us are prisoners here. Sometimes, we end up

here by accident.'

'What kind of accident?' asked Susannah, jumping on the word, wondering if that was how she had arrived.

'For me, a happy one. I chose to stay. A lifetime of reading, of living in other worlds, is a worthwhile life to me. If only I didn't have to endure this stifling heat.' He chuckled to himself. 'But let's not speak of me. I'd much rather hear your story.'

Susannah had been lulled into comfort by his calm tone. But there was something worrying away at the back of her mind. Stories are important here, she thought, but so are names.

'I'll tell you my story,' she said, 'if you tell me your name.'

'Arthur,' he said, without hesitation. 'Arthur Carrington.'

Susannah relaxed. Had he hesitated, refused to give his name, she would have run. The Spinster told her it takes the Man some time to inhabit a character. Though he takes on every aspect, every physical attribute, the name is the last part, the final stitch to seal the skin; the name is the hardest part to own. She was going to have to push her suspicion aside and tell everything. She was going to have to trust someone. It was the only way she was going to get help.

She told Arthur Carrington her story, all that she remembered.

Arthur listened attentively and, when she finished, he stood and gestured for her to follow him. He took her into the dim reaches of the bookshop. Spider webs crackled as they brushed through them and dust settled in their footsteps. There was an air of must and neglect. This was clearly not a shop that sold its books. Was Arthur a collector, too? she wondered.

Arthur hobbled along until he found a particular bookshelf at the back of the hut. He counted along the bookshelf until he came to the number eight and pulled a heavy book from its place. Despite the apparent haphazardness of the shop, he obviously had every book catalogued in his memory. Susannah was envious of his ability, especially when she found herself so forgetful.

Arthur handed her the book. Inscribed in brown leather on the cover were words in gold — *A Book for All Seasons: A Comprehensive Cartographical Study of Egortiye.*

'Egortiye?' she asked.

'It is the name given to the four prisons as a collective land by the old scholars.' His eyes twinkled. 'Interesting, don't you think, that it begins with ego, the sense of self? A world obsessed with identity.'

Susannah dimly registered what Arthur was saying. Her interest was focused on the book in front of her, the book of maps that could be very useful indeed.

It was thick and heavy, and Susannah had to balance it on a nearby tower of books to open it. When she did, she found a beautiful marbled frontispiece but that the rest of the book was entirely blank. She looked at Arthur. 'What are you playing at?'

Arthur smiled. 'Touch a page, any page.'

Susannah looked at it suspiciously and slid a finger slowly down a page. She was amazed when ink appeared to run from her finger and etched a map. It pooled into architectural renderings of buildings, squares, lanes, mosques, castles, towers, and the general minutiae of a precisely drawn city. A deep familiarity went through her as she traced in the designs; she had done this before. In another book, elsewhere. When the map finished drawing itself, Susannah noticed a red line begin to move through the city, up and down the pathways.

'What's that?' she asked Arthur.

'That's you,' he said. 'This book shows where you have been, where you may go, and where you currently are.' His eyes glittered behind his glasses. 'It also shows you where friends are that may need to be rescued, if you only ask it.'

Susannah stared in wonder at the book. The red line began in the desert and then described a roundabout course to a tent. There was a solid circle within the tent, presumably to show the time spent within, and then the red line dashed up and down the many pathways that Susannah had also dashed up and down. It finally came to a stop on the rise of a hill, inside a small hut; here. If the red line was herself, could she then find Brandon, as Arthur had suggested?

'Show me where Brandon is,' she said with authority, and touched the page.

Instantly, a blue line inked itself, beginning from the same place she had entered the season — the desert. It continued straight, not following her path into the city through the gate, but directly over the wall, which she found odd until she remembered the Karkarim had taken Brandon, and they had flown. The blue path continued in this straight line, looping only to settle at a tower the map decreed was "Property of the King".

Arthur gave her a grim look.

'What is it?'

'It is the Vizier's Tower of Punishment. I should have realised. That is the first place dangerous subversives are taken for re-education.'

'Brandon isn't a subversive. He's harmless, and lost, like me.'

'That sounds like rather an interesting predicament,' he replied. 'And that isn't a predicament I'd like to be in, especially with our King.'

'Who's this Vizier?'

'He administers the King's laws ... and punishments. The citizens of summer are closely monitored by the Karkarim to ensure that they do not act outside the character that the King has decreed for them. If they are too interesting he sends them to the tower. They rarely come out the same as they went in.'

This sounded alarmingly like the machinations of the Man with 8 Faces to Susannah, but she decided she had better not jump to conclusions. After all, she had suspected Brandon of being a façade, and she had been wrong.

'I must rescue Brandon!' she cried. She was responsible for killing his father. But she was not going to let *him* be harmed.

Arthur turned sorrowful eyes on her. 'It won't be easy. The tower is heavily guarded.'

Susannah smiled. 'I think it will be very easy.' Her eyes filled with a wicked gleam. 'I think they'll find me very *interesting* indeed.'

CHAPTER TEN
THE TOWER OF PUNISHMENTS

DESPITE SUSANNAH TRYING TO CONVINCE him that she was totally capable — now that she was in possession of the book of seasons (which she carried cumbersomely in a leather satchel he had given her) — Arthur insisted on coming with her to the tower. 'A young girl travelling with an older man who is part of the season will invite less inquiry.' Susannah argued that she was small and less obtrusive, and this gave her the advantage. But he did not listen. Truthfully, she liked Arthur, and she did not want him to get hurt.

The tower was situated on a rocky plateau just outside the fortress walls. It occupied a position of authority over the city below, like a watchful eye. It looked formidable and threatening. Now that she was closer, Susannah could see that it was made of brass, burnished bronze in the sunlight. Though it was in disrepair — the metal tarnished, windows hanging out — it was no less impregnable.

Ten metres away, standing in the shadows by the tower entrance, stood two figures.

'There are only two guards,' said Susannah, surprised.

'Two is enough,' replied Arthur cautiously. 'Look.'

Susannah peered at them. They were dressed in the same scarlet livery as those on the fortress walls. She realised with a shiver that they were not men. They walked upright, and held themselves in the manner that guards should, and held golden spears. But she saw that their faces, which were dark-skinned and hidden beneath their gold helmets, occasionally twitched and opened. Mandibles came apart and clicked together. Black eyes rolled in their sockets, seeing everything.

'They're beetles!' she exclaimed, shivering with disgust.

'Yes,' said Arthur. 'They're fast and very strong. They also have a great sense of smell. This close we shall soon be sniffed out.'

'I want to be sniffed out. It looks like there's only one way into this tower, so we might as well get this over with. Are you ready?'

Arthur placed a hand on her shoulder. 'Are you absolutely sure you want to go through with this? No one has ever come out of that tower unchanged. No one knows what is inside and what terrible punishments await.'

Susannah became stubborn; there was no possible way he was going to stop her from getting inside. 'I know what's in there,' she said. 'Brandon.'

She marched forward to greet the uniformed beetles.

As soon as they saw her they stepped forward, thrusting their spears at her. Susannah faltered at such aggression. They hissed and clacked their mandibles and she squirmed; she disliked insects: their throbbing bodies, their twitching legs. But she had to go through with this.

She stopped, stood legs apart, hands on hips. She

glanced behind her and was glad to see Arthur standing a little way off, leaning heavily on his left leg so he could raise his cane to fend off the beetles should they attack.

She thought for a moment and then said, 'My name is Susannah Alexandra Jane Hattersley. I've heard that your King is the most interesting person in this season.' She paused. 'I do not agree. I've come to tell you that I have found a much more interesting person.' She stared into the dark orb of a beetle's eye. 'Myself!' Arthur cleared his throat. 'Oh, and this man here is interesting, too, almost more than me. He reads a lot of books, which the King would outlaw if he knew how exciting they were.' She smiled sneakily. 'It has changed his character, I'm sure.' She leaned forward. 'I believe that is against the law.'

The scarlet guards chirruped. Deciding that the girl with no shoes and the man in white were a possible threat, they jabbed them with their spears.

Susannah yelped. 'Ouch! Stop that immediately. Stop it! I demand you take us to see the Vizier! Instantly!' She frowned. 'Otherwise I will do something hideously interesting.'

'And I shall do something intriguing,' said Arthur, a naughty twinkle in his eye.

The beetle guards considered, and then motioned to the tower entrance. One of them placed a spear into a small hole in the outer casing. There was a click. The tower clanged from within and slowly a section of metal indented to reveal a door. It split apart, opening up to receive them.

As Susannah went through the brass doors, the ticking of clockwork became louder — the grinding of cogs resounded. She wondered if the sound was the building's mechanics, or the sound of punishments.

The doors closed behind them with a solemn boom and she remembered Arthur's statement: 'No one comes out unchanged.' She had wanted to come inside to rescue her friend, but what changes were now in store for her?

Inside the tower, it was obvious that it was run by clockwork, the inner workings uncovered. Perhaps the Vizier liked the pervasive tick-tick-tick of the cogs as they turned; measuring the hours and minutes of some torture he had devised. She could imagine the steady ticking growing into a torture itself.

Susannah and Arthur were shepherded roughly by the scarlet guards up a winding staircase. The stairs were also made of brass and they had to be careful not to slip on the slick surface. Susannah was aware of Arthur's fragile state and told him to lean on her shoulder when he could. The guards chirruped taunts behind them. Susannah shuddered being this close to their rasping carapaces, their claws, their black mouths.

Eventually they reached a landing littered with broken cogs and wheels. Once again, a beetle guard placed its spear against the wall. A door opened to reveal a small room. Two chairs were set out in the centre, a claw-legged table held a bowl of fruit, and a solid, latched window took up the whole wall at the far end of the room. They were rudely shoved inside. The doors closed with a resounding clang.

'Well, it's not half as bad as I expected,' said Arthur, glancing around, taking an interest in the bowl of fruit. He picked up an apple and bit into it. 'I wonder if the stories have been exaggerated.'

Susannah rolled her eyes. 'I don't think the Vizier is going to offer us tea and ask us why we're here,' she replied. She looked out the fastened window, noticing they were high up, the city spreading like a maze below. 'I think this is to make us comfortable before the torture.'

Arthur spat out his apple. 'I'm inclined to agree.' He placed it back in the bowl. 'Gone bad,' he explained.

'While we wait we may as well explore the tower.'

She pulled the *Book for All Seasons* from her satchel. As she opened it, she noticed that the pages she had touched before were no longer blank but had filled in permanently; the ink was no longer fresh but faded brown with age. She looked inquiringly at Arthur. He had taken a seat in one of the chairs, being out of breath from the climb.

'I forgot to tell you,' he said, seeing the map. 'Once you have asked the book to map a region or a building, or even to follow a person, it stays written, as long as you are the holder of the book. I once filled all but ten pages of it with my enquiries, but that was all erased when I gave it to you. It encourages great adventure, don't you think?'

Susannah was annoyed. To have a ready map of all seasons was far preferable to one she had to actively create by imagination. 'I suppose so,' she replied.

Arthur saw her irritation. 'You can create your own world now, simply by asking it what you wish to see, rather than travelling mine. It will no doubt tell you of secret places I have never known.' His eyes became grave. 'Never let anyone take it from you. If it is out of your possession for longer than a day, everything is lost.'

If it could tell her where everything was, and any particular person she wished to follow, she could keep out of harm's way. She could hide from the Man with 8 Faces.

First things first, she wanted to know where Brundon was. She placed a finger on the smooth vellum and thought about his hooves and hairy arms, his horns and his doe eyes. Ink bloomed beneath her finger, quickly tracing in the architecture of the tower, with precise measurements of each room. Though it looked outwardly like a simple tower, the plans revealed it was more complex. Not fully understanding what she was seeing she showed Arthur.

'Goodness,' he said.

There was a good reason why it was clockwork. Large engines existed beneath, with curved implements attached to burrow into the rock.

'It seems,' said Arthur, surprised, 'that the whole tower is made to move.'

'Or burrow underground,' suggested Susannah. 'That looks like a tunnel to me.' She pointed to a corridor underneath them.

'I wonder why the Vizier wants to tunnel underneath the palace.'

Susannah had a nasty thought. 'Perhaps he wants to tunnel into the other seasons?'

They gave each other a grave glance.

'I don't see your friend,' he said.

Susannah looked closely at the tower's design. She noticed the cleverly concealed cells wrapped around the central staircase. She quickly found theirs when a red dot appeared. There were cells until the top floor, which looked like a laboratory, with its images of grotesque devices. It had to be the Vizier's torture chamber. As she stared at the room and its design began to flow onto a separate page, so she could further explore it, a blue ink dot wet the page.

'Brandon!' she cried. 'He *is* here!' She was almost overwhelmed by relief that her friend was nearby.

Abruptly, a thinner blue line detached itself from Brandon and began to draw from the topmost room, rapidly down the staircase.

'What's that?' Susannah wondered.

Arthur shrugged. 'Something to do with your friend, perhaps?'

'I'm not sure,' she said. 'But it's stopped right outside our door!' She pointed at the large red circle that signified herself, and the light blue line spinning in small circles at the cell door.

Arthur leapt up, surprisingly fast for a man of his years, and went to the door. He put an ear to it and listened. He looked at Susannah warily. 'There's certainly something out there. It's buzzing.'

'A beetle guard,' she whispered.

Before Arthur could reply there was a barrage of hard thumps that made the metal ring. Arthur jumped back, taking Susannah's hand.

'Not a beetle guard, I think,' he said. He glanced at her. 'Perhaps a Changer.'

Susannah slammed the book closed, ready to use it as a weapon.

The attack stopped, and there was an expectant silence. Then a solid *thunk* as though a bolt had been drawn back. The doors began slowly to open.

Susannah drew in breath.

'Whatever it is, it's managed to hit an opening mechanism,' Arthur said, squeezing her hand reassuringly.

Susannah waited, and waited, until the doors reached

their apex and the machinery stopped grinding. She peered out for the thing that had violently attacked them. But there was nothing in sight. She looked up at Arthur, who raised an eyebrow. Unlocking her hand from his, she took a step forward …

A buzzing metallic thing came flying at her from the landing. It darted about her head, the noise of wings startling her. She squealed and tried to brush it away. Arthur brandished his cane. All of a sudden it flew to the window and settled on the ledge. Susannah slowly turned around, willing it to stay there.

It was small and made of metal, with a segmented thorax, the wings long and fine. Its round eyes regarded her. Arthur had crept forward and was raising his cane to strike.

'No!' she yelled, grabbing his arm. The dragonfly twitched, looking from girl to man. 'It's okay.' She smiled. 'It's Brandon's dragonfly. He made it for me.'

Arthur lowered his cane. 'Whatever for?'

Susannah reached out a hand. The dragonfly flew to her and alighted on her open palm. 'So that I would always have a piece of him. So that I could find him whenever we got separated.' She found herself grinning. 'In a way, it *is* a Changer.' She brought the dragonfly up to her eyes, noticing how fluid its metallic movements were, how artfully it was made. 'Take us to Brandon,' she said.

The insect lifted from her palm and was quickly out the door. Pausing only to grab her satchel, Susannah raced after it.

A cry echoed down the stairs as they raced upwards. It was the cry of a boy being punished. Susannah was sure it was Brandon and ran faster, leaving Arthur behind. The dragonfly darted upwards, hovering at intervals to let her catch up. The stairs went on forever. Susannah ran and ran, her satchel banging into her side, until eventually she reached the top.

She entered immediately into the room the book had shown her at the top of the tower. As the pictures had suggested it was a torture chamber, filled with crude, harmful devices. They brimmed with barbs, stained a rust colour from former punishments. The room was large, and the walls were made of brass. It had a wraparound window, like a lighthouse. Cogs and pulleys showed in a roof that rounded in a dome.

There was a cry from the other side of the room. 'Ah, interesting, you've decided to resist,' said a sharp, nasal voice.

The dragonfly settled on her shoulder, quivering. Susannah peered around a deadly device, realising her entrance had not been noticed. She heard Arthur wheezing his way up the stairs and put a finger to her lips. He leaned heavily on his cane to catch his breath.

'You realise it will make the Janus machine probe deeper. And inflict more pain. It's also evidence of a guilty character. They always fight.'

Creeping between the machines, Susannah moved forward until she could see what was being done to her friend.

Brandon was strapped to an upright metal X, wrists and ankles tethered by leather cord. His legs bucked, hooves kicking, but the restraints held. Susannah could tell he was distressed even though she couldn't see his face. For strapped to his face was a Mask of Lies. This one had been altered. Spidery metal legs extruded from the porcelain mask and wrapped around his head. The porcelain took on frightening liquid shapes. Every so often it rippled with obvious glee, and Brandon cried out in terror.

'Intriguing. It seems this is not your normal physical appearance. So who are you hiding beneath? If you're some sort of new Changer I will pull whoever you are out!'

The wicked voice issued from the man who stood over Brandon, a tall man colourfully dressed. His robe was a patchwork of red, green and gold squares, like a Klimt painting. He wore a Mandarin's pointed hat made of the same material. It sat upon a face with cruel eyes under dark eyebrows, a thin-lipped mouth, and cheekbones that could slice with their disdain. For all his get-up, he was missing something to give him the villainous appearance he clearly wanted. It was his pale face; an indoor man, frightened of the sunshine. He looked cold and slimy to the touch. The most frightening thing about him was his two-inch-long gold nails. Nails that stroked the controls of a clockwork device, lovingly teasing out pain.

'Who are you, boy?' he whispered. 'I'll find you out. I am the King's Vizier: I see everything he wants to see. I administer characters to all persons of this season.' He paused, eyes narrowing. 'I did not administer yours. I know you are from another season. But why are you here in mine?' Brandon whimpered. The Vizier stroked his device. 'Oh, no need to answer. I can tear it from you. And once you are broken, you'll be as mindless as those I make into beetle guards.'

The beetle guards were once men! And he was going to turn Brandon into one! Susannah was about to rush forward when Arthur clamped a hand on her shoulder.

'Wait,' he said.

'What do you mean, "wait"? He's torturing Brandon!' She pulled forward. Again, he restrained her.

'He has dangerous powers. You don't go marching in without a plan. Besides, we know he's interested in other seasons. Perhaps we'll find he knows an exit from this one.'

She struggled through a stream of emotions — anger at his callousness, doubt at her cavalier attitude, acceptance of his reason, stubbornness at her need to act. But she did not move. She decided that if the Vizier intended actual physical harm she'd stop him, regardless of Arthur's warning.

There was a part of her, a suspicious part, that wondered why the old man should be so interested in getting out of the season. He told her he'd chosen summer, as though he had a choice, and was content but for the heat. She did not like this distrusting state, but she needed to be on her guard.

The Vizier twisted the clockwork ball in his hand, and thin levers sprang out from within. He quickly moved one into gear, as one might do in a car. 'This is the Janus mask, a clever invention, with modifications of my own, of course. It hooks into your mind and searches out exactly what you are, the very essence of your character.' He delicately pulled another lever. 'It also tells me of your closest friends, your enemies, every little dark thought. Ingenious, don't you think?' He twisted a final lever and leaned hungrily forward to watch.

The mask quivered, and Brandon cried out. Susannah wanted to run forward and stop his torture, but Arthur still gripped her shoulder. The mask slithered on her friend's face, forming strange shapes. Shapes, she realised, that she recognised. Those wrinkles, those folds of skin, that white beehive — that was the Spinster.

'So,' said the Vizier, 'You are acquainted with that irritating woman.' The mask undulated into Brandon's true face beneath, a mirror image, then the hair grew backwards into the skin, the horns into the scalp, leaving the fresh face of a wide-eyed boy. 'The Spinster did this to you! How unkind. You must be a bad boy to have been punished already.' The mask then gave him a vision of Tom, and Susannah felt a pang go through her; there was a pain there that she was going to have for a long time, her own self-inflicted punishment. 'A common man, of no interest to me.' Susannah's pain was quickly replaced with anger. The mask pulsed, as though the next features it sought were difficult. A girl's face: black ringlets framing fiery, intelligent eyes and an arrogant pout; an inquisitive, naughty face. Susannah did not immediately recognise her.

Arthur's grip lessened. 'It's you,' he whispered. 'But … changed somehow. Not as you are now.'

Susannah peered at the shifting liquid representation. It *was* her. But there was something missing, something she possessed now that she had not then. She could not work out what it was.

Underneath the mask Brandon murmured, 'Chloe …'

'Yes!' cried the Vizier triumphantly. 'This is the girl my Karkarim told me of, the one who was seen with you. Since you seem too much a simpleton, it must have been she who opened the barrier.' He considered for a moment. 'I shall have to entice her out with a trap. You shall be it. I need only rewrite your character a little.' He brought his attention back to the clockwork ball.

Susannah broke free from Arthur's hold, raced forward and smacked the golden ball from the Vizier's hand. Such was her aggression that it hit the wall and broke apart, spilling clockwork everywhere.

'You leave my friend alone, you hideous man!'

'My, my, such a result so quickly,' said the Vizier, licking wormy lips. He outstretched his golden talons.

But Arthur was there before Susannah, smacking the Vizier across the face with his cane. He came forward, enraged, ready to challenge the old man, but then the dragonfly swooped about the Vizier's head, darting in to stab at his face. The torturer cowered and retreated to a corner of the room. Arthur went too, covering him with the cane.

'Get him out of that contraption,' Arthur said.

Susannah pulled at the leather straps pinioning Brandon. 'It's all right, Brandon. It's me, Susannah! You're safe now.' She stroked his arm.

Since her destruction of the clockwork device, the mask had solidified and was in its natural porcelain state. She gently lifted it off her friend's face and dropped it to the floor where it cracked from brow to cheek.

'See. I told you. It's me. I came to rescue you.'

Brandon's eyes rolled for a moment before settling on hers. He had been crying and his face was red and hot. Susannah gazed upon his bulky form, his hairy face, his horns, his sweet hooves, and found herself nervous without a single reason why. There was a terrible pause when she thought he might have been too changed by the torture to ever be the Brandon she knew. Then Arthur said from across the room, 'Is he all right?' And, like a switch flicked, intelligence and warmth flooded into his eyes and they locked with hers. She hugged him.

Over her shoulder he said, 'Susannah,' as though it were a new name that he was trying out in his mouth and it didn't quite work yet. To help him she replied, 'Yes.'

'My lady.'

'Susannah', she said pointedly. 'What do you remember?' she asked, still holding him.

'I ... I remember ... pink veins strangling me. A strange dream. Metal eagles. Then ... then a nightmare ... and seeing you ... just now.' He broke into a giddy smile, though it was fraught with too much remembered pain.

She smiled back.

His eyes flicked away, searching the room. He took in the Vizier glaring at them from his corner, the old man in the white suit holding him at cane point, the dragonfly hovering, and then the bronze circular chamber around them with its grotesque devices. His eyes came back to her. 'Is this summer?'

The Vizier answered him. 'Yes, it is. Which season did you expect?'

'Be quiet,' snapped Arthur. 'It's of no concern to you.'

'Oh, but it is,' said the Vizier. 'I am employed to regulate this season with the King's law. And that includes stopping undesirables who breach the season by unknown means, to create subversion and chaos with their uncontrolled characters!' He moved forward, ignoring the warning buzz from the dragonfly. 'I need to know *where* you have come from, and, more importantly, how.'

Susannah took a step toward him. 'You seem very *interested* in us,' she provoked. 'But what if I told the King that his Vizier is becoming too *interested* in getting out of the season.' The Vizier's eyes flashed. 'We know about the clockwork engines underneath this tower.'

'They are merely to keep it anchored on this precipice of rock.'

Arthur harrumphed. 'They are quite clearly digging into the rock, which, I imagine, would not help support the tower at all.'

The Vizier glared at them, and then laughed. 'It does not matter. I may do as I please, regardless of the King's ridiculous paranoid rules. All he cares for is his popularity rating: mere numbers. And I always give him excellent numbers. He is far more likely to believe me than you.'

It was time, Susannah thought, to knock this man from his pedestal. 'Not if we can tell him what you do not know.'

'What do you mean?'

Susannah smirked. 'Tunnelling below the earth is not the way out.'

Arthur turned, giving her a hopeful look.

The Vizier gazed at her intently for a moment, then grinned, showing yellow teeth. 'So, you do know more than the boy simpleton.' He clicked his talons together. 'It is evidently your pretty self whom I must torture instead.' He moved forward.

Arthur's cane came up, but he was off-guard. The Vizier's talons scythed through the air, raking Arthur's face. The old man cried out and fell. The Vizier strode across the room, not taking his eyes off Susannah for a second.

The dragonfly attacked. The torturer ducked, weaved, reached out and plucked the insect from the air and dashed it against a wall. Metal segments flew everywhere; the buzzing stopped.

Susannah stood her ground. They could not run. There was only the balcony behind them and an obstacle course of harmful devices before them. Brandon pushed her behind him, where she began to protest.

The Vizier reached out, talons ready to rend flesh. They were sharp in both the children's vision.

Suddenly he fell, crashing to the ground, screaming in pain. Behind him, the children could see Arthur, gasping after using his cane to lever a machine off its supports. The machine had fallen onto the Vizier's right leg, crushing it, stopping him in his tracks. He had enough wit about him to shake the pain away and rake the ground before the children. He scratched at them vainly, snarling.

Arthur appeared shocked at what he had done.

'Come on,' said Susannah. 'We need to get out of here.' He looked wanly at her, holding his scratched face. 'Arthur?' she prompted. He nodded.

Brandon had gone to a metal hole in the wall and was rifling about in its contents. 'Brandon!' she called. 'Come on!'

He ignored her, continuing his search. Just as she determined to fetch him he snatched up something with a glad cry and shoved it down his shirt.

There was a nasty gurgle from the Vizier's prostrate body. It was probably what he deserved but Susannah pitied him.

'I'm sorry,' she said.

The Vizier heard her and an eye flicked open, stared fixedly at her. 'You … can't escape,' he whispered. And then he opened his mouth wide and screamed: 'KARKARIM! KARKARIM!'

Susannah and Arthur locked worried glances. 'Run!' he cried.

They ran.

At the entrance to the tower were three enormous machine eagles — the Karkarim. Their metal joints wheezed and hissed as gyros wound inside them. Their metal talons, which their master imitated, clawed the ground outside the tower, waiting for something to tear apart. This close, Susannah could see their bodies were etched with intricate runes.

'There must be another way out!'

'The book,' Arthur suggested. 'Quickly!'

She took out the book, gaining a quizzical look from Brandon. She turned to the page with the tower, touched the paper, and commanded, 'Hidden exits.'

The book rapidly did nothing at all. Susannah repeated her request. Still nothing happened. Exasperated, she shook it. 'Stupid thing!'

Arthur stopped her. 'There is only one way out,' he said gently. 'I shall give you both a diversion.'

'But they'll kill you,' said Brandon.

'No. I don't think they will. I am not who they want.'

'Don't you have a Changer you can jump into?' she asked desperately.

Arthur smiled, and his eyes crinkled. 'Alas, no. I'm afraid I don't belong here, so I do not have those natural abilities.'

'But they will take you to the King,' said Susannah, upset.

'Possibly,' replied Arthur. 'But he will find I am only a

man of the season who reads a few too many books and has a few too many interesting if impossible ideas. And he will not need to torture me to discover that.' He gazed dolefully at her, and she wondered whether he believed what he was saying. He came forward and hugged her. 'I have had such fun, Susannah.'

'I will rescue you,' she said.

Arthur smiled. 'I'm sure you will.'

He shook Brandon's hand. 'Take care of her. She's a very interesting young lady, and that alone will get her into much trouble.' He looked at Susannah. 'And take care of that book.'

He doesn't expect to ever see us again, she thought. He's going to ... 'Arthur!' she cried. But he had already walked out into the bright sunshine.

The Karkarim turned toward him, appraising him with their whirring mechanical eyes. Arthur doffed his hat at them. 'I have just been involved in the most interesting adventure. I —'

But before he could say another word, claws were raised and sliced Arthur Carrington into four red pieces. The Karkarim snapped playfully at the parts.

Susannah gasped, horrified. Cold guilt coursed through her at yet another person who had come to harm, because of her.

And then Brandon pulled her away into the painful summer light.

CHAPTER ELEVEN
THE MARK OF SUMMER

SUSANNAH RAN AND RAN AND ran, until all she could feel was the hard, red sand underfoot. She concentrated on running; that was all there was. She would not let her mind tick over, would not let a thought enter her head.

Above, she heard the cries of the Karkarim, searching her out.

It was coming on to twilight and the last brilliance of the sun screamed down on her. Traders packed away their day-to-day offerings to reveal colourful new wares. They were reinvigorated by the prospect of more profitable sales in the cool, sociable hours of the night. They glanced up at Susannah as she ran, wondering why she was in a hurry. She looked an interesting girl, black ringlets flying, in a strange dress with a tail that impeded her run.

At some point she lost Brandon — his hand snatched from hers — and that sudden emptiness would have worried her but now ... but now ...

No-one comes out of that tower unchanged, Arthur said. She had thought herself above the rules of this world, scoffed at the dangers. How could she be harmed? Someone who did not belong, someone who'd been told they did not "fit". But this insidious season had got inside her, sifting through grain by sandy grain. It had filled her up with its cruelty and danger and turned her into an object of harm simply by being herself. She would not let anyone else get hurt. She had to run, hide, make sure that no one befriended her. She had killed two good men.

Her heart was fit to burst, her breathing laboured, her feet aching, her nostrils filled with sand. Yet her physical pain could not override her turbulent thoughts. She stopped and dropped to the sand. She pulled in air.

It had rapidly turned to dusk. The sky was a dramatic orange and green. Along the canyon pathways lamps on poles were lit, giving the city an expectant glow. From Susannah's vantage point high on a hill, they looked like a swarm of fireflies. Stunned by the day's heat, the night took on a more relaxed quality — sociable voices, laughter, the clink of glass. Bells rang from the towers, marking day's end and the unknown promises of the night.

How could a city so cruel by day hold such beauty by night?

Susannah found herself thinking of the Man with 8 Faces, and his ability to take on false appearances. Could he be here? She had thought he was disguising himself as the much-feared Vizier. But she found that man a pitiful villain, tied to the season, intent on his own escape. She'd have known had the Vizier been the Man. He had sampled her, but she also had part of him inside her. She gazed across the city and let her mind wander ...

She found herself infused with the heady sounds and smells of the night — spices and dust, cloth and newly-washed skin; grilled meats, salted fish, fresh herbs; hot pans sizzling, the strumming of sitars, a babble of voices ... Susannah took it all in, feeling as though each sound was made for her alone.

Suddenly her vision telescoped, pulling the horizon close.

She was in the desert. The air was warm, heat radiating from the dunes. There was nothing for miles. She blinked, and a cut appeared. She turned her head. And the cut widened into a shimmering picture. It was the spring season. She could see the maze and the dripping garden; in the distance, the crumbling palace. Memory rushed into her, filling her up. And a name came at her with formidable intent — *Chloe*.

She was slammed back into her body, retreating from it. The name meant something to her. But she did not know who Chloe was. Her name was Susannah.

She blinked. The vision had been an unclear one, though she'd felt a great sense of loss that had frightened her. Was Chloe a character the Man had assumed? Was it a warning? She had seen the barrier, seen how she'd entered the season. Had she left a gap for him to follow after? It was not proof that the Man was here in the season. But it made her uneasy. If he *was* here he was hiding himself well. In any case, she would be wary of girls named Chloe.

She looked up at the wall towering above her and felt deja vu as she gazed beyond to the fortress. Turning, she found her crazy-paving run had brought her full circle. She had slumped down against Arthur's hut. Her guilt had brought her back.

Standing, she lifted the cloth flap and went inside.

The smell of dry, musty books enveloped her as she entered, and she swallowed back tears. It was as though Arthur's familiar spirit had come to greet her. She walked further into the hut, feeling watched; all the books alive, wondering what place she might have in their stories.

A cool, evening breeze blew in. The books crackled their pages. In that small second, Susannah realised someone else was in the hut with her.

'Susannah?' said a deep voice, accusingly.

She turned. Brandon was standing in the entrance. He was dusted with red, and there were rips in his clothing. He had a cut on his forehead, shocking against his pale skin. His hairy cheeks and forearms, his horns and his hooves made him more animalistic than ever. He had lost his enchanting nature in this season. There was a subdued menace about him now.

She was not pleased to see him.

'You ran away,' he said.

'Yes,' she replied. Why was he angry with her?

He took a step forward.

'Don't,' she said. 'Keep away.'

'Keep away?'

'I'm not safe.'

He gave an unattractive snort. 'I know that,' he said. He touched the red weal above his eye.

'How did you find me?' she asked.

He swung her leather satchel from his back. He pulled the book of maps from it. 'I followed your red line.'

Susannah was annoyed at her carelessness. She hadn't even known she had lost the priceless book. She frowned. How had Brandon been able to read it?

'Why did you run away?' he asked fiercely. Susannah bit her lip. Brandon didn't wait for an answer. 'You come to rescue me and then you deliberately leave me out there.' He gestured violently behind him.

'I'm not safe,' she said again.

'I know that!' He gritted his teeth. 'If I'd never met you Papa would still be alive!' For a moment his eyes darkened, then he softened. 'We agreed. Back in spring. To run away *together*.'

All animosity left her. He was right. They had agreed to take the danger away from spring. But it had followed them anyway.

'I'm sorry,' she said. 'But things ... changed.'

'Yes,' he replied, coming forward. 'It's a new season. You've got to change with each one.'

But Susannah's wariness hadn't quite gone. 'Your enchantment isn't working,' she said, gauging his reaction.

'Isn't it?' He looked ruefully down at himself. 'The spell hasn't reversed.'

'Perhaps it's something the Vizier did?'

Brandon shuddered. 'I don't ... know. That man did something terrible to me.'

Susannah did not intend to be kind. 'He put a Mask of Lies on you. He was trying to dramatise you. Like your father, I expect.'

He rounded on her, eyes flashing. 'Why are you so unkind?' He was now close enough to touch her if he reached out. 'You have changed. You look ... different somehow. Harder. Your eyes are ... colder. Almost as though ...' His eyes widened. 'As though you're a character, a mask!'

'How dare you! You're the one who's changed. No

enchantment, a more beastly appearance. And you were never angry before; you always called me "My Lady".' She slatted her eyes. 'Who are you really?'

Brandon suddenly slumped, all anger leaving him. His voice was small when he spoke. 'It's just me — Brandon Tuck.' He paused. 'I told you. That man did something to me in the tower. It … hurt.'

Susannah came forward and hugged him. 'I'm sorry, Brandon. It's this season. It's been so horrid that I'm suspicious of everything and everyone. I don't have anyone to help me.'

'Yes, you do.'

She smiled and withdrew from the hug. Good old Brandon, she thought. Up close she noticed wrinkles under his eyes. They had not been there before.

'Promise,' he said, gazing at her with those dazzling blue eyes, 'never to run away from me again.'

She frowned, full of doubt. 'I can't promise that. I'm too dangerous. If you stay with me you could get hurt again.'

'Not if I can help it.'

'You won't be able to stop it,' she said. 'It's better if you're not around me.'

Brandon was quiet for some time. Then he made a decision. 'In that case, I think there's only one thing to do.'

Susannah saw the wicked twinkle of the old Brandon in his eyes. 'What are you thinking?'

'We've both been hurt by the Man. Instead of hiding, isn't it time we found him and hurt him back?'

'We don't know how to hurt him,' she reasoned.

'Not yet,' he agreed. 'But we know what he wants. He wants you. And by going after him we put ourselves in danger, and no one else.'

She thought about that for a moment. 'You want to use me as bait.'

Brandon raised an eyebrow. 'It's a good way to trap him.'

'If he's even here,' she said. 'I tried to find him before but got nothing.'

'Well, you haven't made yourself known yet.'

Susannah nodded. 'I suppose we could make ourselves interesting to the people in charge. That king, for instance. He sounds like a nasty piece of work.'

'Though you know what will happen,' said Brandon.

Susannah caught his fearful expression. 'It's the only way,' she said. She gripped his shoulders. 'No one gets hurt this time, okay?'

Brandon sighed and nodded. Susannah rubbed his furry cheek.

She took his hand and they walked out into the summer night, ready to cause a ruckus to summon the Karkarim.

It was utterly changed. The alleyways that had been dusty and inhospitable during the day had transformed into friendly, colourful spaces. They were full of makeshift cafes and eating carts, people sitting on stools dragged out from houses and stores. Strings of light smothered everything in a soft glow. Traders didn't break the peaceful atmosphere with loud hawking. Instead, they pulled their customers in by draping silks across their shoulders, or placing antiques in their hands, by shamelessly throwing spices over their heads and offering a bargain wash inside.

There was a gentle susurration of noise — a conglomeration of gossip and banalities, news and deals, plans and cruelties, complaints and resolutions, comments and arguments, talk and chat. The voice of summer, turning in the night sky like a vast entity.

This was the time — the King concerned with the workings of his own house — when the citizens of summer could be moderately interesting and get away with it. The Karkarim still circled the night sky, listening to the conversations, but unless there was an overly raucous party, or fight, the night's revelries were rarely raided. They had simply become a normality, and quite uninteresting to anyone but a newcomer to the season. And, of course, newcomers were not allowed into the season without the King's permission. Susannah and Brandon were about to put this to the test.

Into this dance of light and play they came, arm in arm, sauntering confidently down the alleyways. Susannah had a look of self-importance, as though she were the queen of the season (it was a look she had learned from the Queen of Spring). Brandon, less comfortable with his role, nevertheless brought all his animalism to bear and thrust out his broad chest, marching forward like a showy bull. To say they were noticed was an understatement.

Susannah was in her element, eyes sparkling, daring anyone to stop her fantastic performance. She felt comfortable with Brandon's arm hooked through her own. His hairs were not at all bristly but soft like down. She was thrilled as the crowds parted for them; she could see the people's eyes widen as they passed by, full of curiosity and fright. There was a moment when a voice inside her head rippled up from the depths with a cautionary warning at her attitude, but she stifled it.

Always she looked to the sky, searching for the vicious metal eagles.

Brandon's stony mask broke into a scowl at how easily Susannah was slipping into her imperious role. To him she was changed; she scared him with her new hardness.

He had wanted to see the other seasons with Susannah; there was the promise of new adventures in her purposelessness. But it wasn't as he expected. It was far more dangerous, far more unsettling. For he, too, had changed. The Vizier had placed something new inside him, and he now recognised his beastliness. He could feel the violence within. This season was not good for them; it encouraged bitterness and spite. But in order to break its rules, to become noticed, they would have to be cruel, to be worse than anything the season had produced. That frightened him. He did not want to turn into a villain. It would make him that much closer to the *thing* that had killed his father. He wanted to be good. He only had to look at his stubby hooves, his hairy arms, to see what came of deceit. But he also knew he could go far in this season.

They came to an intersection where four alleyways met. There was a small well in the centre, surrounded by people. They each had a tin basin they had filled with dirty red water. Some were bathing, and the water made their skins glisten in the lamplight. Others were vigorously washing their garments. Children darted in and out of the busy scene, splashing one another.

As Susannah and Brandon marched up, everything stopped. People gazed at Brandon's hooves and horns, at his fierce countenance (he had screwed his eyes into slits). All noise ceased. Then there was a whisper: 'The Devil …'

'And his mistress … Lilith.'

Susannah took a step forward. 'We are not here to harm you.'

A young man, dressed in rags, called up some courage to yell out, 'What do you want?'

'We want to tell you something interesting,' said Susannah, her gaze roving over them.

'That is forbidden,' said the young man.

'That is ridiculous!' Susannah replied. She gestured at the lights, the colour, the sights and sounds. 'This is all very interesting. The King will not like what he sees if he comes down here tonight.'

'The King never comes out of his castle. He has others for that.'

'Would the King send a girl to spy on you?' Susannah scoffed.

The young man looked at Brandon's animal features. 'What about him? Is he a new experiment of the Vizier's?'

Thinking quickly, she turned to Brandon. 'He is my Changer, and my guide through these lands. As you have noticed, we are strangers in this season —' She ran on before they could interrupt. 'Do not ask how we came here. I will not tell you. All I will say is that we are not friends of your king, or your vizier. We are not spies.' She paused meaningfully. 'We want to help you.'

'Help us … do what?' asked the young man.

Susannah grinned with superiority. 'Help you overthrow your king!'

There was a terrified murmur from the crowd.

'You must not say such things!'

'Why not?' Susannah snapped. 'You clearly don't like

him. He is a bad king. He hurts you. His Vizier tortures you and enchants you so you become beetle guards. Don't you want to get rid of him?'

The young man came closer.

Brandon, in response, glowered.

The young man looked carefully at them for some time, measuring the truth in her story.

'And who would you put on the throne, in his place?' he asked.

She took a step forward and looked into the young man's clear brown eyes. 'Someone who would be kind to the people. Someone who knew what they wanted, someone who would pull down the Vizier's tower, and melt it for scrap!' Her voice was rising. 'Someone who would let the people gossip about him, and laugh, who would never make a man a beetle guard again. Someone who would make this a season where people smiled and loved and lived their lives happily without this unkind, incompetent —'

'Susannah,' said Brandon, warningly.

'King of Numbers!' she finished grandly.

The crowd before her, glistening wetly, had become animated at her speech, their eyes wide at her disobedience. Some even shyly tested smiles. She looked at them now, and saw their faces fall back into grimness and shock. It was what she wanted to see, but she still felt sad.

There was a gust of air at her back.

Brandon cried, 'Susannah!'

And though she had expected it, had deliberately made it happen, it shocked her how quickly the eagles came, and were in the midst of the crowd, pecking and scratching and flinging people bodily from the melee. She put on her bravest face and stood her ground. She shouted at the eagles so they focused on her. She would not allow a single death. The crowd ran as she attracted the birds' attention. Their talons scratched the ground and they turned their beady eyes upon her. Beaks snapped viciously open and shut. She wanted to run, fear sizzling along the top of her skin. These inhuman monsters had killed Arthur. But they would not kill her. The King would want to speak with her.

The metal eagles whirred forward till they were looking eye to eye.

She took Brandon's hand, squeezing it hard. He was shaking. 'It's all right,' she whispered, not taking her eyes off the birds for a moment.

'I want to see your king,' she said, and was surprised when her voice sounded solid and unwavering.

The foremost eagle rotated its head, gears grinding, considering. Then it screeched a machine cry and darted forward.

Susannah flinched.

But it only gripped her dress in its beak and gently lifted her up. When her feet left the ground, her stomach lurched. Brandon was similarly lifted up and gave a cry. With the two children held fast in their beaks, the Karkarim rose into the sky. With broad sweeps of their wings, they headed for the King's fortress.

CHAPTER TWELVE
THE SUN KING

A SANDSTORM ARRIVED FROM NOWHERE, barrelling over the horizon, the clouds reaching them in minutes. From above, it magically condensed from nothing. Susannah doubted it was a natural phenomenon. Had the season become unstable?

The sand moved as though seeking prey. Yet it parted like water as the Karkarim flew through it. Susannah was reminded of the protective runes on the hands of the spring clockwork women. Clearly the runes in the metalwork of the giant eagles had the same effect.

The Karkarim increased their speed and swooped down to the fortress, their precious cargo tightly held in their beaks. Though the initial ascent and the rapid sinking of the ground into miniature were dizzying, frightening moments (Brandon yelled for some time), Susannah found the actual flight exhilarating.

Just as they were about to land Susannah noticed a strange sight below. The sand at the base of the fortress heaved upward and deposited a red shape on the surface. Sand fell from it to reveal silver beneath. She had only a second's glimpse, but she was certain it was a train carriage. Something told her this was important, but she didn't know why.

Now, she gazed out the floor-to-ceiling windows at the red storm. It scraped against the glass, looking in.

Beetle guards had manhandled them along corridors. Knowing they were once men made her less repulsed, even sympathetic toward them. Yet they were still brutes, mindlessly prodding her with their spears.

They had been left in a small waiting room, like naughty children waiting for the headmaster. The floor was red slate, and the walls gemstone blue. A tracery of gold figures was etched around the room, telling some obscure history. Both doors at either end of the room were shut tight; despite its glamour, it was meant to confine them.

Susannah wondered what was going on in the city below. Were the traders hustling produce indoors, anchoring their tents? Were they huddling inside huts as the wind harried them in the canyon pathways, lifting chairs and tables, throwing them across the city? Why was there always this wreckage behind her, erasing everything she had done? Did she have something terrible inside her that attracted devious, manipulative people, and dark thoughts? Her reflection gloomed back at her; it seemed to think so.

Brandon was slumped in a corner, head down. The experience had been too much for him. She kept forgetting that he had been forcibly removed from his season. Simply by being with her he was enduring traumatic experiences. But she was the only one who could get him home to spring. They'd made a pact. Now they were here in the King's fortress, where they wanted to be, they would have to make plans.

She sat beside him on the cold floor. 'Brandon?'

He lifted his head and she saw that he had been crying. He savagely brushed away his tears.

'It's okay,' she said, comforting him. 'We're here.'

'Yes,' he replied dumbly. He didn't want to admit that the flights with the Karkarim had frightened him almost witless. He had discovered another new thing about himself: he did not like heights. He was a ground animal, hooves married to the dirt. Throughout this flight the absurd thought that he was not as important as Susannah, and would be dropped suddenly to his death, kept going through his head. But the eagle held him firmly. As they hit the ground shame coursed through him at his childish tears.

'I was scared too,' she said.

His eyes snapped at her, nostrils flared. 'I wasn't scared.'

She bit her tongue, not wanting to start an argument.

'Well, I think we were noticed.'

'Yeah. But what do we do now?' he asked gruffly. 'You don't even have a plan.'

Susannah was shocked by the change in Brandon. She had expected to find him the same as ever — a kind, charming boy. She had expected that they would fall into their old ways (it felt so long ago that he had saved her from the Miss Chiefs). She wanted his friendship. But his spring courtesy and kindness had been ripped away by this season.

'What did the Vizier do to you?' He stiffened at her question. 'Please,' she said, remembering politeness convinced more easily. 'We're friends, aren't we?'

He hid his eyes. 'He ... he hurt me. The ... pain. I've never known anything like it before. Not even when the Spinster's spell changed me. There was darkness, something slithering into my body.' He paused, gathering his words. 'It was like I'd been invaded. And it was telling me I wasn't who I was.' He glanced at her. 'I saw someone else.'

Susannah leaned forward, absorbed. 'Who?'

'A different boy. Someone I was supposed to be.'

'A character for this season,' she surmised. 'Then what?'

He looked away, then back at her. 'Then ... you. I saw your face. Ever since, I've felt different. Like ... like he stole something from me.'

'He stole your enchantment,' she said. 'Maybe this is the real you.'

'No,' he replied, a growl in his tone. 'I wasn't born with this fur. This isn't the real me.' He rubbed at the grouting in the floor.

Susannah stared at him. He wasn't telling her the whole story. He was keeping something back.

'Strange,' she remarked after a pause.

'What?' he asked, tensing. 'Don't you believe me?'

He was definitely hiding something. 'Of course I believe you,' she said, waving his worry away. 'It's just ... it sounds so much like what the Man with 8 Faces would do.'

'But you said the Vizier wasn't him.'

'I know. That's why it's strange. I would have known.'

Brandon's eyes glinted. 'Maybe your link isn't working in this season? Maybe you've changed too much since spring.'

'What do you mean?'

'The seasons change us, that's all,' he said. 'I lost my enchantment. Perhaps you've lost something too.'

'And what exactly do you think I have lost?' she demanded.

'Ever since you rescued me, I've noticed you were different.'

'You can talk!' she cried.

He ignored her outburst. 'When I was in the Vizier's chair, I saw a different boy. But I saw a different girl too. She looked like you, but neater, not so rough.'

'You idiot, that was just a character the Vizier put into your head.'

'Was it?' replied Brandon. 'I don't think so. I think I knew this girl already. I think she might be the real you.'

'There's only one real Susannah.' Her eyes blazed.

'Exactly,' said Brandon. 'That's just it. It's taken a while but it has come back since spending time with you.' He paused. 'I never knew you as Susannah. I knew you as Chloe.'

She drew a sharp breath. *Chloe*. The name tied to the Man with 8 Faces. She was instantly on guard. How did he know that name unless he was somehow involved?

'My name is Susannah,' she said, iron in her tone. Yet there was the smallest doubt that niggled.

'It is now,' Brandon replied, growing more confident as he saw her doubt. 'It wasn't before.'

'How do you know?' She played her trump card. 'Only the Man or one of his servants would know such a thing.'

'Because I've remembered a girl named Chloe from spring. I saved you from the Miss Chiefs. I took you to my father's cottage.'

She frowned. 'Yes. But that was Susannah. This Chloe is something the Vizier has put into your head to confuse you.'

Brandon's eyes lit up with an idea. 'I know who'll have proof!' He stuffed a hand down his shirt and pulled out a silver hand mirror. A thrill of recognition went through Susannah.

'That's mine. The Man took it from me,' she said.

'I found it when we were inside the barrier.'

'You found it?'

'The Blank must have thrown it in after us,' he said, defensively. 'The woman in the mirror has helped me before.'

'Woman in the mirror?' she asked, memory tickling her brain.

'Yes. She's the one who told me how to find Chloe in the Miss Chiefs' maze.'

'Stop it! There is no Chloe!'

'She's the one who'll tell you who you really are.'

'I'm Susannah Alexandra Jane Hattersley!'

'You're not.'

'I am!'

He paused, his eyes searching hers, looking for the sweet, feisty girl he knew. 'If you're so sure, ask the mirror to confirm it.' He knew she couldn't resist a challenge like that. He felt guilty at putting her through this, but he was also certain that he was right. She needed to break through this barrier to her true personality.

Finally, she said, 'Fine,' and snatched the mirror from him.

She held it out as though it were a harmful object, wary of what she might see within. But it was just a mirror speckled with black dots. There, nothing, she thought, until she realised she should be looking at her reflection. She looked deeper, thinking of her name. The edges of the mirror rippled, as though it were liquid. She felt her mind harden and focus on the glass. Images flickered across it: a long black box; a woman in a red dress, eyes closed, hands clasped on her chest; people gathered around her, whispering, wanting to help; running to her bedroom, opening the door to find … a look, a touch. The proof of her father's deceit, only glimpsed before, a year ago (running to mum to blurt it all out) and starting a terrible story that would split her world apart. New black brogues; a silver train rushing through green fields; Aunt Lavinia's strained, guilty smile. Then the mirror let her go and she bounced back into her body.

Gradually a face faded into view. A woman stared out at her. A wrinkled woman with deep-set blue eyes, dark hair piled high upon her head, and a large friendly mouth. *Mum?* She dropped the mirror.

The woman swore. 'Pick me up instantly, Chloe Susannah Alexandra Jane Hattersley!'

Such was the commanding tone in the old woman's voice that Susannah did as she was told. She looked into those eyes, twinkling with wise old age. *No, it couldn't be mum.* A subtle pain hardened around her heart.

'You called me Chloe Susannah,' she said, her voice cracking.

'Because it is your name,' replied the old woman. She continued sternly, 'You forgot yourself, which is the one thing I warned you about! Thank goodness Brandon had the sense to grab me, otherwise Chloe might have been completely lost to this season.'

'I don't understand,' she said. 'I'm Susannah. I've always been Susannah.'

'No,' snapped the old woman. 'You are Susannah now only because you have been adopting the character this season has given you. In spring, you were Chloe, and while you may wish to stay here as Susannah — indeed it may be impossible for you to go back to being Chloe — you *must* remember who you were. Otherwise, the Man will easily erase you and slip into your skin. He is gaining more control of the plots and the characters in every season. You must not let him steal any more of you.'

She sat back within the mirror, her lecture ended. She could see doubt eating away at the girl. 'Surely you've had misgivings? Hasn't something felt as though it were missing?'

Susannah slowly nodded. 'Yes.' She looked at the woman, then Brandon. 'I was Chloe?' They both nodded. 'Okay. I accept that. But I'm not now. I'm Susannah.'

The old woman smiled. 'You are Susannah. But you are also Chloe. Accepting that means you have power over the Man. He cannot dupe you. You must hold onto your identity. Especially now you are in this wicked place. You will be tested with many lies about your character here.'

Susannah looked at Brandon. It was as though a curtain had fallen and she saw that he was not a beast, intent on harming her, but that he cared for her. She instantly felt more comfortable in his presence. She looked into the mirror only to find that the old woman had vanished.

'Put it in your satchel,' Brandon suggested. 'Keep it near you where it's safe.'

She did as he said, feeling the tension in her fall away.

The sand scratched at the windows, reminding her where she was, and what the old woman in the mirror had said. 'We need to come up with a plan to make the King show us the way out. If he knows about the Backstage Door, then the Man will be watching.'

'Any ideas?' he asked.

'Well ...' she started, but got no further, for the gilded doors at the end of the room opened with a crack. A strange creature appeared between them.

It was a dwarf dressed in a severe black suit. Its dress only made its revolting features more pronounced. Though it was humanoid, it had a face like a pig: fat cheeks and tiny eyes behind thick-rimmed glasses. It was bald, and its skin shone unhealthily with oil. In one hand it held a heavy book, in the other a silver-feathered quill. Its pinprick eyes roved over them. A nauseating stink wafted from it.

Susannah stepped forward. 'I want to see the King.'

'How dare you speak!' it snapped in a squeaky voice. It wrote something in its ledger. It stared at them. 'I am Catarrh'l, the King's adviser. You will follow me, and you will only speak when the King or I advise you to, and you will answer all questions.' It straightened its glasses. 'You are both in serious trouble.' It turned and marched officiously away, expecting them to follow.

Susannah glanced at Brandon.

He raised his eyebrows and shrugged.

'Come on, then,' she said, 'Serious trouble can hardly be worse than what this season has thrown at us.' She didn't quite believe that, her heart thrumming with trepidation, but thought she should say something to boost Brandon's spirits.

They went to face the King of Summer.

Susannah had steeled herself for the unpleasantness to come, but the grandeur of the King's throne room let down her guard.

The length of it was obscene. The chamber stretched into the distance, long as a train platform and deep as a cathedral. It was bathed in the light of a hundred lanterns. The roof was a vast dome above their heads, robin's egg blue, painted with a fresco in which snakes, eagles, bears and humans fought. A colonnade of red-tiled pillars lined the path to the empty throne at the end of the chamber. Behind the throne was a stained-glass sun, colours glowing in the light. Red lace curtains fell from the ceiling; the King's violent personal colour. They reminded Susannah of those in Zahir's tent.

Beetle guards lined the path to the throne, their eyes rolling. They held spears and any movement they considered dangerous would be dissuaded with a sharp point.

The stinky pig turned and looked at them. 'Hurry up!' it squealed, and Susannah realised it was female. 'You will not keep the King waiting!'

Susannah looked at Brandon. 'There's a punishment for that too, I suppose.'

'There certainly is!' snapped Catarrh'l, 'and one for facetiousness as well.' She glanced at two beetle guards. They left their post and took up at the children's side. Susannah and Brandon were marched smartly down the long chamber to the throne.

Susannah noticed mosaics on the walls between the pillars, of ancient battles and complex histories. She wondered how long these prison seasons had existed, and how long the King had been master of this one. She wondered what his crime was.

As they neared the end of the chamber, the pillars gave way to tiered wooden benches on either side, as though for a jury.

They arrived before the King of Summer out of breath, and Susannah saw the point of the long nave. An excellent ploy, she thought, to make the enemy weak. She was determined not to appear cowed before the King and pulled herself together.

Catarrh'l bowed, and said in an obsequious manner, 'The two trouble-makers, Your Majesty, for divine punishment.'

The beetle guards prodded them to their knees.

Susannah gazed up at the monarch of this cruel season. He was seated not in the throne but reclined in a whale-shaped bath that steamed gently, tiled in jade. But the first thing she noticed about the King was that he was a very large man. His stomach protruded from the water, and his face settled back into a frame of fat. Despite being immersed, he was dressed in a red velvet robe that dripped and flapped around his arms as he splashed. His head was wound in a gold turban. His lips were red and moist, and he licked them hungrily. His eyes took in everything, raking over Susannah's body as though he could tear her apart with his gaze. His villainous appearance was topped off with a neat, pointed goatee that did not hide the sneer of his mouth at all. Cruelty, gluttony and unkindness radiated from him.

'Spiteful children!' the King yelled in a baritone that resounded around the chamber. 'Gossiping harpies! Foul pestilential cankers!' He crooked a finger at Susannah. 'I shall enjoy devising the most painful of punishments for you.'

Another performance, thought Susannah. Here we go again.

The King's attention swivelled suddenly from her. His eyes rolled around the chamber. 'But first ... Miss Chiefs!' he yelled far louder than was necessary, shocking his cowering servant. 'Where are you? You have not changed the water this evening! Do you want me to boil to death? Do you?!'

A shiver went through Susannah at the mention of those vicious girls. There was a shuffling sound from beneath the bath. Two Miss Chiefs appeared either side of the King. They were bare-chested but wore metal harnesses, the steel shocking against their pale skin. Their flowing red skirts trailed across the sand-dusted floor. They both had long curly red hair and, like their spring sisters, it stood upright so they both looked permanently shocked. But their eyes told a different story — they glared penetratingly at Susannah.

'What were you doing under there?' cried the King. 'Some form of sabotage I'll have to punish you for later, no doubt.' He leered, relishing the idea of punishment. 'Water!' he snapped, making everyone but the Miss Chiefs jump. He nodded to the taps at the end of the bath.

The Miss Chiefs glanced slyly at one another behind the King's back, uncaring if his audience saw their insolence. Catarrh'l fumed. Together they came forward, each taking hold of a tap.

The King held up a dripping hand. 'And if a single drop is splashed outside this bath, you shall regret it.'

The Miss Chiefs twisted the taps on full, blasting cold water into the tub with a roar. Then they sat either side of the bathtub. The King sighed as the warmed water was replaced with a surge of cold. His pleasure did not last long. He sat up and cried, 'Catarrh'l! You've neglected to tell me my ratings? Quickly! Report!'

Catarrh'l bowed low, abject. 'Your Majesty, I am sorry.

I had many duties —'

'Is that an excuse?' he asked with menace.

'No, not at all, most wise and benevolent Majesty.' His adviser scraped the floor with another bow. 'But you did ask me to bring these insidious, gossiping children to you for —'

'Are you now suggesting I have been asking too much of you?'

'No, no, no, your glitteringly splendid Majesty. I am obviously neglecting my proper duties with frivolous ones. I apologise unreservedly for my ineptitude and shall see the Vizier this very night for my punishment.'

At the mention of the Vizier Susannah shuddered.

The King thought about this response, then sat back, satisfied. 'Well then, inform me of my popularity rating.'

Susannah began to feel sorry for the adviser. Power had clearly corrupted the King of Summer as much as it had the Queen of Spring.

Catarrh'l fumbled with the book she had held throughout this exchange, flipping pages rapidly. She opened her mouth to reply but the King shouted, 'Water!' As the Miss Chiefs did not move, Catarrh'l squeaked, dropped the book, and dashed to turn off the taps. The King flopped his heavy body around in the bath. The water brimmed to the edge of the tub, but no matter how hard he tried it did not spill over. He glared at his adviser, displeased he could not follow through on his promise of punishment.

Susannah came forward to pick up the book. 'You shouldn't put up with that,' she said gently.

'Be silent!' said the pig, snatching the book from her. 'It is an honour to serve the great Burnidial, glorious majesty of summer.' She took her quill and wrote in the book.

'Another black mark against your name. Your punishment will indeed be most interesting.'

'Interesting?' provoked Susannah.

'… Interesting for the King to devise.' She turned back to the King, who was following the conversation.

'Indeed, it will be,' he replied nastily.

Catarrh'l smiled, having regained Burnidial's approval. She referred to her ledger. 'It is no doubt due to this girl that your popularity ratings are down. She has been stirring foment throughout the redlands with this beast of hers.'

Brandon growled. 'You had better be careful what you say. If I am a beast then I might get angry and you won't like that.'

Catarrh'l took a step backwards, but the King ignored him. He waved frantically from his tub. 'What do you mean they're down?'

Catarrh'l shoved her head into her ledger. 'Oh!' she cried, 'they are only slightly down, my most exquisitely loved King. The disagreeable comments are only a tad larger than the satisfied ones.' Then she shot out a fat finger; her face scrunched into ugliness. 'It's *her* fault! She has been spreading vicious lies about you, Your Majesty. The Karkarim heard them all over the redlands; nasty whisperings about you.'

'Exactly what have the people been saying about me?' he enquired in a dangerous tone.

Catarrh'l flinched, not wanting to repeat the slander. She hummed and ahhhed, and flipped pages in her ledger, looking to Susannah and Brandon in the hope they'd provide distraction. But the King was not to be fooled.

'Catarrh'l,' he oozed, 'bring me your ledger.' His eyes gleamed dark with harm.

Catarrh'l whimpered and shuffled forward unwillingly. She held the book over the bathtub.

Susannah, tiring of this charade, seized her moment and raced forward. The King saw her coming and his eyes widened. Before he could say a word, she gave Catarrh'l a push, and the ledger slipped from the adviser's hands into the water with a heavy *plop*. As she stepped back, ready for the outrage, she wondered why she'd done that. Was it to save Catarrh'l embarrassment or bring herself to the King's absolute attention? Perhaps she had not liked the idea of the King devising punishments for innocent people.

The King splashed comically at the book as though it were a venomous bug that had come to share his bath.

Susannah smiled, until she was manhandled back to Brandon, and forced to her knees by a beetle guard.

Brandon was horrified. 'Now we'll get the worst punishment of them all!' he hissed.

'I know what I'm doing,' she whispered, as the King flapped and splashed, and Catarrh'l fished ineptly for the ledger.

'*YOU!*' screeched Catarrh'l. She had managed to extricate the sodden book from the bath, but its slanders were irretrievable. 'All my gossip notes, all my reports ...' She gasped. 'The ratings!'

The King calmed his frantic splashing. He glared at Susannah with such force she felt needles prick her skin. His voice was low and threatening. 'No one has ever dared attack me in my throne room.' He shook his head. 'I will devise the most exquisite, prolonged, painful punishments for you, my girl.'

Catarrh'l smiled, showing short brutish teeth. 'Yes!

And since my evidence has been destroyed, there is only one course of action.'

The King frowned.

But the Miss Chiefs stood, smiling coldly. Out of their mouths came a terrible whisper, 'A trial.'

Catarrh'l fumed at their interruption.

The King's face broke slowly into a leer. 'A TRIAL!' he yelled as though he'd thought of it himself. 'Let it begin immediately, Catarrh'l.'

Swallowing her annoyance, the piggy servant clapped twice. Instantly the throne room rushed into activity, as unseen doors in the walls opened to emit a flurry of courtiers and servants. They filed into the wooden benches either side of the room, and then sat, all eyes on Susannah and Brandon. The Miss Chiefs were pressed into reluctant service, hauling the King's bath into prime viewing position.

'Here we go,' she said to Brandon. 'A trial means we get to ask our questions too.' Brandon's doubtful look did not give her reassurance. She took his hand.

The King noticed. 'Confine the accused!'

Catarrh'l clapped three times. The red lace curtains hanging from the ceiling whipped into action, swirling round Susannah, ripping her free from Brandon. She was hoisted in the air, squeezed into an inescapable lace cocoon.

Brandon gazed up at her forlornly. His beetle chirruped a warning to ensure he did not move.

Catarrh'l spoke, her voice rising grandiosely from the floor below, 'My court, the accusation is gross gossip against our most beneficent king, despicable premeditated vandalism of the court records, and, most alarmingly, the obvious aberration of this girl existing in our glorious summer season.'

'There she is,' said the King, pointing. 'Find her guilty and let the most inventive of punishments be meted out to her!'

Catarrh'l straightened, as much as her short stature allowed, and clasped her fingers behind her back, getting into character. She paced for a few steps, then paced back, letting the proceedings fill with sombre silence. Then she shot her first question out, 'What are you doing here?!'

Susannah raised an eyebrow. 'Your machine eagles brought us here.'

Catarrh'l clicked her fingers. The curtain tightened about Susannah. She let out a squeak.

'Don't be facetious,' the stinky pig snapped. 'It will only add to your punishment.'

'Not if I am found innocent,' breathed Susannah.

Catarrh'l smiled nastily. 'That is unlikely. The evidence against you is damning.' She composed herself. 'I ask again: What are you doing here?'

It was time for the truth. 'We're looking for someone,' she answered. 'The Man —'

'A man? What man?'

'No. *The* Man. The Man with 8 Faces.'

There was a short silence in which the King's bathwater sloshed, the court shifted, and Susannah gasped in a breath. The Miss Chiefs looked at her as though she had just revealed she was poisonous.

Catarrh'l shared a glance with the King, who prompted her with a nod. With some distaste she said, 'What do you know of the Man?'

'Well he's not very nice, and he seems to want me —'

'You? Why should he want you? You're completely unimportant. You're nothing.' Then her eyes flared behind her spectacles. 'A-ha!' she exclaimed triumphantly. 'You are looking for him because you are his disciple! You wish to bring destruction and chaos to our season! That is why you destroyed my records, isn't it?! To allow for the coming of the Man. To allow cracks to appear in the workings of the season. Isn't it? ISN'T IT?' Her voice rose throughout this tirade, finally ending in a high squeak. 'That is your purpose, is it not? To destroy our season so you can take it over yourself!'

The court gasped and began muttering.

Susannah rolled her eyes. 'ABSOLUTE POPPYCOCK!' she shouted. It was something she had heard her mother say to her father during one of their arguments. It had the desired effect. The court was silenced.

Catarrh'l raised a knowing, unkind smile. 'Oh? And do you have any evidence to refute me, young lady?'

Susannah thought fast but nothing came to mind. She had, to some small extent, brought chaos to this season, but was that a cause of her investigations into finding the Man, or was that simply because she was Susannah Alexandra Jane Hattersley? She had to admit that Catarrh'l had touched upon a point that she could not really deny. Since entering this strange world she had been the catalyst for terrible upheaval and change. But there must be something she possessed that could show them she was not colluding with the Man but trying to ensnare him. But it was not wise for her to tell these people everything. Though she had not sensed the Man among them, she could not be sure he didn't have his Blanks impersonating someone within the court. Her agonised frown told Catarrh'l everything she needed to know.

'I gather from your silence that you do not,' said the advisor.

Susannah's courage rose, and she shot back, 'Your guesses are hardly evidence!'

'It is evidence enough,' snapped the King, splashing about his bath. 'You are guilty until proven innocent here. There is much guilt on display. And we have witnessed no evidence of your innocence.'

'That is because she has none, my wisdom-soaked Majesty,' replied Catarrh'l. 'And I have yet to call the chief witness to her disturbing, divisive and most violent behaviour ...' She let the statement hang, building suspense. Susannah's heart raced. There could only be one person she meant. She glanced at Brandon for comfort, but he had shut down, the trial too much for his pastoral spring nature.

And then Susannah's worst fear was realised.

Catarrh'l brandished a hand to the wings. 'I call the Vizier of Summer, meter of the King's punishments, arbiter of the Karkarim's records, and official seer of the season!'

A door opened in the wall, and for a moment an ungainly shadow was silhouetted, like a large spider. Then, slowly, the Vizier moved into the light. Under his mandarin hat his face was pale, and he gritted his teeth and licked his lips in obvious pain. He clattered forward on crutches, dragging a broken leg. It was braced in a metal cast and pins pierced the bone; it looked like scaffolding lopsidedly holding him up. For a moment Susannah felt shame at what she had done to him, and pity at this poor specimen he had become. Then she remembered what he had done to Brandon.

Looking down at her friend, she saw recognition dawn in his eyes. This crippled man had hurt him. Darkness came over his face, and he stepped forward. The beetle guard clamped a claw to his shoulder, which brought Brandon painfully back to himself. He cowered. Susannah knew what was coming next and steeled herself for accusations.

The Vizier pulled himself conspicuously into the centre of the room, displaying his disability like a wound to the court. It was a deliberate and silent attack on Susannah. It was also effective; the looks of sympathy on the faces of the court further added to her guilt. Only the beetle guards shrank from him, chirruping alarm. The Vizier bowed his head to the King and Catarrh'l.

Catarrh'l swept into prosecution mode. 'Who did this to you?' she asked gently.

The Vizier, leaning on his crutches, stabbed a talon at Susannah. 'She did this to me!'

'You were torturing my friend!'

'You had both breached the season without permission! It is my job to find out why. I am allowed to use certain methods to do so. In any case it is obvious that your character is subversive, with plans to destroy this season.'

'How is it obvious?' she demanded.

The Vizier smiled his thin-lipped smile. 'Why, anyone who was innocent would have entered in the usual way and not through a Backstage Door.'

Susannah leapt on the statement. 'How do you know about the Backstage Door? Only the Man uses them!'

Catarrh'l and the King again shared a glance.

'Indeed he does,' said the Vizier with dangerous insinuation.

Susannah frowned angrily at him. 'If you must know, we were escaping from the Man himself.'

Catarrh'l piped up. 'You said before that the Man wanted you. Why?'

'I … I'm not sure,' she lied.

But the Vizier snatched at her uncertainty. 'Because she is, like him, a source of chaos and unrest!' he cried. 'It is evident just looking at her that she is unlike us. She has no purpose here. She is a corruption, a foul pestilence on our society.' He sneered. 'And as she has no purpose, she does not exist, and we can do anything to her!' He clicked his talons together.

'Yes!' cried the King. 'We must give her a purpose!'

'Oh, you are indeed most astute and judicious, Your Majesty,' fawned Catarrh'l. She turned to the court. 'Why, she could be this very Man herself! We know he is a master of disguise. And a character assassin, stealing skins for his own devious ends.'

The King shifted in his bath. 'A murderess,' he breathed.

'The charges are set,' said Catarrh'l solemnly. 'Slanderous gossip against the King.'

'Utterly proven beyond a doubt by my own Karkarim,' replied the Vizier, knocking in the nails of Susannah's coffin.

'Wanton destruction of the court records and daily ratings,' listed Catarrh'l, barely hiding her upset.

'Witnessed by all in this very throne room.' Bang, another nail.

'Unforgivable subversion by her very existence in this season without a clear purpose.'

'Evidenced by the former two utterly proven crimes.'

'And, most heinous of all, the murder of —'

'Excuse me,' interrupted Susannah from up high, her voice reverberating throughout the chamber. 'You can't try me yet! I haven't presented my evidence.'

The Vizier glared at the interruption as though he could

inflict torture through his stare. 'It has just been proven that you have no purpose in this season, and therefore you do not exist. As such you cannot possibly defend yourself.'

'That's ridiculous,' snapped Susannah. 'Besides, what if my purpose is to be subversive, as you said? What if I have been sent by someone from another season to spy on you, to find out all your horrid little secrets?'

'Such as?' asked the Vizier, worriedly.

'Such as your attempts to tunnel under the season, to escape,' she needled.

The King frowned. 'What is this?' he asked, turning his gaze on the Vizier.

'Your Majesty, this is simply another lie from the accused to spare her guilty skin.'

'Yes, I am inclined to agree,' replied the King, dismissing it. 'Carry on, to the punishment.'

'It is not a lie! I was there!' Susannah was becoming desperate. The trial was not progressing in her favour. She had not had the chance to discover answers to questions she had wanted to put to the King. Now was as good a time as any.

'You're all criminals acting like you own the seasons. But if you don't help me to find the Man with 8 Faces he will get rid of all of you! He's like a cold; you don't know you've caught it until it's too late. His influence on the seasons is becoming stronger and stronger and no one knows how to stop him. Except for me. That's why I'm here. I have to find him and stop him. Only I can! If you punish me you will be doing something very stupid indeed. You must tell me how to get out. Where is the Backstage Door to the world beyond the seasons?!'

Her impassioned speech shocked the court into silence,

eyes were flared, mouths turned down in disgust.

Then Catarrh'l spoke: 'Shut up,' she said. 'You don't exist.'

'I most certainly —' Susannah started, but the stinky pig clicked her fingers and the lace curtain tightened, squeezing the breath from her.

The Vizier turned to the court. 'What punishment should be meted out to her?' he asked.

There was much discussion and debate as everyone began to babble.

Suddenly a small but clear voice cut through the hubbub. It did not shout as everyone had been doing, it did not add to the melodrama. It said, 'Stop', and everyone stopped. Then it said, 'I have evidence.'

Through the tears that had been squeezed from her by the curtain's tight embrace, Susannah saw Brandon shrug off his guard and walk forward. What did he mean? What evidence did he possess? His bearing was suddenly powerful and assured. She found herself hopeful that he could present indubitable evidence in her defence. He was, after all, a part of this world and could use its systems properly. Simultaneously she was afraid he was bluffing and was going to get them into the most awful trouble. But most of all she was pleased that he had broken free of his fear and was doing this for her.

Brandon stopped his slow, careful walk at the King's bath. The Vizier and Catarrh'l waited expectantly. He reached into his vest and drew out a thin bottle. There were a few drops of yellow in the bottom. They threw out shards of golden light as he held it up. His face was lit up and the chamber suffused with a warm benevolent glow.

'Is that —?' the King started, awed.

'Sunshine from this season,' finished Brandon. 'This is how we were able to enter. There was nothing wrong in how we came here. We only wanted to get away from the Man. We thought we could hide in another season.'

'The art of capturing the sun has been lost for many years,' breathed Catarrh'l. 'Only one person knows how.'

'How did you obtain this?' asked the Vizier.

Brandon shrugged. 'I stole it from the Spinster.'

There was a sharp silence. The rays of golden light played over everyone's faces. Then the King roared. 'You stole my sunshine! My sunshine!' For a moment he was speechless with apoplexy. 'That alone is worth a thousand punishments! A million punishments! Stunning, torturous agonies! I cannot think of anything worse that has ever been perpetrated in this season! Stealing the very lifeblood, our most perfect symbol, our everything!'

Catarrh'l turned to him. 'While this does provide evidence, of a sort, to vindicate your entry into the season, it has placed you in a worse position than your friend.'

The King splashed and railed in his bath, letting out cries of rage. 'Oh, punish him!' he cried. 'Punish him now and severely!'

Brandon stood his ground. 'I will gladly take on all the punishment. You will transfer all of it to me.'

'No!' cried Susannah, from above. 'I was the one who spread the gossip, not him! I told everyone you were the incompetent King of Numbers.'

The King's eyes rolled with rage, his meaty fingers clenching the sides of the bath.

But the Vizier calmed him before he broke. 'Your

Majesty, do not listen to such lies. She is trying to save this boy, whom she cares about a great deal. I suggest his punishment is necessary to effect her own.'

Brandon looked up at her. 'It is all right, my lady,' he said. 'I know what I'm doing.'

Susannah looked into his beautiful blue eyes and saw strength and resolution in them. His furred cheeks made him more a man than a boy.

Catarrh'l wrung her hands. 'Your Majesty, you cannot possibly be considering this. The girl must be punished too.'

The King frowned, irritated with events. 'I hope you are not giving me advice on what to think and do in my own throne room,' he said, throwing his advisor a look of disdain.

'Certainly not, my most intelligent and large-brained King. I was merely —'

But the King waved her puny reasoning away. 'The proceedings have become confusing. I must retire to think things over. Punish the boy immediately. I put you in charge of that, Vizier.'

'And the girl?' questioned Catarrh'l lightly. 'What delights of pain have you thought of for her?'

The King eyed his advisor. 'I believe I just told you, Catarrh'l, that I need to think it over.'

The Vizier interrupted, 'I wonder, Your Majesty, if I might be allowed to conduct some experiments upon her.'

At which point the Miss Chiefs stepped forward, flanking the King. They leaned in and, each with a hand cupped to her mouth, began whispering suggestions in the King's ears. His eyes flicked comically right and left as he listened. His frown grew severe. Then he splashed his water angrily, 'Enough!'

Susannah watched his mind working behind those beady eyes, digesting what the Miss Chiefs had told him. He turned to the Vizier. 'You may experiment on the boy. As for the girl, confine her in my harem. I may wish to see unspeakable acts of torture performed on her later.' His gaze trawled the court, attempting to catch any arguments against his pronouncement. Catarrh'l opened her mouth but shut it quickly as his gaze sharpened on her.

'The trial is ended. Go!' The King beckoned the Miss Chiefs. 'Quickly, push, push! I am drying out. Give me water instantly! I said instantly!' And with that he was pushed down the long chamber, shouting his demands to the puffing girls.

Catarrh'l clicked her fingers and the curtain unwound from Susannah, dropping her to the floor. She looked up, hoping to see Brandon and his reassuring gaze, but he had been led off by the beetle guard to await his punishment. Her vision filled with the grimaces of Catarrh'l and the Vizier.

'Oh dear,' gloated the advisor, 'that didn't go well for you, did it?'

Susannah shot back, 'As I obviously don't exist, nothing you can say will hurt me.'

'If that's the case, you shan't be able to feel anything we do to you either.' The Vizier smiled. 'And that is something I'd like to put to the test.'

His talons reached for her.

CHAPTER THIRTEEN

EYE OF THE MIRROR

SHE WAS TAKEN BY BEETLE guards and marched down long red corridors. The Vizier and Catarrh'l had gone to attend to their respective business: the pig to caress the King's ego after Susannah's damage to his daily routine; the Vizier to calibrate his torture equipment for Brandon's punishment. Susannah had resisted the urge to spit in his face.

The beetle guards set a swift pace, and the journey seemed endless, with twists and turns and corners and staircases and large doors and small doors and ups and downs and always a corridor at the end of each.

Eventually they arrived at a door made of blue marble. One of the guards placed the tip of its spear in the lock. The door opened. They threw her inside, and the door shut at her back.

The chamber was large and covered with small blue tiles. Three walls boasted mosaics: to the right a yellow sun, herald of the season, though this one looked distinctly unfriendly with rays rippling outwards like snakes; to the left, one of the Karkarim, swooping with talons outstretched; and, as she turned, Susannah saw the doors come together to make the stern, watchful face of the King of Summer. On the fourth wall, directly in front of her, was a mirror, the width of the room, with a bevelled gold frame. It reflected everything that was happening in the room with bedazzling excess.

Women lounged indolently on cushions at the edges of the room. They ate from platters piled high with fruits and delicacies. Susannah saw one take a grilled scorpion and place it in her mouth, crunching down on the brittle body. Each one appeared to be absorbed in her thoughts and, though they shared space among the cushions, they did not speak to one another.

The centrepiece of the room was a large pool, water spilling from aqueducts at each corner. A few of the women splashed through the clear blue water. Light shot down from shafts in the ceiling, reflected by the pool into glittering threads across the walls. There was an overpowering musk to the room that made Susannah woozy.

The women eyed her, sizing her up as a possible rival. There were all ages — young girls, middle-aged women, even the elderly. Some of them wore pantomime makeup to enhance their cat-like eyes and pouting lips; others wore none at all, having a remarkable natural beauty.

Well, she wasn't going to act the passive slave. She had to save Brandon. He had been brave to take her punishment, but stupid, too. She knew they wouldn't find her innocent; she'd be punished alongside him and his death would mean nothing. But how could she think that? He was *not* going to die.

She pressed against the marble doors to see if they would budge.

'It's no use,' said a voice.

Susannah turned to find an old woman had come forward. She had curly dark hair streaked with grey; her face was a canyon of solemn lines, yet her eyes were vibrant and a warm brown. Unlike the other women's disdainful frowns, hers was one of sympathy.

'That way is locked and guarded. And I do not think you have knowledge of the spells required to open it.'

'You might be surprised,' Susannah snapped, trying to ignore the woman and turn her attention back to the door.

'If you attack the door all you will do is bring the beetle guards, and then someone will get hurt.' She sighed. 'Do you want that?'

Susannah hesitated. She had caused too much harm and death. 'No,' she replied.

'It's all right,' said the woman in a soothing tone. 'You're safe here, at least for a while. The King never visits at this hour.'

She offered a hand. 'Come and sit down. Are you hungry?'

Susannah paused, afraid of kindness in this embittered season. Everyone who had been welcoming to her had been punished for it. Arthur, she thought, and pain swelled like a thorn in her chest. But she couldn't do this alone. She needed help to find and free Brandon from the clutches of the Vizier.

She reached out and took the hand.

The woman led her to a back corner where cushions were piled high on soft matting. She cleared a space in the centre and motioned Susannah to sit. The woman folded herself down with difficulty. She took the tray of fruit and grilled bugs and placed it in front of Susannah. Susannah picked and prodded, avoiding the insects, until she found something that looked like a plum. She rubbed it clean on the edge of her dress, and bit into it. It wasn't a plum, but it was sweet and juicy and her mouth tingled with delight at the evidence of food. The old woman smiled.

'So,' she started, 'what have you done to upset the King?'

'Why do you think I've upset the King?' asked Susannah around a mouthful.

'You are here.'

'What is this place?' she asked.

The woman's eyes looked old and tired. 'Like this season, it is a pleasurable prison cell, though on a much smaller level.' She sighed, letting go of painful memory. 'The King places here any woman he is displeased with. To do with as he wishes when he feels like it. I have survived longer than most.'

Susannah bit her lip. 'Does he hurt you?'

'Only if you are stupid enough to let him,' replied the old woman.

'He is an idiot,' Susannah said.

The old woman laughed. 'Oh, I shouldn't laugh, but that is very true.' She hid her smile with a well-manicured hand. Her eyes flickered around the room, glaring quickly at the other women who might impeach her. Her gaze settled back on Susannah.

'I do believe I like you, young lady. Do you have a name?'

Susannah hesitated, weighing her guilt with prospects of hurting a future friend. The offer of kindness won. 'My name is Susannah Alexandra Jane Hattersley,' she said, and nodded to confirm the friendship.

'Goodness,' replied the old woman, 'such a decadent name. One might almost think you a princess of the seasons with that name.' She smiled grandly. 'My own is the very modest Aranae. I am pleased to meet you despite the inauspicious circumstances.'

They shook hands.

Aranae gazed at Susannah gravely. 'Now that we have decided to be friends, can you tell me truthfully why you are here?'

Susannah's smile slipped. Should she tell Aranae the truth? Could it reach out and harm her if she knew that Susannah was the most wanted girl in all the seasons? Could the Man use Aranae to get to her? But that was the problem — the Man could use anyone who wasn't strong enough to resist his pull. Was taking a chance on the truth worth it? She made a decision.

'I was pulled into the seasons by the Man with 8 Faces. I'm trying to find my way out. The only way is to find the Man first and confront him. So my friend and I got ourselves noticed by spreading gossip about the King. I thought that the Man had to be here somewhere, but I can't find him. Now the King has taken my friend, the best friend I have here, and he is going to be punished because of me.'

And with that she had selfishly reached out and brought Aranae into her dangerous orbit. Why couldn't she have just lied? As she'd spoken she'd felt a willingness to slip into a comfortable deceit. But she would not give in to the season's habits.

Aranae's face had gone white.

'Are you all right?' asked Susannah, worried that her

curse was working on the woman already.

Aranae blinked and turned her gaze on the young girl. Her eyes held a deep understanding. 'I know of the Man,' she said. She shot a steely gaze at Susannah. 'I will help you get out of here.'

'We can go together,' replied Susannah.

Aranae smiled weakly. 'No. It is too late for me. I have only my mental strength left. I am not as young as I once was when I came to this awful place. I cannot escape now.'

'Of course you can,' argued Susannah.

'You do not understand, dear girl.' She looked up. 'Do you smell that faint perfume in the air?' Susannah nodded. 'It is pumped in to keep us docile and inert, to keep us from making plans against the King, whom we all hate. But it is not just a simple perfume. It kills the desire to escape in us. A potent spell, concocted by the Vizier.' Susannah screwed up her face at his name.

Now that it had been mentioned Susannah did feel a daze falling upon her. Laziness enveloped her limbs, a paralysis deadly to freedom. 'It's happening to me!'

'Yes. But you are young and strong. We must get you out before it takes you over completely.'

'You said that door is always guarded,' said Susannah.

'There are other ways out of here, if you have the right knowledge, and the right equipment. What do you have in that satchel?' Aranae asked.

Susannah frowned and glanced down. Her satchel was hanging at her side. She had forgotten she carried it, though it swung heavily against her. 'I wonder why they didn't take it from me.'

'They were probably more concerned with your

unexplained presence in the season rather than the threat of anything you carried. Quickly, give it to me.'

Susannah handed it over. 'How do you know I'm not from this season?'

Aranae opened the satchel and peered in. She glanced up. 'Well, are you?'

'No,' said Susannah after a pause.

'There you are then,' said Aranae. 'You don't have the cruel attributes of this season. I gather that is why everyone is so alarmed by you. You're different. Which is no bad thing. But they don't see it that way. They want everyone to be the same, to obey, to be insipid, to be controllable. That is the way of these totalitarian types.'

Susannah looked at the woman, who was trying to glean a means of escape in her satchel. 'Why aren't you afraid of me?' she asked.

Aranae stopped her fussing, gave Susannah a measured look. 'I was much like you, once — a strong spirit, never letting anyone tell me what to do, deciding things for myself, disobeying the order.' She smiled wistfully. 'It was wonderful.' Her smile fell. 'But then I came here, and all that changed.'

'How did you come here?' asked Susannah, suspicion getting the better of her.

Aranae heard the doubt in the girl's tone. 'It's all right, Susannah. I am not the Man, nor one of his Blanks.'

Susannah narrowed her eyes. 'That is exactly what he would say.'

'No. He wouldn't want you to doubt him, which is what you're doing.' The old woman's eyes blazed with intelligence, but there was no malice in them, nothing to be wary of.

'Will you trust me?' she asked.

'Only if you tell me how you know about the Man,' Susannah replied.

Aranae sighed and dropped her eyes. She was silent for a long while. Then she said, 'Like you, he was after me, years ago when I was young. He tried to steal me.' She looked directly into Susannah's eyes, telling the absolute truth. 'This was the only place where he could not use me; there is apparently nothing for him here. I imprisoned myself so effectively he had no advantage.'

Susannah felt a great sorrow. 'Then I'm sorry. You shouldn't help me. He will find you because of me.' She breathed in to calm herself. 'Someone who helped me has died already.'

'He won't kill me,' said Aranae. 'There's no point in him using me but to get to you. And since he doesn't inhabit me now, it would be stupid for him to inhabit me elsewhere as I never leave the harem. If you see me anywhere else, you will know it is him. So again, my escape is impossible, as I am safe if I never leave this room.' She smiled, and the flesh crinkled at the corners of her mouth. 'You see, we have him there.'

Susannah suddenly felt much better. She allowed a surge of pleasure to run through her at thwarting the Man through nothing more than simple logic.

'Now what is this?' asked Aranae, taking out the *Book for All Seasons*.

'Oh!' cried Susannah, causing a number of women to frown at her exclamation. 'It's a book of maps,' she whispered. 'It shows every season and all the places where secret passageways are hidden. Perhaps there's one in this very room!'

She took the book and stroked the leather cover. The weight of it comforted her, as though it were an old friend who knew her well, accepting her completely into the world within its pages. She was about to open it when Aranae gasped. She was looking into the hand mirror, eyes wide, as though seeing something wondrous.

'Never mind the book,' said the old woman. 'This is your escape.' She held the hand mirror aloft. 'Wherever did you get this?' she asked.

Susannah shrugged. 'It was on a dresser in my bedchamber in the spring season.'

Aranae's eyes flashed. 'But that's impossible.'

'Why?'

'This mirror doesn't reflect anything here.' She gazed into Susannah, measuring her for lies. 'Which can only mean ...' Tears glistened in her eyes. 'My dear Susannah, come here.' She reached out.

Warily Susannah stood and went across to the reclining woman. As she knelt, Aranae enfolded her in a hug. 'It's been so long since I met someone from the world beyond the seasons.'

As Aranae held her, Susannah became aware of a smell. It was coming from Aranae, her hair and her skin soaked in it. It was a smell of the sea; a surging, wintry sea. With a jolt she was sent back to her room in the spring palace. She remembered sifting through the oddly named perfumes — *An Autumn Storm*, *The Duke's Velvet*, *Summer Bazaar*, *Sea in Winter*.

Susannah realised with a shock that Aranae's tears were those of someone who knew where she came from, who had fallen through just as she had, who had been trapped here for endless years, pursued by the Man and his Blanks. She was not the only one this had happened to. The Man had brought others into this world and crushed their spirit with his lies. And they had not been able to find a way out. Terror coursed through her and, though she was a strong capable girl who thought tears were childish and unnecessary, she found her resolve breaking and a sob escaped her throat. Then she let go and the tears poured down her cheeks and wet Aranae's shoulder. Susannah cried for all the harm she had caused others, and the indignities she had suffered, and all the mean, petty sniping of the seasons. For a moment she was utterly self-pitying, and it was good to let out such a rage of tears. Then she found the sobs quietening and her chest was less full of strain. A calm emptiness settled inside her. She composed herself, released herself from the hug and looked at Aranae.

'Oh, my dear Susannah, my dear, dear Susannah,' said the woman.

'Did he pull you in through a Backstage Door, too?' asked Susannah.

'I did ... something stupid. He was able to pull me into Egortiye because of what I'd done.' She smiled. 'But I'm safe now. There's peace and silence here.'

Susannah wasn't sure what Aranae meant. But she decided not to question her. A deep understanding existed between the two of them now. Not a single doubt was left. They trusted one another completely.

Susannah looked about the chamber at the reclining women, at the dazed, careless faces and felt sure that she would overcome this. This was not to be her end. She turned to Aranae.

'Tell me how I can escape,' she said.

It was the mirror. All this time, she had possessed the most powerful tool of escape and she hadn't known it. The seasons' strange spell had induced forgetfulness in her, tamed her to the rules of the world.

'This mirror should not exist in Egortiye,' said Aranae. 'It comes from the world outside the seasons. This makes it special, as the rules that govern mirrors here can be subverted by a mirror that is not governed.' Her eyes widened as she told the story. 'You can use this mirror to enter any other mirror within the season, and then exit through another.'

Susannah said, 'There's already a woman in that mirror. She has spoken to me.'

'Really?' said Aranae, eyes gleaming. 'I wonder where she comes from?'

'What do you mean?'

'I mean, whether she is from one of the seasons or ...'

'Or from the world beyond the seasons,' finished Susannah, excited.

Aranae paused. 'Does she give you sound advice?'

Susannah nodded, 'Always.'

'What does she look like?'

'Old, black curls with grey in them, a friendly face, though she does get grumpy quite often. She keeps telling me not to forget her. I don't know whether to trust her. She knows a lot about the seasons.'

'Black curls, you say?' Aranae looked pointedly at Susannah.

'Do you know who she is?' Susannah asked.

'No,' she answered after a pause. 'Perhaps you can ask

her when you go through.'

'I can meet her in there?'

'Oh, yes.' She gestured to come close and whispered. 'But you must be careful. There are things that get trapped in the mirrors, and if you spend too long in there they can ensnare you. That is why even those who know about them scarcely use them.'

'Things?' asked Susannah, wide-eyed. 'What sort of things?'

'Echoes of yourself, and others. Just don't linger. Now quickly, it's time for you to go. You have already spent far too much time here. You are young but any moment the perfume will affect you.' She proffered some of the strange fruits. 'Put these into your satchel. You should always be prepared.'

Susannah picked a few of the plum-like fruits and stuffed them into a spare compartment in her satchel, hoping they wouldn't get squashed.

'How does it work?' she asked, intrigued as to how someone might slip through a mirror's shining face.

Aranae held up the mirror reverently, and then turned it and pressed it against the large wall of glass behind her. There was a *clink*, as though ancient machinery long disused had recognised the key to open its lock. The hand mirror appeared to sink into the glass, merging, coagulating, and Aranae quickly pulled it out. It trailed liquid strings. Aranae winked at Susannah and turned the hand mirror to her. The smooth glass had become a shifting pool of silver. Where it had touched the mirror on the wall there was now a shimmering liquid surface.

'There,' she said, pleased, motioning to the large

mirror. 'Quickly, step through.'

Susannah frowned, uncertain; there could be anything inside.

A shadow fell across them.

'That looks interesting,' said a voice dangerous with insinuation.

Susannah glanced up at a woman, still plump with youth, long blond hair, jealous, flashing eyes, and a mouth that spoilt her beauty with a sneer.

'Go away, Jennamine,' said Aranae. 'This is none of your business.'

'None of my business, but perhaps the King's.'

Aranae smiled. 'You will never be his favourite,' she said, staring squarely at the younger woman.

'Your jealousy at my youth is sickening.'

Aranae let out a bright laugh. 'My dear, I am not jealous but much obliged by your youth. It gives me my superior status here. You must be stupid indeed if you have not realised that the King despises youth. He only wishes to spoil it.'

Jennamine stiffened with annoyance. She forced an ugly smile. 'And I am much obliged by your treason in helping this girl to escape.' Every eye snapped onto them at the mention of this scandalous word.

'Escape? And how will she do that?'

Jennamine glared. 'Don't deny it. I have been listening to your every word.' She struck out a hand. 'Give me that mirror!'

Aranae thought for a moment, and Susannah readied herself to snatch it away from the woman should she be prepared to hand it over. 'No,' she said. 'It is not yours.'

With that she dismissed the younger woman, who stood fuming impotently, not daring to physically challenge her.

'Susannah, are you ready?'

She wasn't, but she nodded.

'I will call the guards!' Jennamine cried.

Aranae ignored her. 'Goodbye, my dear. And good luck. If you could give an appropriate greeting from me to the Man when you next meet him, I would be grateful. I doubt we'll meet again.' Susannah felt sadness wash into her at Aranae's acceptance of her fate.

Jennamine let out a shrill scream.

Instantly the door with the King's face cracked down the middle. Susannah saw the red-liveried beetle guards hoarding the doorway and shivered. She took up her satchel.

Aranae pressed the hand mirror into Susannah's hand. 'Do not lose this,' she said.

As the beetle guards swarmed into the room, clicking and chirruping alarm, she gave Susannah a quick hug, then shoved her into the undulating wall of glass.

CHAPTER FOURTEEN
THE GLASS WORLD

It was utterly cold, what she imagined it was like to be dipped in liquid nitrogen; a slippery, oily cold that did not wet but cut straight to the bone. The first few moments were indescribably unpleasant, and her stomach lurched and folded into knots. She felt herself falling down and then up, direction askew. Her skin tightened.

Then she was suddenly still and, when her senses returned, she found herself lying with her cheek pressed against a smooth floor. All the parts of herself felt scattered; she gathered them mentally to her again. She stood, joints aching, and looked warily around. Her breath came out frosted.

Mirrors, black-spotted, rust-speckled mirrors, surrounded her. Every conceivable space was made of mirror — walls, ceiling, floor — though this in itself was something of a miscomprehension as there was no physical sense of dimension. She may well have been standing on a ceiling and looking down to a floor. There were mirrored staircases that stopped in mid-air and rooms that were not only made of mirror but contained collections of frameless mirrors stood upright or on angles. There was a smooth glass surface everywhere she looked, and endless reflections of mirror upon mirror upon mirror that if concentrated on too closely might drive anyone mad.

Then a frightening thought struck her. She was standing in a place of mirrors. So where was her reflection? She turned about, flung out her arms, trying to catch a glimpse in a mirror, any mirror, of some movement that told her she existed. She stood in front of one and glared into it. For the smallest moment she thought she saw something — a distorted reflection of herself, or a girl very like her. She looked out accusingly as though Susannah had stolen her skin and was living her life. But then the image faded, and Susannah wondered if she had imagined the whole thing.

She raced up a staircase and halfway up it found herself racing down a staircase, ending in a large chamber.

She stepped gingerly into the new room. The mirrored floor was covered in tiny pieces of broken glass. She picked up a slice. It had been a phial of something. She sniffed it. The scent of a dark, bitter fruit. A perfume? A spell?

Where was she? Was she between mirrors? What had Aranae done? How was she supposed to navigate? She hoped Aranae was all right; she couldn't remove a vision of beetle guards tearing into the room, and Jennamine's horrible smile.

Someone cleared her throat. Susannah looked down at the noise and found the silver mirror clenched tightly in her hand. She carefully turned it so she could peer in. Its surface was calm and flat. The familiar old woman was looking out with an expression of reproach. Susannah instantly got her back up.

'There's no use looking at me like that, young lady,' said the old woman. 'You're in a great deal of trouble in here, and I'm the only one who can get you out, so you just be civil.' She sighed. 'I'm also becoming tired of being forgotten, only dragged up to help you out of some dreadful situation you've got yourself in.'

'I didn't ask for your help,' replied Susannah peevishly.

'You most certainly did. What else did you think was going to happen when you were playing with mirrors, eh?' Susannah opened her mouth, but the old woman went on. 'Yes, well, recriminations aside, now we're here we had better find the appropriate exit mirror.'

'What is this place?' asked Susannah.

The old woman blinked. 'A temporary stop, on our way to get your young male friend. Now, hurry, it's not good to linger in here. There are things ...'

Susannah remembered Aranae had said the same. 'What things?' she demanded.

'You'll know when you encounter one.' She raised a knowing eyebrow. 'And let's hope you don't.' She stared Susannah in the eye. 'Let me know the instant you see a reflection.'

Susannah shivered at the implication.

'Now, come along.' She turned around in the mirror, startling Susannah with an unnatural view of her back in the glass. 'That way.' She pointed towards a doorway to the left.

After walking for some time, the absence of a reflection had Susannah's perception completely bamboozled. She didn't know if she was up or down or sideways; she had no relation to the mirrored place around her. The old woman kept up a steady stream of directions, occasionally having to explain how Susannah was meant to find a way to the top of a nine foot wall, or where to touch out the cracks of doors in smooth glass. Susannah tried to ask how she knew so much about mirrors, but the woman answered cryptically, 'I can see a lot more than you can imagine.'

After about half an hour of walking, Susannah was exhausted and frightened. The complete absence of self within the mirrors was beginning to get to her. She had fought hard in this world to justify her existence.

'Can we stop for a moment?' she pleaded.

'Stop?' The old woman frowned. 'I wouldn't advise it.' She glanced about warily.

Susannah sat down on a glass step. 'We've been walking for ages, and I haven't seen anything.'

'That doesn't mean they're not there!' the old woman snapped. 'You don't have eyes in the back of your head, do you?' She harrumphed. 'That's where they watch and wait.'

Susannah felt a cold thrill run down her spine and turned sharply. There was nothing there. But had there been, just a second before she turned her head?

After a while she said, 'I think I've rested enough now,' and stood.

'You'll have added to the journey now,' mused the old woman. 'The pathways keep changing. Let me get my bearings again.'

There was a flash of red in Susannah's peripheral vision. She spun around, following it.

Silence and emptiness.

'That way,' said the old woman. When Susannah did not reply she turned in her mirror. 'What is it?'

Susannah's eyes were wide. 'Something moved.'

The old woman visibly stiffened and gulped. When she spoke, her voice was a hush, 'Quietly but quickly move toward that mirrored alcove at the other end of the chamber.'

Somewhere, glass tinkled.

Susannah stepped hurriedly across the room. Glass snapped and popped underfoot.

'Quietly!' hissed the old woman.

She was almost there, had almost made it to the alcove, when, for just a moment, she saw a blur of red beside her in the mirrored wall. It leapt from the mirror.

'Get down!' yelled the old woman.

Susannah dropped to the floor, but not before she felt a sharpness rake across her back. She cried out.

She lay still and waited. A piece of curved glass rolled back and forth nearby.

The old woman said, 'Very carefully, place me over your shoulder. I want to see if it's behind you.'

Susannah brought the hand mirror up and over her left shoulder. Her hand was shaking. She could feel the thing's presence behind her. She twisted her head round to see if she could peer into the hand mirror. For the smallest moment she saw, beyond the old woman, a hideous face reflected in the glass, looming over her with a rictus grin.

'Don't move,' said the old woman, unafraid. Her assured tone was the only thing that was keeping Susannah from leaping up and sprinting. Then the face was abruptly gone.

The old woman breathed a sigh of relief. 'They don't like to be seen.' As Susannah relaxed she cried out, 'Keep me over your shoulder! I have your back covered. But don't forget to look ahead to dark corners.'

As Susannah stood with her arm held across her chest, a strange gesture to ward off evil, there was a sharp twinge of pain from her back. She drew in breath.

'I'm sorry, my dear,' said the old woman, 'It got you.'

'What was it?' Susannah asked.

'A reflection, of course.'

Susannah's eyes widened in terror. 'Not the Man with 8 Faces?'

'Oh, good gracious no!' replied the old woman. 'I doubt anything would keep him away. He's far too adept at rearranging the rules here to suit himself.'

She swallowed. 'It wasn't me, was it?'

'No, my dear, that wouldn't be possible.' Before Susannah could unpick that reasoning, the old woman sighed. 'I had hoped to avoid this. I'm afraid it's *her* reflection. Look, in the alcove.'

Susannah stared, and could just make out eyes watching them from the dark. It was a figure dressed in red. She was waiting for them, barring their escape. Aware she was observed she hitched her skirt up — a sinister whisper of cloth — and crept into the light.

Despite her mouth, dripping with lipstick, her eyes staring madly with hate, her dress savaged and trailing roots of silk, she was instantly recognisable. Her lips quivered as though finding voice for the first time in months. Suddenly she spat, and a lurid red mark appeared on the floor. She unpicked a sliver of glass from between her lips. Susannah frowned; she had been chewing on it. The woman stared coldly at her. Finally, she spoke in a high, cracked voice: 'Look what you have *done!*'

It was the Queen of Spring.

Susannah was aghast at the spectacle the Queen had become. In spring she had been meticulous with her appearance. Now she was a ragged figure, her dark beauty twisted into despair and madness. There were cuts on her face and her hair was wild. Her eyes were the worst though — a hard, cold white that stared and stared, unblinking, at Susannah.

The Queen held her tattered skirt in both hands, as though at any moment she would launch herself across the room.

Susannah shifted, preparing to run.

The Queen took a step forward and dropped her shredded dress. She opened her mouth wide to show red teeth. Her bloody smile made Susannah shiver in disgust.

'Missssssssssss Hatterssssssley,' she said. 'I don't imagine how you are here. But I am so pleasssssed to ssssee you.' Every lengthened "S" was a stab to Susannah. It was clear the Queen was finding it hard to control herself and not simply walk over and hurt her. Her chest was rising and falling, rising and falling, with obvious restraint.

Before she could stop herself, Susannah snapped, 'Well I'm *not* pleased to see you. I thought we'd got rid of you once and for all.'

The Queen snarled and took two quick steps forward. Glass popped underfoot.

'Stop!' yelled the old woman in the mirror. At the commanding tone, the Queen faltered.

Susannah thrust the hand mirror into her face.

The Queen gave a wretched screech and threw up her arms. Susannah bravely held her ground, listening to the Queen's gasps turn into sobs. Her heart suddenly went out to the woman; she had done terrible things, she had allowed the

Man's corrupting influence in, had been unkind to Susannah and put her in great danger; and yet she didn't deserve this, to be imprisoned in a glass world to go slowly mad.

'Oh, oh, oh,' the Queen sobbed. 'It's so much worse than I feared.'

Susannah frowned. Then she realised; the mirror had shown the Queen her own reflection, something this glass world could not do.

'Columbine,' the old woman said gently.

The Queen uncurled from her self-pity and looked at Susannah.

Susannah looked into the mirror. 'Could we take her back with us?'

The old woman's eyes widened as though Susannah had suggested something obscene. 'Certainly not! That would be overturning the Spinster's judgement, and we do not have the authority to do such a thing.'

'But it was because of me that she was put here.'

'It was the Queen's selfishness that put her here.'

'I still think she should be sent back to the spring season,' argued Susannah. 'She can't do anything bad here.'

The old woman blinked. 'Did I not just tell you that is not for us to decide? Now please stop arguing with me, young lady! We are in enough strife as it is.'

Susannah was about to push the point when she realised the Queen was looking at her. There was a calculating gleam in her eyes.

'Your Majesty?' she said, reverting to obedience in the face of such a crafty gaze.

'What is it?' asked the old woman. Susannah turned her to face the Queen's red grimace. 'Oh dear.'

The Queen's lips parted with an audible wet smack. 'You can … get out?' She looked from the little girl to the hand mirror.

'Oh dear,' said the old woman again.

'I have just decided what I am going to do with you, Miss Hattersley.' The Queen's eyes narrowed with cruel delight. 'It is fitting that my gaoler becomes the prisoner now!'

Susannah puffed out her chest. 'But I was arguing for you!'

The Queen wasn't listening. 'Yes, I know exactly what to do with you. A deceitful, two-faced child. Author of my woes. Imprisoning me here to slowly decay. Oh, I have thought of a million tortures for you. But none of them were good enough. No, not one of them. They were all too quick.' The Queen paused, savouring the moment. 'Now you are here in my clutches. But nothing I can think of would be a reasonable, just punishment.

'But I know what to do, yes, yes I do! I will take your mirror and I will leave this place to wreak a terrible vengeance on the Spinster. But as for my revenge on you …' She laughed; it echoed callously around the room. 'I will unleash *her* onto you!'

She grinned like a mad child and, tilting her head away so as not to look at something awful, pointed over Susannah's shoulder.

Susannah swivelled, feeling a hateful presence behind her. Before she could turn, she felt claws slice across her back.

Everything goes slow motion:

A flash of red in the mirrors.

The Queen: smile like a knife.

Susannah, crying out, falls, cheek slapped to floor.

Someone shouts, 'Get up! Get up!'

Movement in her peripheral vision: the Queen's reflection screaming in for another strike. Susannah rolls, ignoring glass cuts, the reflection barely missing her.

A grimace chases itself from mirror to mirror.

'Get to the alcove!' yells the woman in the mirror. The only place of darkness in this place of light.

Susannah runs, shoving the hateful queen aside, sprinting for the darkness. The flash of red in the mirrors comes in for a renewed attack. Ducking and weaving, another sharp slash across her back. Falling again, pain blooming like a firework, but getting up, racing on ... Reaching the alcove: 'What now?' she yells into the hand mirror.

'Do as Aranae did!' cries the old woman.

The Queen, picking herself up, turns, finger pointed, screeching for justice.

Susannah places the hand mirror against the wall.

The wall shivers into liquid.

Susannah takes one look back as the red devil reflection races through the mirrors, talons outstretched.

The Queen's look of rage falters as her quarry escapes.

'You deserve this,' Susannah says.

The Queen opens her mouth and screams. The mirrors shatter. And just as the Queen's reflection, outrunning the destruction, is within striking distance, Susannah steps into the liquid wall.

She closes her eyes and thinks of Brandon and is instantly transported elsewhere.

CHAPTER FIFTEEN
THE BEETLES' LABYRINTH

WITH DISCONCERTING ABRUPTNESS SUSANNAH WAS thrown from a mirror and smacked into a wall. For a moment she lay crumpled on the floor. Her forehead smarted where she had cracked it. Her vision flared white at the corner of her eyes, adjusting from the bright, mirrored place to this new subterranean gloom. The only light came from a single flambeau throwing flickering shadows on the walls.

Susannah picked herself up and started as she saw a face flash back at her. But it was only the mirror on the wall.

I look a mess, she thought. Her green dress was hanging tatters; her face bore many cuts, one quite deep along her chin that showed pink and fresh. Her skin was grubby with white silica. She brushed herself down.

As she turned she noticed a streak of red running from her right ear to her shoulder. She reached up and felt a gash that travelled halfway down her neck; she traced the fleshy split and shivered with disgust, thinking of slit fruit. The Queen's reflection had clawed her savagely. It had stopped bleeding, which was comforting, but she wondered if she should bandage it. But there was no time; she had to find

Brandon and stop his punishment. She had thought of him, had hoped the mirror would take her to him. And this place certainly looked promising.

She was in a short corridor hewn from rough red stone. She must be deep underground as the stone had many striations, eventually turning to a blackish crimson. Now that her eyes had adjusted to the gloom, she noticed mirrors hung at intervals down the length of the corridor. The corridor had a dry earthy smell and was quite airless.

This is a dungeon, she thought.

There was light coming from beyond the corridor; Susannah could see it reflected in the last mirror. Carefully she made her way down the corridor, noticing as she did how her reflection appeared before her in the glass. It was unnerving, but she was pleased to see it again after her strange sojourn inside the mirrors.

The corridor led into a T-intersection. To the right were more mirrors and a flambeau with a corridor branching off at the end. To the left was a dead end, with a small, barred window up high that opened onto the exterior, and let in a small amount of light.

Intrigued, Susannah went to see if she could figure out where she might be in the fortress. She had to stand on tiptoe to see properly, and even then her eye-line was only just at the bottom of the window. She made out a short tunnel carved out of the stone, and at the end of it another window, also barred. Beyond the window was air, and no sense of perspective. The air was filled with whirling red sand. With everything that had happened to her in the fortress she had forgotten the storm outside. It still raged beyond the window. It was as though the city below had never existed, was a figment of her imagination. She wondered for a dizzying moment whether everything was being erased behind her. But that was silly, that was submitting to the theatrical rules of the season. The Queen still existed, trapped in that frightening mirror world, so the Spinster must exist. The old woman would be looking for her. She wouldn't have let her wander out into the delicately-calibrated seasons to create havoc, surely?

There's no use thinking like that, she thought. You'll only scare yourself. But the thought of help had given her an idea.

She walked to the other end of this new corridor and, sure enough, another one awaited her. Knowing the insidious nature of the season and the unpleasant machinations of the King and the Vizier, Susannah wondered whether these corridors might well turn out to be a labyrinth under the fortress. It could go on for days, and she didn't have days to spare. She had the impression from the Vizier that Brandon's punishment was to happen as soon as his torture equipment was ready.

She sat down and opened her satchel, pulling out the heavy book of maps. Closing her eyes, she allowed her fingers to flip and search the pages, until a strong impression made her stop. She opened her eyes and placed her index finger on the soft vellum. For a moment nothing happened, and Susannah frowned, then ink blossomed beneath her finger. It spread into a dark stain. Susannah remembered what she had to do and said confidently, 'Show me Brandon.' The stain stopped, and a single line began to draw a complicated path with twists and turns and many corridors (she had been right when she thought it a labyrinth). Susannah's heart sank at the path she had to follow; it looked as though it might take some time. Then the ink stopped and split in two, quickly etching in a room with a dark hole in its middle. Susannah wondered what that was supposed to represent. The ink was immobile, but Susannah waited, and a blue mark appeared. Brandon! It had to be; the book had coloured him blue in the tower.

Picking herself up she slung the satchel over her shoulder and, with the book as her guide, she set out to rescue her friend.

The red corridors eventually gave way to black stone. Light became scarce, the dark closing around her like a hand. The flambeaux still burned strong, reflecting off a hard, secreted resin that covered the stone.

At least someone keeps the light going, Susannah thought, or something.

The resin was cool and slippery to the touch. It made her think of insects: bees and termites and beetles. Was this a hive, home of the beetle guards? She was repulsed by the thought of being inundated with crawling, skittering beetles. But, she reminded herself, they're just men; just men.

It was, as she had thought, a long journey, or it certainly felt that way as she went deeper and deeper into the rock underneath the fortress. But the book was easy to follow, though on occasions she had to stop and reorientate it to fix her direction. It was entirely silent but for the crackling of the flames and her soft footfalls. She wanted to hurry but caution made her wary; there were too many corners to stumble around and come face to face with a terror. Even so, Susannah felt every minute, and had to drive unpleasant thoughts of Brandon's tortures from her mind.

Step by step she followed the path drawn by the book. She made it such a rhythm, absorbed in anxious thoughts, that by the time she realised there was something different about the corridor ahead, she'd almost reached the end and blundered out into the unknown.

She dropped to the floor and scuttled against the wall. There was a shiver of light dancing in the final mirror. It was sharp, unnatural light. Susannah glanced down at the book: beyond this corridor the single line broke and etched in the room with the hole in the middle. As she sat there, breathing hard, noise slowly crept in, as though she had been submerged and now, rising, could hear. There was a low hum of machinery operating, a shudder from below her feet, something dreadful she was sure; a chorus of chittering from beetle guards; and a high voice talking, then a laugh that made Susannah's eyes widen with alarm. She knew that spiteful laugh: she could see the pale skin, the gilded cloak, the talons. It was the Vizier. Pure rage made her want to leap up and charge in, and only a small piece of reason kept her still. A cry came floating up to her, a boy's cry, pained and alone and scared. Brandon!

She packed away the book in her satchel. Then, steeling herself against the probable danger she was about to get into, she walked to the end of the corridor and turned the corner.

She was in a circular gallery of black stone that overlooked a central chamber below. Other tunnels ended here too. She could see openings around the gallery exactly like the one she had stepped from. There were no visible beetle guards, despite the chirruping she heard before, but that didn't make her less nervous. There could be guards on the other side of the gallery. But she couldn't see to the other side because of the enormous golden clock that hung in the centre of the chamber.

It was a marvel of engineering, detailed and refined, every cog and ratchet and pinwheel made of gold. The face was as large as a church rose window and was an enormous golden plate without any glass housing. It was gaudily dressed in gold filigree and tiny engraved spirals in the rococo style. It was anchored to the chamber roof, which went up at least forty feet, by a solid golden spire. Susannah could see the minute workings of the clock as it ticked and tocked, as delicate wheels connected, as cogs spun, as pulleys and counterbalances shifted and fell. She wondered what it was counting. For it wasn't an ordinary clock. It possessed four small hour hands and four small minute hands, and four thin second hands. They all operated on a central pin, winding round one another like planets in orbit. The number clicked in her head and she realised, *This is a clock that keeps time for all four seasons*. It was wondrous and yet it was worrying — what was the Vizier using it for?

There was another plaintive cry, cutting through her awe. What was she doing standing here gawking? Brandon needed her help. She made her way to the balustrade and peered over.

It was some sort of operating theatre. In the centre was a medical stretcher. Lights on stands washed everything out, so that nothing had the right detail; everything unformed. Two machines throbbed in the centre of the room, both connected to the stretcher.

Brandon lay on the stretcher, his wrists and ankles cuffed. His horns had been shorn off, much of his facial hair shaved, and round plastic discs with wires attached to his neck and forehead. His eyes darted. The Vizier lurched — dragging his injured leg — around his patient, flicking switches on the equipment.

To one side, in a steel medical basin, lay the Vizier's Mask of Lies. He must have repaired it, she thought, displeased. The lips leered at her, as though it knew she was there. She saw why there were no beetle guards in the gallery. They were clustered around the experiment below, chirruping and rasping their carapaces, huddled in the shadows at the edges of the circle. The great clock hung over them like a presage of doom.

The Vizier shambled back to the boy. His talons clicked together. 'It's very painful, so I'm told. But these tests are necessary. I haven't made someone so young into a beetle guard before. Everything must be calibrated correctly, otherwise who knows what will happen?' His eyes gleamed.

Brandon whimpered.

'What? Don't you want to become a beetle guard? Don't you want to see what horrible things lie inside you?' Brandon's eyes went wide. 'Oh yes, the process turns you inside out, brings all your animal nastiness out. I think you'll be a particularly vicious one.'

He went back to his equipment. 'Of course, I would rather a more prolonged punishment, leaving you to burn to a crisp in accelerated sunshine for instance, but a vizier must obey his king,' his nose crinkled with distaste, 'however dim-witted and unimaginative he may be.'

Susannah was horrified. They were going to turn Brandon into a beetle guard! This was how it was done. No wonder the beetles shivered and agitated in the shadows, remembering the men they had once been before their transformation. She would not let him go through with it! But before she could leap up and challenge the Vizier a priggish voice echoed throughout the chamber.

'I hope I didn't just hear you slandering our most worshipful, magnanimous king.'

A shape appeared in the opening of a tunnel below. The figure came forward and the light covered it and brought it into focus. It was the obsequious servant, Catarrh'l. Dressed primly in her black suit she looked out of place, yet she spoke with authority.

The Vizier turned, surprised. He sneered a greeting to the pig. 'You must have misheard me. I have only the highest reverence for our king.'

Catarrh'l gave a small grunt. 'We both know that is not true.'

The Vizier narrowed his eyes. 'Do we?'

'Come now,' said the pig. 'The Karkarim are the King's in name only. You have supreme control over them. They're your spies.'

'What are you suggesting?'

'Our most enlarged king cares only for his ratings and his title. He does not care to rule the season … as you do.'

The Vizier laughed hollowly. The sound echoed in the chamber. 'We both know *you* are the one who wishes to rule the season. But the Miss Chiefs will never allow it.'

Catarrh'l flinched at the statement. Her eyes grew colder. 'You're lucky I do not have my new ledger with me to record your traitorous comments. You are also lucky that my memory is not so good.'

The Vizier gave a short mocking bow in acknowledgement of her pardon.

Susannah couldn't help feeling pleased at the Vizier's comeuppance. She had not realised there was rivalry between these two. They had been in agreement at her trial, united in proving her guilt.

'However, the King wishes to see you,' snapped the pig.

The Vizier visibly held himself from snapping back. 'I am in the middle of a punishment.'

'Are you suggesting the King should wait for you to finish?'

The Vizier breathed in, trying to remain calm. 'Of course not. I am merely wondering why the King needs to see me now. These experiments cannot be rushed. The machinery needs to be delicately calibrated. I am —'

'These are vapid excuses. I know you love your work, Vizier, but the King's summons must be obeyed instantly.' She smiled, showing yellow teeth. 'I know of your work. I can take over.'

The Vizier snorted. 'You? You're a mere lapdog to the King. You know nothing of the skills of refined punishments.'

Catarrh'l's smile was a little too knowing. Her eyes glittered with threat. The Vizier had gone too far. 'I think you'd be surprised by how much I know.' She let out a snuffle. 'I think perhaps your disloyalty requires a taste of your own punishment.' She motioned to the beetle guards. 'Kill him,' she said.

The Vizier's shock was something to see. His eyes widened to saucers. 'You exceed your authority,' he cried. 'The beetle guards obey only me!'

Catarrh'l picked at her teeth, foraging for a morsel from a previous meal. She didn't even look at the Vizier.

'Yes, they do. But you'll find that these four aren't beetle guards.' The pig found the piece of meat in her teeth; she sniffed it then chewed it.

The Vizier frowned, uncertain at Catarrh'l's assured tone. 'Then, what are they?'

Catarrh'l stopped chewing and, with an expression of distaste, spat the meat onto the floor. 'They're Blanks,' she said.

Susannah's heart sank. That could only mean ...

'... and I am the Man with 8 Faces!' She reached up and pulled her face off.

Susannah turned away, hand over mouth, bile rising in her throat. This close to the Man she was nauseous.

When she next looked she saw a figure she knew all too well stepping from Catarrh'l's rubbery skin, now piled at its feet. It was far taller than the short figure had been, somehow squashed into the skin through some spell. It was the Man from the spring masquerade, reborn, somehow stitched into a skin that she had seen destroyed. He brushed back his long poet's hair and pulled his green velvet jacket into shape, fitting the shoulders to this new body.

The Vizier began to stutter uncomprehendingly, pleading for his existence. 'But sir, I have been waiting for you. I've been tunnelling under summer to find you. I am your greatest ad —'

The Man waved a hand and the Vizier suddenly had no voice. His mouth opened and shut comically.

'Shhh,' said the Man. He stretched, his back cracking, and shot his cuffs. Then he turned to the stunned Vizier and said, 'No hard feelings, old man, you're simply in my way.'

He and the four beetle guards came in for the kill.

CHAPTER SIXTEEN

THE TORTURE ROOM

SUSANNAH SHUT HER EYES, CLAMPED hands over her ears, but it did not stop the sounds of ripping flesh and the Vizier's screams. For some time afterwards there was a wet slurping as of something being eaten, or absorbed, and a sinister giggling that put Susannah's teeth on edge. Nausea spread in her stomach: it was the Man seeking her out through their connection. She wondered how she had been unable to see it in Catarrh'l, the obvious power behind the throne. Had she been so changed by the season that neither one of them could search out the other? Had he found some more secret way to hide? (Even the book of maps had refused to show him when she had asked it). Well, she had found him now. She wasn't going to become timid. She was going to get Brandon out of this and if she couldn't destroy the Man she could at least hurt him. She was the prize at the end of this game, so she knew she had some bargaining power by using herself as bait.

The hideous gurgling ceased in the chamber below. 'Delicious!' said the Man. 'Though villainy always tastes a little over-flavoured to me. A bit too salty.'

Susannah peered through one of the holes in the

gallery balustrade. The Man was picking at his teeth; just as Catarrh'l had been doing moments before. It was a gesture that now had frightful meaning. There was no sign of the Vizier, not a scrap, but Susannah saw, with horror, that the beetle guards were not just beetles anymore, but each had parts of the Vizier's physiognomy. An insect leg was now a damaged foot; a pincer transformed into gold talons, a white arm protruded from a thorax, twitching spasmodically.

The Man noticed. 'I think you missed some,' he said disapprovingly.

The beetle guards chirruped and before Susannah's eyes the disparate parts of the Vizier were absorbed completely. One of the Blanks screeched and pointed a claw at the Man. The lower half of his velvet jacket had become a patchwork of colourful squares. He shook the jacket roughly until the pattern faded back to green.

'The villainous ones are remarkably persistent though,' he sniffed.

'Now ...' He beamed at his surroundings. 'My favourite type of theatre.' He gave his attention to the boy strapped to the stretcher. 'Medical theatre!'

Brandon appeared to be in a shock-induced trance.

The Man tapped him on the forehead, and the boy jumped, trying to wriggle away. 'It's all right. I have no intention of turning you into a beetle guard.' The Man smiled. 'Nothing so mundane for someone who tried to harm me.' His dark eyes glittered maliciously. Then he spread his hands showman-style to present himself.

'How do you like it? You see I had another made. Thanks to my connection with your friend, she kept this skin alive. Not quite as good as the original, there's something wrong with one hand, but I must admit I grew fond of this persona. It is, after all, a remembrance of my first meeting with her, and it's only right that I should present her with a memorable face for her enemy.' He rested his chin on his hand. 'I don't actually know if I have a true face. Would you like to find out?'

Brandon shied away.

'Perhaps you're right. We could be here all night.'

A tiny squeak came out of Brandon. 'What are you going to do to me?'

The Man clapped his hands. 'An excellent question, young man,' he cried. 'I do believe the Vizier was right in his opinion of moulding the punishment to the crime. So what do I do to the boy who tried to destroy me with sunshine?'

'The Spinster …' Brandon quavered.

'The Spinster did not throw the bottle!' yelled the Man. He controlled his rage and proposed more quietly, 'I'd like to burn you up with concentrated sunshine, but unfortunately I need you alive as bait for that tricky girl.' He cocked his head. 'Still, a little torture might pass the time.'

Brandon whimpered.

The gleam of an idea entered the Man's eyes. 'You know, I could dabble to see how much of her influence has rubbed off on you. And you are out of season, an unnatural element, which is powerful enough.' The Man rubbed his chin. 'Yes, it may work, and if it doesn't then I am rid of you anyway.' He made a satisfied noise. 'I shall connect you to the clock!'

'No!' Brandon finally found his strength. A primal fear had entered him, and he bucked and thrashed on the stretcher.

'No?' frowned the Man. 'But you don't even know what the clock does. It might be far more pleasant than being turned into a beetle guard.' He sniffed, and his charm fell, unable to keep to the obvious lie. 'Don't you want to know how you're going to die?' he said, his tone blank. He glanced up at the clock hanging over them.

'This is a clock that measures time in all four seasons, every minute known, every second captured.' He smiled. 'Though the thing that makes this one special is my own clever addition,' he paused for effect, 'as this clock is two-faced!' He gave a quick, mad laugh. 'For the other face measures the time of the world beyond the seasons.'

Susannah, hiding in the gallery, sat bolt upright at this revelation. She remembered a clock face in a tree, the taste of dirt in her mouth.

'What does —'

'— that have to do with you?' finished the Man. 'We shall see. Perhaps not a great deal. As I said, it will depend on how much of her influence has rubbed off on you.' The Man stretched again, closing and opening his difficult right hand. 'You see, when this clock is aligned in exactly the right position, there comes a moment, like a cliff hanger, like the end of an act, when a Backstage Door opens, and I can reach out into the other world and entice someone down into the seasons.'

'Susannah,' breathed Brandon.

'Yes. Chloe Susannah Alexandra Jane Hattersley! The girl of my dreams! Everyone else has been a dismal failure, dying to keep their persona, or, on extremely rare occasions, outsmarting me. But she is perfect, four names, one for each season. She is the ultimate escape.'

Throughout this exchange, Susannah edged round the gallery to look at the other face of the clock. Sure enough, there was another golden face, this one with only three hands — hour, minute, second. Without hesitating she began to climb along the heavy chain that connected the clock to either side of the chamber. As soon as the Man had mentioned this other clock-face she knew what she had to do. She had been excellent at gymnastics at school, not to mention climbing trees, and she shimmied along the chain with ease. When she reached the clock she was over-awed, standing in the golden face as it ticked around her. It was ten minutes to eight. To see something that meant so much to her, something familiar in this crazy, incomprehensible season, made her feel like bursting into tears of joy. Which made it all the harder for what she had decided to do. She reached out and took hold of the slender minute hand.

'Susannah? Why don't you come out now!' cried the Man.

She stiffened. How did he know she was here?

'I've known ever since I took off Catarrh'l, my dear. You don't think we can be in the same room without me knowing?' He tsked. 'Did you like my performance though? It must have convinced you. I can feel your anguish and surprise. Come out and say hello.'

Susannah was still, fixed to the face of the clock.

'You aren't going to be tediously heroic, are you?' he said. There was a dense pause; the air gathered around Susannah as though it were trying to pull her away. 'Very well, be it on your own head.'

A sizzle of electricity and a scream from Brandon.

Susannah wouldn't put him through any more harm.

'Stop!' she yelled with such anger, a startling echo, that she sensed the Man pause. She inched her way around the clock face until she was in view of the chamber below.

The Man looked up at her with an expression of amusement. His eyes were spidery orbs, pouncing on her the moment he'd spied her.

'Susannah!' yelled Brandon. 'Don't —' But he stopped; she had not even glanced in his direction, her attention on the Man.

'My dear, it is wonderful to see you. Let me help you down from there.' He puffed out his chest and began to orate:

'The elusive Miss Hattersley has come down under
To rescue young Brandon, but oh what a blunder,
For in order to save her faithful friend,
It will mean her submission, her face and her end!'

As the Man finished speaking, Susannah felt a leadenness envelop her limbs. Her head was fuzzy with cotton wool. To her horror, an arm wrenched itself from the clock and floated above her head. She had absolutely no control over herself! Her other arm followed. With her arms raised, marionette-fashion, she overbalanced.

She fell backwards off the clock.

… into the arms of a waiting beetle guard. Pincers closed around her legs to stop her struggling. Her head felt like it was submerged in water; there was pressure on her skull. She knew that it was because of the Man's spell, but she also realised the Blank must be exerting some influence, straining at her character, pulling at her memories. It must be willing itself to hold back, with her easy pickings in its arms. Its eyes rolled wildly. Its mouth pincers snapped and drooled. She barely stopped herself from screaming in revulsion.

'Goodness, look at you. Have you been in some adventure I don't know of? Your dress is in tatters. A riches to rags adventure perhaps?' He smiled. 'Let her down,' he said. His voice had the assurance of someone in control. It was rich and mellifluous, and she was drawn into its embrace. The Blank obeyed, releasing her.

Susannah felt unsure on her feet. She took a step forward, but her legs were like wooden posts and she fell flat on her face.

'Whoops,' said the Man.

Susannah's arms went up over her head, and she was wrenched backwards, impossibly, to a standing position. What was happening to her?

'Poor Susannah, you don't remember, do you?' The Man's right hand came up; a showy spread of five fingers. His eyes were like teeth. 'I have a piece of you. It may be in this very hand. I have Chloe inside this skin.' Susannah cowered at the thought. The Man waggled his right thumb and she found her own hand come up from beside her body and limply wave back.

There was a pause; the clock ticked above them.

Brandon's white face followed every word.

The Man inclined his head. 'Don't tell me you're lost for words.' He smiled unkindly. 'I can always put some in your mouth if you are.'

Susannah found she had to summon strength to speak. 'They'd ... only be lies,' she spat.

'But a lie in the mouth of a child can be so deceptively truthful. And, my dear, it would be a better lie than the one you're living now.' His eyes bored into her. 'I can save you from the lies of the world above. I know you. I can cherish your character.' He spoke tenderly, 'You would never have to be an adult, Susannah. You wouldn't grow up into that unkind, lying world. I can stop that time from ever happening. You would be fixed, as perfect as you are now.' His voice coaxed her into submission.

Again, she had to force a response, his slippery influence invading her thoughts. 'You won't control … me.'

'No?' He gave a flick of the hand and she was spreadeagled on the ground. It had happened so suddenly she didn't have time to fight it. The Man tsked.

'Dear Susannah, you have only one role

And that is your person at my control.

We are linked, that you cannot deny

So whatever you do you'll become my lie.'

Susannah, lying on the floor, her limbs heavy, branched and useless, was struck by what he said. We are linked, she thought. So why shouldn't that give me just as much control? This disobedient thought gave her strength. She forced herself to think of deep memories that the Man could not know, things she had hidden: as a reproach to her father, after scolding her for talking back, sneaking his cigarettes from his desk drawer and scissoring them in half; putting pebbles and honey into Mrs Pembroke's letterbox for a prank, and watching the next morning, only to feel guilt at the old woman's alarmed cry, her letters ruined; ripping the barcode from a library book she wanted to keep, a book of photographs of Inca paintings, yet the security screens still screaming alarm as she passed nervously through them, being taken to the Head Librarian's office for a calm but firm talking to that was a hundred times worse than anger; the thrilling realisation afterwards that she'd *wanted* to be caught.

With each private thought she felt blood begin to course through her numb limbs, waking them up with pins and needles. The fuzziness in her head cleared. She slowly wiggled a finger at eye level.

Susannah gathered in her limbs and rose to all fours.

'What's happening? What are you doing?' squeaked the Man.

With effort, she stood. She glared at him; this terrible man who had done so much harm to so many people, who was the cause of her being here, murderer of Brandon's father, the vile worm in the ear of the Queen of Spring, bringer of destruction and chaos for his own selfish escape. Well, she — Susannah Alexandra Jane Hattersley — was *not* going to let him get away with it! She was filling with rage, a feeling she had always had within her, but had kept quiet because she was scared of it. Now she let it out, directing it at the Man.

She raised a hand.

'You haven't the will power to fight me!' he declared.

She crushed her hand into a tight ball. The Man doubled over and shrieked, high, like a child who had never been hurt before.

'You're the one who isn't real,' she cried. 'But I am, so I can do anything to you!'

The Man whimpered, hugging his chest. 'Blanks!' he breathed through the pain.

The Blanks came to get her. As they closed the circle, she felt herself wavering, unable to fight against them all at once. Their pull was immensely strong. The first pincer touched her and she gasped as waves of delusion poured over her. Who was she? What was she doing here? She was a little girl lost and these were her friends who were going to take her home.

The Man walked up to her, his face close, his breath like dead flowers. 'I already have Chloe,' he said. 'Now I'm going to take Susannah.'

'Wait,' she said. Her voice sounded as though it were far away, in another season. 'Take me but leave Brandon alone.'

The Man's eyes were the dark face of the night. 'Why, thank you, my dear,' he said. 'Not that you would have had any choice, but that is exactly what I intend to do.'

He took her in his arms. Her mind melted, and she fell into bottomless depths of non-existence.

CHAPTER SEVENTEEN
THE BREAKING OF THE CLOCK

SHE WOKE GRADUALLY, GRIMACING AS white light speared under her eyelids. Was she dead? Worse, was she unreal?

Her surroundings etched into the white like ink stains blooming on paper. Large black shapes moved around her. She tried to sit up and found she couldn't. Her wrists and ankles were cuffed with metal. As her focus came back she saw she was on the medical stretcher. Her first thought was exuberant — *the Man hasn't commenced the operation yet!* She could still implement her plan. She stopped a smile; she was exactly where he wanted her to be. But that show of force had been dangerous; what if she had provoked him into such a rage that he had stolen her skin there and then? It had to be done though; the Man would never have believed her to come quietly.

She rattled the metal cuffs to attract attention. A face leaned over her — long, elegant poet's features and cold, dark eyes. 'It's no use struggling, my dear.' The Man chuckled. 'I do so like these villainous clichés, don't you? They give such piquancy to the proceedings.'

'Can't think of anything better?' she baited.

The Man seethed. 'That petulant, feisty smirk! How I long for the moment when I can destroy it!' His hair touched her face and she jumped, disgusted at the oiliness of it.

'Why don't you just do it now?' she said.

'Everything must happen at the right time.' He looked up at the clock. Susannah saw it now said five to nine. Had she really been out for almost an hour?

'Where's Brandon?' she asked.

'Don't worry. He's here. I have allowed him to watch your death. It will be a painful experience for him, and appropriate punishment.' A beetle guard Blank pushed the boy into the light, to stand at the side of the stretcher.

He looked exhausted, black underneath his eyes, his face and head shockingly bare, stripped of persona, like a criminal. He took her hand, and frowned, so strong and sturdy, yet impotent in the face of the Man's power. Susannah made sure the Man wasn't looking and gave Brandon a wink. His frown began to clear so she shook her head imperceptibly. He brought it back, more brooding and worried than before, but there was the hint of an optimistic smile at the corner of his mouth. She needed him to be aware for her plan to work. She was gambling on a lot of things, and they were all falling in her favour. Was it her connection with the Man allowing her some precognition of his actions? But this last play was the most dangerous.

The Man leered over her again. 'It'll all be over soon. In two minutes, exactly.' His face fell. 'You know, I thought it might feel different. I had wanted great drama, threats, a fight. It's almost too easy.'

Susannah couldn't have him thinking like that. 'Shouldn't you be happy you're escaping?'

'You're quite right, Miss Hattersley! In a few minutes I will have the world beyond the seasons open to me. To think, no more hiding from the Spinster, no more searching for you, no need for disguise, no more censorship of my great ideas!'

'No disguise?' Susannah scoffed. 'Who will you be then? They're frightened of difference up there. You can't wander about like a Blank. You'll have to blend in.'

'Something I am fortunately very good at,' he sneered.

'You'll never be able to be yourself.' She smiled the smile he hated.

He looked up at the clock. 'In ten seconds, neither will you.' He darted forward, leaned over her chest. 'Listen. Your heart is tick-tocking away, readying itself to align with my great clock. Shall we?' He began to count down her destruction, leaving expectant pauses between each number, dragging it out for his pleasure. '10 … 9 … 8 …'

With the Man and his Blanks' attention on the countdown, Susannah waggled her hand in Brandon's. The minute hand she had snapped from the clock slipped from her sleeve and into his hand.

'4 … 3 … 2 …'

She braced herself. She knew this would hurt.

'1!' cried the Man with relish, a grin from ear to ear.

The delicate clockwork clicked to a sudden stop. The silence was complete. Then there was an almighty toll, gigantic and deafening in the small chamber.

'The Backstage Door opens!' said the Man, gesturing upwards.

And then there was pain, as time reached into Susannah

and began to wind her organs around it. She would have screamed if she'd had the breath for it, but all she could do was open her mouth wide, as though her very being was silently drawn from her. Her heart felt as though it had *opened*.

It shocked her how quickly the seasons rushed into her, colours and feelings, loves and hates, filling her. With every new sensation a piece of her was erased. Her brain throbbed with fire. She was terrified that she couldn't control this. He was overwhelming her with *so much information*. Another memory — falling asleep in a boy's room, mobile twirling overhead — was brutally destroyed. She had to stop this. She had to calm down and remember. Remember who she was. Remember what had happened. Keep the focus on her, not him. She must resist. She must piece herself back together. A logical sequence of events to overwrite his chaotic influence. He loved melodrama and the surreal. She would combat it by thinking in opposite. She owed it to the seasons, to the woman in the white wig. To the boy who was her friend.

The boy …

Brandon. He shone in her head like hope. She grasped the image of him. His hairy cheeks, his yellow horns, his hooves and kind blue eyes.

She forced herself to remember. Everything they had done, all they had been through. It passed by with excruciating slowness. Her head throbbed with spasmodic images. She lived it all again, and in the living lost her old self, became someone new.

And then she remembered she had a plan. A clever, dangerous plan. But it had to work. Her plan had to work.

Brandon watched on worriedly. Had her plan worked? He had already used the minute hand to lever her cuffs open. Susannah's hand was clamped in a hard fist, veins standing out a startling blue.

The pealing of the clock continued, crashing inside his skull. He could see something happening behind the clock-face. The pins and wheels and cogs were operating like tumblers in a lock. He looked at Susannah's wide eyes, her mouth an O of inconceivable pain. The clock was destroying her! He looked at the tubes puncturing her arms, thought of ripping them out but didn't know whether it would kill her.

Just as he was about to give in to despair, the clock gave out a strange sound. It was the sound of metal tautened to breaking point — there was a distinct metallic *chink*; a chink that shattered the equilibrium and began to splinter the rest of the mechanism. Golden cogs slipped out of place with a clank, pins clattered, delicate machinery collapsed in on itself. The clock's pitch fell, became slow, leaden.

With a great resounding *crack,* the clock split.

Cogs spilled from the innards.

Something vital tore within the mechanism. The chains holding the clock snapped. With the tension released, the golden spire that anchored it to the roof began to shiver. Suddenly there was another immense crack. Slowly, the clock began to tilt sideways and fall.

Brandon hurriedly pushed Susannah's stretcher out of the way, as the gargantuan clock made a heavy arc to the floor.

The crash knocked him off his hooves.

Metal workings flew from the timepiece. There was a great crunch and squeal of splintering machinery.

The clock rolled once in its new resting place. Then there was silence. Dust clouds swirled in the chamber.

Slowly Brandon got to his feet and gazed at the destruction. The timepiece had come within inches of them. One of the medical machines was crushed beneath it.

He was distracted by a gasped breath. Susannah was breathing hard, recovering from her trauma, but she was alive! Brandon smiled and smiled and smiled. He took her hand again, transferring the clock hand into it. The action galvanised her. Her eyes opened. They were bloodshot and frightening.

'You!' screeched the Man, who had been shocked into silence by the destruction of his dream. 'You have destroyed my escape! How? How can a mere child break the clock?'

Susannah sat up groggily, and with difficulty used the minute hand to lever off the second metal cuff. She held it up. 'I think ... you need this ... for your plan to work.' Her voice was slow, exhausted.

The Man's eyes narrowed. 'You stupid girl, you realise you've trapped us both here forever.' There was an anger building within him that made his figure grow with each word.

'I'm not letting you out ... beyond the seasons.' She nodded solemnly, at ease with her decision. 'It's the price ... I have to pay.'

There was a pause, full of threat. 'Then I am going to pull you to shreds with my own hands,' the Man said. He took a step forward.

Brandon yelled, 'Susannah!' as she sat there and did nothing.

She let the Man come to her. As he reached her, hands

hooked into claws, he appeared to change into the real Man with 8 Faces — an embittered persona of hate and cruelty.

Susannah sat there because she wasn't quite herself. The opening of the door had disrupted her workings, had thrown her minutes out; everything was in wild superimposition.

She watched calmly as the Man screeched down on her. But she had enough sense left in her to recognise him as something harmful. When he was within striking distance, she slashed with the minute hand.

He stopped instantly, as did his Blanks. His mouth was open, but no sound came out. A thin line appeared on the Man's face and then traced its way to his groin. With a burst, the Man's stolen skin split open, and a fierce light shone from him, striking them all.

Susannah rather mechanically shielded her eyes.

The four Blanks fell to the ground as though their strings were cut, shedding their beetle guard skins, which quickly decayed.

The light faded, and Brandon gasped.

'Susannah, look!'

Within the Man's split skin Susannah could see, shimmering and unreal, a forest of bare trees. Orange and red and yellow and brown leaves curled at their feet. A chill wind blew into the chamber.

'Is it autumn?' asked Brandon. He took her hand, trying to elicit some happy response. He pulled her down from the stretcher. She took a few steps toward the season within the Man. How had she done it? he wondered. Had the clock worked, aligned all seasons as the Man had wanted? Perhaps the minute hand had enabled her to open a season within the Man? Whatever had happened he wasn't going to stay in this barbaric season a moment longer.

He looked at his friend. 'Are you all right?'

She looked at him vacantly. He knew she wasn't all right. She seemed blank, as though she didn't know who she was. He wanted to get her out of here. He picked up her satchel from under the stretcher and placed it gently over her arm.

'You found a way out. Come on,' he said, and he urged her forward.

That was when the light within the Man flared.

Brandon screwed up his eyes at the brilliance.

Even so, he still saw Susannah reach out with the minute hand and point it at the light.

The light shot out a tendril that wrapped itself around Susannah's wrist and pulled her into the Man.

His skin sealed, the light shut off, the body dropped and crunched swiftly into decay.

Brandon was left stunned and alone, with only a few dead leaves on the floor to mark Susannah's passing.

CHAPTER EIGHTEEN
THE WORLD OF LIES

SHE PUSHED UP THROUGH WET earth, tasting it in her mouth, feeling it press against her eyes. For a frightening moment she was stuck, but then felt loose soil and air at her fingers. She gathered all her little strength and her hand broke free, found traction on the dirt, and she levered herself bit by bit from the ground. She spat mud and wiped her eyes and lay there, discovering how to breathe again.

The rain tapped against her head. She was very cold. But she could not make her body move. She wanted to lie there forever.

There was a white light coming from somewhere. She managed to turn her head, cranking it like old machinery, and saw: the leafless tree, the clock face cut into its trunk edged with fading light; she looked down and saw that withered roots entwined her ankles.

Was she home? Her head jangled, as though it had a loose part in it. She couldn't remember how she'd come to be here.

There were voices nearby, crying urgently in the darkness. Then a different kind of light, crawling over the ground, finding her, holding her safely in its beam. Then people who exclaimed (she must look like some swamp creature covered in bog) but who lifted her gently and carried her to the antiseptic-smelling ambulance that was waiting on a side road, telling her that everything was all right, that she was a very lucky girl. That she was safe, and not to worry anymore.

'Brandon!'

She woke with a cry, not knowing where she was, frightened.

There was a touch on her arm and she flinched.

'It's all right, Chloe,' said a calm female voice, and the hand returned and covered her own, pressing it down to the coverlet. Holding it steady.

Chloe — was that her name? — got her breath under control and looked at the woman beside her. She was a nurse, in regulation blue-and-white uniform, and white cap with red cross, folded so it looked like a paper boat on her head. She had an open, pleasant face, though Chloe noticed a hardness about her eyes and lips that brooked no argument.

Peering beyond the nurse, Chloe saw a darkened hospital room, lit only by her lamp, and the hall light eking in. It held four beds, two opposite and one beside hers. The two opposite were unoccupied, but the one beside her had its curtain pulled across, and she heard a stuttering snore.

The nurse gave a slight smile. 'Do you remember why you're here?'

Chloe screwed her face up in thought. Then, like the shocking suddenness of the event itself, she remembered.

'The train crashed.'

And she was there: experiencing the violent jolt, battered by bodies as she was flung down the carriage, terror striking as the metal, with a noise like death, split, and she was thrown into the dark.

'Yes. I'm afraid so,' said the nurse. 'You're a very lucky girl.' When Chloe frowned, the nurse went on, 'Apart from a few scrapes and bruising, only your arm was broken.'

Chloe looked dumbly at her arm encased in plaster. It was like something that did not belong to her. She waggled her fingers and was disappointed when nothing happened. She felt sure there was a reaction to that gesture.

The nurse stood. 'You'll be good as new. All you need is time.'

'Time?' Chloe asked, fixing on the word.

'Time for bones to knit together, time for skin to heal.' She gently eased Chloe forward, plumped up her pillows, then lay her down. 'And time for sleep, which is the best restorative.'

She turned Chloe's lamp off with a dry click, sending the room into darkness.

'Indeed, I think you're well enough for visitors.'

'Visitors?'

The nurse tut-tutted. 'Tomorrow. First, sleep.'

She stood over the girl a moment more, watching until Chloe closed her eyes, then went from the room to other duties.

But Chloe could not sleep. Her mind was awhirl with thoughts, most of which she did not understand. Whenever she closed her eyes she saw: an elderly woman with a tall white wig dressed in rolls of fat; a grimacing red reflection in a mirror; a thin pale man in a patchwork cloak who flicked his talons at her; a beautiful man with long dark hair, sensitive features but malicious eyes; and a young boy with furry cheeks, yellow horns, dirty hooves and the kindest eyes she had ever seen.

A name came at her: Brandon. Was he the boy? Then her mind righted itself — surely she meant Bradley, her friend, far south now, who had given her a walkie talkie for the trip north, who appeared dishevelled even in his Sunday best, who put on his cap with its wolf ears and floppy snout and growled at their back door to be let in. No, it couldn't be him; he did not have horns. He also did not have those enchanting blue eyes.

Why was her memory so jumbled? Had she bashed her head during the crash? She felt lost and wished there was someone who could explain everything to her. But there was only the snoring man in the curtained bed. Perhaps she'd have visitors tomorrow who might help.

Feeling exhausted by her thinking, she decided the nurse was right, so closed her eyes, hoping her visions would not tumble her into nightmares.

The visitors, it turned out, were Aunt Lavinia and her father. As soon as they entered the room she had her back up; it was natural for her to despise these two. Though her memory was fuddled, she remembered every single pain that her father had caused. Every day of that terrible year when she had to be on the lookout for him — when he waited for her at school, trying to entice her into his car on adventures, or when he'd turn up in the backyard and start pleading with her just to walk with him to the shops — knowing that if he got her alone he'd never let her go back to her mum. He was a ragged man by then, his shirts creased and grubby, and he stank of cigarette smoke and drink. She knew he was living on the houseboat his friend loaned him, after her mum threw him out, and she knew he spent most of his day gambling. And then it got much worse, when her mum was diagnosed with cancer, and, even with the treatment, Chloe saw she died a little more day by day. Ironically, as though he'd passed on his weakness, as her mum got sicker, her father found his feet, got a little money, and Aunt Lavinia, the jealous sister who could now have everything, took him back. And then it was as though her mum's death was inevitable, and Chloe had to wait out every week, every day, every hour, every minute, every second, until her mum was gone. Then her father could claim her, alongside the lounge, the books, the kitchen knives.

But when they came into the room — her father looking dapper and assured in a stiff green blazer, with his long dark hair and his soft, thoughtful features; her aunt in a new floral dress that accentuated her thinness, her pleasantly made-up face — Chloe wondered how two apparently ordinary people could cause such harm. Still, she was determined not to be kind to them.

'We were so worried,' said Lavinia with genuine relief, wringing her hands. 'We thought you'd never wake up.'

Her father bent and kissed her forehead. She shivered but if he noticed he did not show it. 'My dear, dear girl,' he said, and there were tears in his eyes. 'I thought you were lost.'

Chloe glared at him. There was anger in her chest, waiting to be unleashed. He had caused so much chaos and disruption in her life.

Lavinia sat on the edge of the bed and smiled, hands

in her lap. Her father stood and gazed at her with his dark eyes, breathing hard. She saw he was concerned, and it was so odd an expression on his face that she wilted.

'Are you … hurt?' he asked.

'Just my arm. And my hand tingles a bit.'

'It could have been much worse,' said Lavinia primly, as though she wanted someone to blame. 'You're a very lucky girl.'

Chloe frowned. 'So they keep saying.'

Her eyes had not left her father's. He registered her irritation and gently asked her aunt if she might go and fetch them some lemonade. Lavinia tensed, aware she was being sent away, but smiled and graciously left the room.

Her father took a seat on the bed. They looked at one another for a long moment, letting the past, letting time pass between them. There was so much to say that it was hard to find a place to begin. Chloe refused to speak first. She held her father's gaze for as long as she could, then, finding something cold at the back of his eyes, she turned her face away.

Eventually he said, 'I'm sorry.'

'What?!' she cried. 'Is that it? Do you think that's all you have to do, and everything will be all right again?'

'Of course not.'

'Good,' she spat. 'Because sorry is not good enough, after what you did.'

He stiffened at her anger but nodded. 'You're right. I did some terrible things. But I was not myself then.'

'Oh? Who were you?' she asked sarcastically.

He frowned. 'I did love your mother. I did.' He held her gaze to show her the truth. 'But she was so … accomplished at everything. And I, well, you know how my ideas usually fared … not a book published, not a table sold, not a single role out there in the world for me.' He clasped his hands as though in tight prayer. 'It broke me, Chloe, to think that I was such a failure … at everything I tried. It affected my mind. It was like someone unknown was censoring me. I became sad, and, yes, I took our money and stupidly gambled it away. And then, when your mother could not live with me anymore, I did stupider things, trying to snatch you away.' He had tears in his eyes again. 'But you know why, don't you?'

She shook her head.

'You're the best thing I ever did. You're proof I'm not a failure. I mean, look at you: you're strong-willed and knowledgeable and clever and pretty. I had to have you. I needed you.'

'So that's why you kissed Aunt Lavinia?'

He hardened at her cruelty. 'That … that was something that just happened, at the time.' He wiped the tears from his eyes. 'But it's something I can't apologise for. It was not a mistake. Lavinia understands me.'

Chloe looked at him, pouring all himself out, hoping that she'd reach out and take his hand. But she blazed with fire at his heartlessness. She sat straighter in the bed, feeling strength come into her, knowing that what she said next was the truth.

'You're my father. I can't deny that. I even accept that you're with Aunt Lavinia now. You can take me to Edinburgh, and I'll live with you both, and go to the new school you choose for me, and do my homework, and do the dishes, and do everything you say.' She paused. 'But I can never, *ever* forgive you for running away and letting mum die. Yes, I know it was the cancer that killed her. But you didn't come back to lift a finger to help. You just stayed away, waiting for her to die, doing disgraceful things with her *bloody sister!*'

He hung his head and took a deep breath. 'It needn't have happened,' he said, 'if you could have kept our secret.'

She was shocked at his seeking to blame her, and yet knew what he said was true. 'You mean if I'd lied,' she said, her voice calm. 'To mum.'

He glanced at her, saw her anger, averted his eyes. 'Yes. If you'd lied.'

She breathed hard. 'I can't forgive you, dad.'

He let out a sob, and then a gentle smile. She realised why a second later. Had she really called him — this dreadful, selfish man — *dad?*

He stood, making the bed springs creak. 'You can,' he said. 'It will just take time.'

He reached out a hand, saw her wary eyes, and brought it back to his side. 'Everything will be all right,' he said. 'You'll see.'

Then he turned and walked from the room.

But everything was not all right. They would take her, her father and her aunt, into the cold embrace of the north, where the towns were grey and the weather mean. She would be the "new girl" at school, prone to teasing, having to steel herself against insults, having to fight back.

And what was there to look forward to? The ordinariness of times tables, science, geography, history, all those silly physical education activities. Only English and

Art promised joy. But even they had been superseded by her visions. She had dreamt last night: of copper towers and minarets, a grand throne room full of sand, a red stone town, huts stacked the length of a canyon; she had seen a garden filled with overlarge flowers and green plants dripping with wet, a crumbling palace with fading portraits and dusty, luxurious furniture; she had seen a sweet little redbrick cottage with a green door, smoke pluming pleasantly from its chimney, and a library with shelves going up into the sky, each holding hundreds of stories.

There was such colour and vibrancy in everything; it was more real than this world. She glanced out the window beside the bed, seeing the rain spattering the glass, and beyond, the deadened winter fields where nothing grew. Her reflection looked moodily back at her.

There was a movement in the glass, and, for a second, she thought she glimpsed a different girl, a harder, rougher girl. She looked familiar. There was a name that went with her. She opened her mouth to speak it; it was almost on her tongue.

There was a wheeze from beside her. A voice said, 'Alex … andra.'

She glanced quickly around. Saw the curtain moving around the bed across from her. She slipped from her bed and pulled it open. An old man lay there, white-haired, sagging jowls, and clearly ill for he was pale as milk and sickly thin. His eyes were closed but he was breathing fast, as though running. Chloe came near, concerned for him. She wondered if she should call the nurse. As she leaned over him, the old man reached out and took her unplastered wrist. His hand was cold and dry as paper. But as he touched her, scenes went through her head. She knew who he was. It was the man from the train.

'Arthur?' she said.

His eyes snapped open.

His mouth tremored. He whispered, 'You ... must go back. Must go ... back, Alexandra.'

'I think you've mistaken me for someone. I'm Chloe.'

He grasped her wrist tightly. 'No. Go back ... get your ... other names.'

Despite his rambling, she gleaned some of his meaning. 'I can't go back,' she said sadly.

'You can,' he said, his voice stronger. 'This is a lie, a lie. You mustn't ... believe it.'

His hold on her weakened. His eyes yearned to tell her more, but his spirit was unable to hold out. His lips moved silently. She put her ear to his mouth to catch his last whisper, 'Your names ... Chloe Susannah ... get them ... back. From ... him.'

He sighed and closed his eyes. For a terrible moment she thought he was dead. Then his chest slowly inflated, and his breathing became calm and regular with sleep.

She knew, as soon as he spoke, that the name she had been searching for when she looked in the glass, was *Susannah*.

She went back to the window, searching it for her reflection. But the rain was harder, throwing itself at the glass, making it difficult to see.

She felt as though a piece of clockwork in her head had found its correct place and, pins aligning, had slotted gently into position. She was Chloe and she was Susannah, or she had been. Those names did not agree with her, did not tell the world who she was now.

Get them back ... from him, Arthur had said.

And suddenly she saw *him* in the window, smiling with ghastly glee, as though he was winning the game of masks. The Man with 8 Faces. How could she forget him? He had put her through such pain. His cruel smile ate into her, but it also made her stubborn.

She had to take back the names he'd stolen from her. More, she had to go back for the others she had left behind. Brandon! she thought. They were all in danger. They needed her. She was the one the Man wanted. She wouldn't let anyone else come to harm because of her.

But how to return? She recalled the clock face cut into the dead tree, and the minute hand she had levered off the seasonal clock beneath summer. Time, she thought; she must align herself with Egortiye somehow. Could she find her way back to the forest by the crash site? No, she had no idea where she was, or how to get there. She remembered her satchel, with all its wondrous, helpful things.

She searched under the bed, in the drawers beside her, then more urgently around the room, looting the contents of Arthur's bedside table. But she found nothing. Where was the golden minute hand? She was certain she had brought that back. Had they taken it from her? She felt anger fizz inside her.

She rang and rang and rang the buzzer for the nurse.

The pleasant-faced woman arrived quickly, showing no sign of irritation. 'What is it, dear?'

'Where is it?' asked Chloe dangerously.

The nurse frowned, politely. 'Whatever do you mean?'

'My satchel. You've taken it,' she said. 'I want it back.'

'Now, that's not a very nice thing to say.'

'Give it back. Now.'

The nurse took two steps forward, her face stern. 'I think you need to go back to sleep.'

'I've slept enough. I want to leave.'

'You can't leave. Not until you're better.' The woman snapped her fingers, and suddenly there were two burly male orderlies in the room. They looked blankly at Chloe. 'Now, are you going to behave, and go back to bed?' the nurse asked.

Chloe backed away, thinking of what Arthur had said — 'This is all a lie.' But what did he mean?! She had to get away. She couldn't let them put her back to sleep. If she went to sleep *he* would be there.

As they closed in, she leapt for the window, fumbling the latch.

But they were too fast, and they took her and pinned her down on the bed, and the nurse administered a needle that quickly numbed her.

Her protests weakened. But she held on to one fierce thought: *I must find the way back; the tree, the clock …*

Then, as though she had wished it, there was a white light and the sound of ticking, and something strong held her, like the branches of a tree. She felt herself falling into the mud at the bottom of sleep, and she said a single word before she was lost in that other world.

'Brandon,' the girl murmured.

The nurse made a soothing noise, and brushed Chloe's hair from her eyes. 'There, there. You'll find him. Though not at first. Poor girl, I'm afraid you won't remember much of this. But that's the price of going back.' The nurse scratched idly at the skin under her ear, then, irritated, peeled a strip of flesh from her face. It revealed a blank white surface beneath. 'Fortunately, my master does not want you for your memory, only your skin. Your very pretty skin.' She stroked Chloe's cheek.

Chloe frowned in her sleep, murmured again.

'Shhh,' said the nurse. 'There's nothing to worry about. Everything will be all right.' She smiled. 'You'll see.'

ACKNOWLEDGEMENTS

I'm indebted to many people over the years it has taken to get this book published. Paul Magrs (for insisting I "Write. Just write."), Tiffany Hutton (for being a steadfast friend, emotional support, and excellent editor), Caroline Candusso, Prashant Miranda (for the superb illustrations), Matthew Bright (for the excellent cover and help navigating the self-publishing world), Paul Zorzi, Kevin Holley, Richard Taylor, Ant Whelan, Daniel Mitterdorfer, Joe Curreri (who understands everything I write better than me), Alf Mappin, Grace Guerzoni, Shane Wolfe, Brad Wolfe, Stuart Douglas, Nick Tsirimokos, Moray Laing, Dan Hall, Gary Russell, Steven Talbot, Laurel Cohn, Helen Williams, Stephen Townsend, Elinor Sheargold, Mum and Dad.

This is for Scott-Bradley Pearce, who gave me time to write.

Printed in Australia
AUOW01n1609220818
301814AU00001B/1

9 780646 989723